Murder at the Abbey

A Redmond and Haze Mystery
Book 2

By Irina Shapiro

Copyright

© 2020 by Irina Shapiro

All rights reserved. No part of this book may be reproduced in any form, except for quotations in printed reviews, without permission in writing from the author.

All characters are fictional. Any resemblances to actual people (except those who are actual historical figures) are purely coincidental.

Contents

Prologue 5
Chapter 1 8
Chapter 2 12
Chapter 3 19
Chapter 4 31
Chapter 5 39
Chapter 6 43
Chapter 7 49
Chapter 8 55
Chapter 9 62
Chapter 10 71
Chapter 11 78
Chapter 12 84
Chapter 13 93
Chapter 14 96
Chapter 15 112
Chapter 16 118
Chapter 17 127
Chapter 18 130
Chapter 19 136
Chapter 20 147
Chapter 21 154
Chapter 22 162
Chapter 23 170
Chapter 24 185
Chapter 25 190
Chapter 26 210
Chapter 27 215

Chapter 28 224

Chapter 29 229

Epilogue 233

Notes 236

An Excerpt from Murder at the Mill 237

Prologue

The morning was cool and fresh, the cloudless sky promising the kind of day that made Davy happiest. There was just a hint of autumn in the air as the sun shone above the still-green trees and the pleasant smell of hay drifted on the light breeze, the golden stacks dotting fields like giant beehives. Davy reached for the leather flask that rested next to him on the bench of the wagon and took a long pull of ale. He'd left early, not bothering to eat, and now he was hungry and planned to enjoy a hearty breakfast of fried eggs, buttered toast, and a generous helping of beans.

Davy tensed as the ruins of the Benedictine abbey came into view. A tall arch, part of the eastern-facing wall of the church, still framed a bit of sky, its peak crumbling but stubbornly refusing to succumb to the elements, and several jagged columns lined what would have been the nave, their uneven tops rising from the earth like accusing fingers. A few low sections of wall and bracken-covered stone were the only remnants of the buildings that had housed the monks who had made this corner of Essex their home back in the thirteenth century but were driven out two hundred years later by an edict from Henry VIII. No one knew, or cared, what had become of the monks, but there were some whose land had once belonged to the priory that said they heard cries in the night and the mournful echo of the monks' chants. Others said that druids had worshipped at that very spot long before Christianity spread through the land and that their Pagan gods still haunted the holy place, angry that the old religion had been wiped from the face of the earth and hungry for vengeance.

Logically, Davy knew the ruins were nothing more than bits of broken stone, but he hated the place. Some part of him feared its malevolent atmosphere and had done since he was a small boy. He found himself holding his breath every time he drove his wagon past the moldering remains, desperate to get away as quickly as possible. Hunching his shoulders, Davy sucked in his breath as the wagon came to the bend in the road that afforded the clearest view of the abbey. He hadn't meant to look, but his gaze was drawn to the ruins, as always. He peered at the lush meadow before the church, curiosity quickly replacing superstition. Something was lying in the grass, something long and white. Davy pulled on the reins and the horse drew to a stop, instantly lowering its head to nibble at the grass beside the road. Davy jumped off the bench and cautiously approached, hoping he wasn't about to be lured to his death by some cruel Pagan deity.

It was eerily quiet, as if the ruins were holding their breath. Waiting. A woman lay in the tall grass, her fair hair spread about her head like a golden halo. At first, Davy thought she was asleep, but as he drew closer, he noticed that her eyes were open, her gaze seemingly fixed on the lone bird wheeling above the stone arch. Her arms were outstretched, and a paintbrush was held loosely in her right hand, her elegant fingers still wrapped around the polished wood.

Davy knelt next to the woman and took hold of her wrist, searching for a pulse, but there was none. He reached out hesitantly and touched her face. Her skin was still warm, and as soft as a rose petal. He might have thought her some ethereal being had the acrid smell of vomit not assaulted his nose, destroying the illusion. The tip of one boot and the hem of her gown were stained, bits of her breakfast clearly visible on the expensive fabric.

Davy stood and backed away, studying the woman from a safe distance. There were no signs of violence that he could see, but why would a seemingly healthy woman just die? She looked as if she'd been struck down where she had stood. What had she done to anger God so? Davy took a step back, and then another. Before he knew it, he was hurrying back to the wagon, now terrified. He'd be damned if he'd hang around the old abbey with only a corpse for company. He grabbed the reins, startling poor Horace. The horse took off at a trot, the bottles of spirits Davy had purchased in Brentwood clinking in their crates as the wagon lurched and trundled down the lane.

As soon as Davy reached the safety of the Red Stag, he called out to Matty, who'd come out of the stable to greet him. Normally, Matty helped Davy bring in the crates before seeing to the horse and wagon, but today, Davy had a different job for him.

"Matty, fetch Constable Haze to the old abbey. Tell him there's been a death. A suspicious one, I reckon. And be quick about it, boy."

Davy marched into the tavern, helped himself to a tankard of ale, then turned to Moll, who was watching him, her eyes wide with curiosity.

"What's 'appened, Uncle Davy?" she asked once Davy had drained the tankard and set it on the counter with a bang. "Ye look like ye've seen a ghost."

"A woman is dead. At the old abbey. Someone should tell 'is lordship."

Moll smiled prettily at the mention of Lord Redmond, the American captain who had arrived in Birch Hill only this June to claim his grandfather's estate. Lord Redmond was the oddest nobleman Davy had ever come across, but he had to admit that the man's medical skills had come in handy since Dr. Miller had passed three months ago. Lord Redmond didn't mind getting his hands dirty, nor did he treat only those of his own social class. He was a radical, to say the least, but Davy had a grudging respect for the man, and secretly liked him—as much as he could like any rich cove, that was.

"I'll send someone over," Moll said dispassionately. Women held little appeal for his niece, especially dead ones.

Davy helped himself to another pint, gulping it down despite the early hour, then went out to unload the shipment of spirits before someone with sticky fingers decided to take advantage of the situation and help themselves to a bottle of whisky or port. He had to make ready. News of the death would spread like wildfire. The Red Stag would be packed tonight.

Chapter 1

Friday, September 7, 1866

Daniel Haze lifted his hand in greeting when he saw the tall figure of Jason Redmond striding across the grassy expanse of the abbey grounds. He held his medical bag in one hand and tipped his hat with his other when he spotted Daniel.

"Good morning, Constable," he said. "Welcome back."

"Good morning, Captain," Daniel replied, surprised at how pleased he was to see the man, even if they were meeting over a fresh corpse. They'd graduated to first-name basis when investigating the death of Alexander McDougal, but nearly three months had passed since they'd seen each other, and Daniel felt a little awkward using the captain's Christian name as if they were lifelong friends.

"How's the head?" Captain Redmond asked, referring to the injury Daniel had sustained during the investigation that had nearly cracked his skull.

Daniel's hand instinctively went to the spot where he'd been struck, but all he could feel was his hair, which could use a trim. "It's fine. Good thing I have a thick skull," he quipped.

"I'll say. How was your trip? Is Mrs. Haze well?"

Daniel felt heat rising in his cheeks. The trip to Scotland had been wonderful, a second honeymoon after years of grieving and hiding behind cool politeness, a reconciliation of hearts and bodies that had filled Daniel with the kind of buoyant hope he hadn't felt since before Felix's death. The loss of their little son had brought him to his knees, but it had nearly killed Sarah, who'd felt responsible for the tragedy and couldn't forgive herself for not being able to prevent it. It had been Daniel's injury that had brought them back together, reminding Sarah that she still had something left to lose and jolting her out of her impenetrable grief.

The captain smiled and nodded, his keen powers of observation telling him everything he needed to know.

With the pleasantries over, they turned their attention to the woman at their feet, taking a moment to study the scene and learn anything they could from the position of the body and the surrounding area. The woman was lying on the grass, her eyes wide open, as if she were simply daydreaming while watching the wispy clouds float overhead, an expression of surprise on her lovely face. An easel stood a few feet away, the canvas still in its place. A brown leather satchel lay next to the right leg of the easel, its flap thrown back to reveal tubes of paint, extra brushes, and a stained rag. Daniel could see no sign of a struggle or any evidence that anyone had been there at the time of her demise. A gold chain encircled the woman's graceful neck, an oval locket engraved with flowers and vines glinting in the morning sunlight, and a delicate gold wedding band was still on her finger. Both items were valuable enough to fetch a good price if fenced, so robbery didn't seem to figure into her death. In fact, her death seemed natural, if untimely.

"I don't see anything that would lead me to believe this was a suspicious death," Daniel said. "Except for the paint palette, nothing looks out of place, but given its position in relation to the body, I'd say she dropped it when she fell. And the paintbrush is still in her hand, as if death occurred suddenly."

"Yes, I think you're right," Captain Redmond replied. "May I examine her?"

"Please."

Daniel watched as Captain Redmond bent over the young woman, studying her face for a moment before carefully turning her onto her side to see if she might have sustained a blow to the back of the head or her back. He then rolled her back and carefully checked her arms and legs before standing up and turning his back to the onlookers who'd gathered by the road and were craning their necks for a better look at what the two men were doing. News spread quickly in a place like Birch Hill, and those who could afford to take time away from their work or chores had come to see the scene for themselves, eager to have something to tell their friends and neighbors over a pint later.

"I can't examine her properly here," Captain Redmond said softly. "But she seems to have been sick before she passed."

"Of course. We'll need to move her somewhere private."

"I can use one of the outbuildings on the estate to perform a postmortem," Captain Redmond suggested.

"We'll need permission from her family," Daniel replied, speaking in hushed tones as if the woman could hear him.

"Do you know who she is? I haven't seen her around."

"I do. Her name is Elizabeth Barrett. Wife of Jonathan Barrett. His country estate is very near here. I think the land might have even belonged to the priory at some point but was sold off after the Dissolution of the Monasteries." Seeing the blank look on the captain's face at the mention of one of the most well-known events in British history, Daniel decided to stick to the more pertinent facts. "The Barretts reside in Brentwood for most of the year but visit their country estate every summer and usually stay through at least part of September. You wouldn't have seen them because they keep mostly to themselves while here and attend church in town."

"I see. Well, we can't very well leave her here until the family is notified. I can have the body moved to Redmond Hall for the time being."

"While I perform the unenviable task of informing her husband," Daniel finished for him.

"Precisely."

"You mean, you need to undress the woman completely in order to perform a thorough examination, and this will give you enough time to do that before Mr. Barrett refuses permission and claims his wife's remains?" Daniel asked, grinning at the captain, who grinned back.

"Take your time," the captain said. "I will need at least an hour."

Daniel sighed. "I'll be off, then. I'll give you as much time as I can."

"It's good to have you back, Daniel," Captain Redmond said, clapping Daniel on the shoulder.

"Thank you, Jason. I'll come and find you once I've delivered the sad news."

Jason Redmond tipped his hat and waved to his coachman, who'd been standing at the edge of the gathering crowd, watching the proceedings with a frown of distaste.

"Joe, let's get her into the brougham," Jason called to him.

Joe strode toward the woman's body and lifted it off the ground with a gentleness that surprised Daniel. He'd known Joe all his life and had always thought of him as something of a brute.

"I've got her, sir," Joe said quietly. He wrapped his arms around Elizabeth Barrett as if she were a child and carried her toward the carriage, shielding her face with his arm as if to protect her from the curious stares of the gawkers.

Jason opened the carriage door for him, and Joe settled the body on the padded seat, half-sitting, half-lying it to make it fit, then waited for his master to climb in before jumping on the box and setting off. He looked straight ahead as the brougham began to move, walking the horses at a sedate pace so as not to disturb the dead.

Chapter 2

It was with a heavy heart that Daniel approached Rose Cottage, as the Barrett country residence was known. He assumed it had been named after the flowers that climbed the brick walls of the Georgian manor, or perhaps it was a reference to the color of the brick that turned a shade of rose when lit up by the morning sun, as it was now. The window frames and door were painted a gleaming white that matched the white arbors, which were smothered with fragrant yellow primroses. It was a charming home, and within it lived a family that was about to be confronted with tragedy. Daniel lifted his hand and used the knocker to announce his presence, suddenly wishing he could just go home and spend the morning with Sarah instead of delving into the lives of people numb with grief and shock.

A young maid, who'd grown up in the village and attended Sunday services at St. Catherine's, opened the door and looked at him expectantly. "Constable Haze," she said, her brow furrowing with concern. "Is aught amiss?"

"Dulcie, please inform Mr. Barrett that I must speak to him," Daniel said.

Dulcie nodded and invited Daniel into the foyer. "Wait 'ere, Constable," she said. "I'll tell Mr. Barrett ye're 'ere. 'E's at breakfast."

"Tell him it's of the utmost importance," Daniel called to her retreating form.

Jonathan Barrett appeared a few minutes later, pointedly taking his watch out of his pocket and checking the time even though a grandfather clock occupied the wall directly opposite the front door and showed that it had just gone ten.

"I say, what is this about?" he asked, taking in Daniel's tweed suit and bowler hat and staring him down as if he were a cheeky tradesman who'd dared to come to the front door instead of using the servants' entrance.

Daniel used the opportunity to study the man, since he'd never seen him up close. Jonathan Barrett was around thirty and had curling brown hair that was cut short and swept back from his high forehead. His brown eyes were wide and thickly lashed, and his face was clean shaven, the sideburns neatly trimmed. He wasn't very tall, but he was lean and wiry and gave the impression of someone who possessed physical strength. Despite the early hour, he wore a crisp white shirt, a dark tie, and well-cut jacket and trousers.

"Mr. Barrett, I'm Parish Constable Haze. May we speak somewhere more private?" Daniel asked, hoping his hushed tone would convey the delicacy of his call, but Barrett ignored the request.

"I'm sorry, old chap," Jonathan Barrett answered irritably, "but I'm rather pressed for time. What was it you wanted?"

Daniel took a deep breath and plunged in. "Sir, I'm afraid Mrs. Barrett was found by the old abbey just over an hour ago."

"What do you mean, 'found'? She's not a stray dog," Jonathan Barrett snapped.

"She's dead, sir," Daniel said as gently as he could. "Davy Brody, the publican of the Red Stag, came across her body this morning."

Jonathan Barrett's mouth went slack, his eyes opening wide. "What? No, that can't be. Elizabeth is upstairs, asleep. She likes a lie-in in the mornings."

"There was an easel with a painting of the ruins and a palette of oil paints," Daniel said. "She appears to have been painting the ruins at sunrise."

Running a hand through his hair, Jonathan Barrett looked at him with all the shock and disbelief of someone who'd just been given the worst news of his life. "No," he whispered. "It can't be her. Not my darling Elizabeth." His eyes filled with tears. "Are you sure it's her?"

"I'm quite sure, sir, but I would be happy to wait if you'd like to check her room."

"Jonathan, what's going on?" A woman was coming down the stairs, her face full of concern. "What's happened?"

"Deborah," Jonathan moaned. "It's... It's Elizabeth. Constable Haze says she was found dead. By the ruins."

"No, that's quite impossible," the woman said, shaking her head. "Lizzie was perfectly well when I saw her this morning."

"You saw her?" Jonathan Barrett asked.

"Yes. I woke early and came downstairs to read a while. Lizzie came down just before sunrise. She was going to the ruins to paint."

"Miss...eh?" Daniel faltered, unsure who the woman was since they hadn't been introduced. Given her resemblance to Elizabeth Barrett, she was likely a sister or a cousin, but he didn't wish to presume.

"Mrs. Silver. Deborah Silver," the woman said helpfully. "I'm Elizabeth's sister."

Daniel nodded. Mrs. Silver had the same golden hair and blue eyes as her sister, but her beauty wasn't as delicate, her figure not as trim. "So, you saw Mrs. Barrett just before she set off?" he asked.

"I think we'd best step into the parlor," Jonathan Barrett said. "This is not a conversation for the foyer."

Daniel followed him into the parlor and accepted the proffered seat. Deborah Silver and Jonathan Barrett sat across from him, watching him as if they expected him to say it'd all been a mistake and he'd take his leave now.

"How did Mrs. Barrett seem?" Daniel asked Deborah Silver. It wasn't a very astute question, but he didn't want to open with a difficult or intrusive inquiry for fear of being asked to leave before he had learned anything that might be helpful. He'd seen that happen as a young bobby in London when he'd accompanied an inexperienced detective to question a witness in Seven Dials. The detective had instantly put the witness on his guard with his abrasive manner and could get nothing out of the man save his name and occupation.

"She seemed fine," Deborah said, shaking her head in disbelief. "She'd been itching to paint the ruins at sunrise but had overslept the past few days and missed her chance. She was drawn to that place. Lord only knows why. I always thought it sinister."

She pulled a handkerchief out of her sleeve and dabbed at her eyes. Jonathan Barrett patted her hand, and she rewarded him with a watery smile.

"How did she die?" Jonathan asked. "Did she suffer?" His voice caught and he looked like he was fighting back tears. "Was she set upon by someone who'd intended to rob her?"

"I found no signs of violence, Mr. Barrett," Daniel said, hoping to reassure the man. "Death seems to have come quickly."

The man nodded and averted his gaze, as if needing a moment to compose himself.

"Did Mrs. Barrett often go out alone?" Daniel asked.

"She didn't like to be disturbed while painting," Jonathan Barrett said sadly. "I thought she was quite safe so close to the house."

"Did no one help her with the supplies? Carrying the easel must have been difficult, especially for such a slight woman."

Jonathan Barrett instantly flared at the implication. "If you think I should have offered to help her, I did. Every time. I also suggested that she ask Dulcie, or one of the grooms, but she said she was quite capable of carrying her own things. I had the easel made especially for her. It's exceptionally light and the legs fold, making carrying it less cumbersome."

Daniel nodded in understanding, not wishing to incense the man further. Instead, he turned to Deborah Silver. "Did your sister have anything of value on her? Money? Jewelry?"

Deborah sniffed. "She always wore a gold locket, and her betrothal and wedding rings. I don't believe she took any money with her, only the easel and paints. She carried the supplies in a brown leather satchel. Was it still there?"

"Yes, it was," Daniel said, trying to summon forth the memory of Elizabeth Barrett's hand. "Did you say betrothal ring?"

"Yes. It was an oval sapphire surrounded by diamonds and set in gold," Deborah said, watching Daniel intently. "Was it not there?"

"No, I don't believe it was, but I can't say for certain. I would need to check."

"She must have been robbed," Deborah Silver exclaimed. "That's the only explanation that makes sense."

"But it doesn't explain how she died," Daniel pointed out gently. "As I have already said, there were no signs of violence or any evidence that a struggle had taken place. If, indeed, Mrs. Barrett had been robbed, she had not been hurt in the process."

"Then explain to me, Constable, how a twenty-six-year-old woman who's in good health dies suddenly and with no warning," Jonathan demanded, his grief turning to anger. "Someone must have attacked her, hurt her. She was such a gentle soul. Who would do this to her?"

"Mr. Barrett, I know this is extremely painful, but I must ask for your permission to perform a postmortem on the body, so that we can determine how your wife died."

Jonathan turned a mottled shade of plum. "A postmortem? Are you mad, man? Where is she? Where is my wife?" he cried. "What have you done with her body?"

"Sir, your wife has been taken to Redmond Hall. Lord Redmond is a surgeon. I've asked him to examine your wife's body for signs of violence," Daniel finished lamely.

"What? The American?" Jonathan Barrett sputtered. "You mean, you instructed him to see if she's been interfered with?" he thundered.

"Among other things."

"No! I won't have it!" Barrett raged. "I want her here, where she belongs. I will see to all the arrangements. I won't have anyone touching my Elizabeth." He buried his face in his hands. "Dear God, how could this have happened?" he cried, looking up at Daniel, his eyes blazing. "I never imagined she wasn't safe. She liked to walk around the countryside. She loved it here," he wailed. "She loved this house. How could I have known this place would bring about her end?"

"Sir, we don't know what happened, which is why it's important to find out the facts."

Jonathan Barrett looked up at Daniel. His nose was red, and his eyes were swimming with tears. "I need to know what happened to her. I need to know if she suffered before she died. If she was scared," he added on a sob. "Please, find out what happened to her."

"Does this mean I have your permission to perform an autopsy?" Daniel asked.

"Of course not! You can find out in other ways. Do your job, man. Ask questions. Surely someone must have seen something. These villagers are busybodies, one and all. They're always hovering, watching," he said with distaste. "They'll know what happened. I'm sure of it." Jonathan Barrett suddenly sprang to his feet.

"Jonathan, where are you going?" Deborah asked, looking at him with concern.

"I'm going to Redmond Hall. I'm going to bring Elizabeth home."

"Shall I come with you?" Deborah asked.

"No, my dear. You stay here. I will be back shortly."

He glared at Daniel, who stood, sensing the interview to be at an end. He'd question both Jonathan Barrett and Deborah Silver again in the coming days, but for now, he'd allow them some time to deal with the shock. He was about to ask Mr. Barrett if he might get a lift to Redmond Hall but immediately changed his mind. The poor man needed time alone to come to terms with his loss, and given his state of mind, he'd probably refuse anyway.

Chapter 3

By the time Daniel arrived at Redmond Hall, it was nearly noon. Dodson, an old Redmond family retainer, opened the door and invited him in, smiling as if Daniel were a long-lost relative.

"It's nice to have you back, Constable," Dodson said as he took Daniel's hat and coat. "And you've returned just in time, it seems."

"Yes. We arrived back only last night," Daniel replied. "I believe the captain is expecting me."

"He's in the library."

Daniel was glad Dodson didn't feel the need to stand on ceremony with him. He was perfectly capable of finding the library on his own, having visited Redmond Hall several times in the past.

The door to the library stood open, so Daniel walked right in. Captain Redmond sat behind a desk, a thick volume open before him. A gas lamp cast a pool of mellow light on the text and the captain's dark head. He'd been reading but looked up when he heard Daniel's footsteps.

"Have you eaten, Daniel?" he asked without preamble.

"I've come directly from speaking to Mrs. Barrett's husband."

"You must join me for luncheon, then," he said, gesturing for Daniel to have a seat. "Mrs. Dodson always makes enough food to feed a family of six."

"Thank you. I will gladly accept your invitation," Daniel replied. He'd missed breakfast, on account of Matty Locke coming to fetch him to the ruins, and was ravenously hungry. "Where's Micah?" Jason's young ward was conspicuously absent, and from what Daniel knew of the boy, he never willingly missed a meal.

"Out with Tom Marin. I gave him the day off from his lessons, so they went fishing. Mrs. Dodson packed them a picnic lunch, but he'll turn up once he's hungry again," Jason said,

19

smiling affectionately. He was very fond of the boy, their bond stronger than that of some fathers and sons.

Once, late at night, while Daniel was spending several days convalescing at Redmond Hall after being brutally attacked, Jason had told him about his time in the Union Army during the American Civil War and how he'd come to meet Micah Donovan, who'd been "the best damned drummer boy any regiment could ask for." He'd also spoken about his time at Andersonville Confederate Prison, where he'd spent nearly a year alongside Micah and his father and brother, who'd taken young Micah along when they had enlisted rather than leave him on the family farm in the care of his sister.

"It wasn't because they didn't trust Mary to look after Micah, but because Micah had worn them down with his pleas and promised not to get in the way. He'd offered to carry messages, help nurse the wounded, and generally make himself useful in any way he could," Jason had said, shaking his head with incredulity. "Imagine, taking an eight-year-old boy to war. Madness. But they did, and he was taken prisoner along with Liam and Patrick Donovan and wound up in Andersonville with the rest of us. He's eleven now, but he still carries the scars of the war years and will probably do so for the rest of his life, most especially of the time he had spent in prison."

"What was it like?" Daniel had asked. And Jason had told him.

The place had been a hellhole, the Southern governor's ultimate goal to kill off as many Union soldiers as possible without firing a shot—unless they tried to escape, in which case they were often shot in the back. The lack of adequate food, sanitation, and medical assistance, combined with the unnecessary brutality of the guards, had resulted in the governor's execution for crimes against humanity, but his death had done little to comfort the families of those who'd been lost, nor would it provide a family for a boy who'd been left alone in the world. Jason had stepped into the breach, taking Micah into his home and treating him as he would a little brother. Or a son.

"Luncheon is served," Dodson announced with all the pomp of someone addressing the royal family.

"Please ask Fanny to set a place for Constable Haze," Jason said.

"Already done, sir. We assumed he'd be staying," Dodson replied smugly.

"Shall we?" Jason asked as he stood.

Daniel followed Jason into the dining room and took a seat, his stomach growling loudly enough for Fanny to hear. She did her best to hide her smile and served them consommé before discreetly leaving the room and giving the men a few minutes to speak privately before she returned with the main course.

"Has Jonathan Barrett come by?" Daniel asked once he swallowed a spoonful of soup. He found that dealing with death did nothing to diminish his appetite.

"Been and gone. He's taken his wife's remains," Jason replied. "He didn't even ask to see me; simply demanded that Dodson direct him to the body. He had his coachman to help him, so I decided not to intervene. The man was in no mood to speak to me—not that I can blame him. I caught a glimpse of him from the window. He seemed distraught."

"He is. Did you have enough time to examine the body?"

"Not as much time as I would have liked, but enough to make a determination as to the cause of death."

Daniel leaned forward in his eagerness to hear what the captain had to say.

"I believe Elizabeth Barrett was poisoned."

"Poisoned? Are you certain?"

"I am."

"Could she have taken the poison herself?" Daniel asked. There'd been no evidence of another person's presence at the scene, and given the abbey's reputation for being cursed and haunted, he thought it might appeal to an unhappy young woman—if Elizabeth Barrett had indeed been unhappy—as a place to commit suicide.

"If you were to kill yourself, would you do it in a place where you weren't likely to be discovered for some time? Left to the elements and animals, who wouldn't take long to start feeding on your remains?" Jason asked. "Besides, why bring an easel and paints and begin painting a picture if you're about to top yourself? I can't pretend to know what Mrs. Barrett had been thinking at the time of her death, but that sort of behavior doesn't seem consistent with a suicidal person's state of mind."

"I suppose you're right," Daniel said. "Have you any notion which poison was used?"

"Cyanide."

"How can you tell just by looking at her?" Daniel asked, genuinely perplexed.

Jason finished his soup and leaned back in his chair, looking thoughtful. "Generally, cyanide will kill within a few minutes, if the dose is strong enough. The victim would experience weakness, confusion, headache, dizziness, and vomiting. I can't be sure that Elizabeth Barrett experienced any of those symptoms, not having been there at the time she ingested the poison, but there were traces of vomit on the hem of her dress and her shoes, and a small amount was still present in her mouth. The fact that the vomit on the dress and shoes hadn't had a chance to fully dry means she was sick shortly before her death. She dropped the palette, which tells me the symptoms came on quite suddenly, and her pupils were dilated. She appears to have staggered backward, possibly in her confusion."

"That's hardly conclusive evidence," Daniel argued.

"You're quite correct. However, when I bent over her and opened her mouth to check for vomit, a scent of bitter almonds was clearly discernable. That particular odor is synonymous with cyanide poisoning. I wouldn't have smelled it had I not opened her mouth and brought my face close to hers. It would have gone completely unnoticed."

Daniel was about to comment when the door opened and Dodson entered, carrying a platter of roast chicken surrounded by potatoes. He ceremoniously deposited the platter on the table and asked if he should carve. Fanny appeared a moment later, bringing a dish of vegetables and another flagon of wine. As soon as they retreated to the kitchen, Daniel returned to his line of questioning.

"Where would one obtain cyanide?"

"One would either purchase it or make it," Jason replied. He speared a potato and popped it into his mouth.

"How would one make cyanide? From what?" Daniel asked, taken aback by Jason's answer.

"Cyanide is found in many common fruits. It can be made by crushing cherry stones or apricot pits."

"There's lethal poison in fruit?" Daniel asked. He was inordinately fond of fruit, and this news came as a shock.

"Yes. Each pit contains a miniscule amount. You'd need quite a few pits to obtain enough cyanide to kill someone," Jason replied calmly.

"And how would one go about extracting the poison from a pit?"

Jason shook his head. "That's what I was trying to figure out when you came in. I was reading up on poisons. Unfortunately, the method of extraction wasn't specified. I'd need to find a more descriptive guide or consult someone with practical knowledge."

"Such as?" Daniel asked.

"Such as a knowledgeable chemist. Would you know of such a person?"

"Can't say that I do," Daniel replied.

"Have you ever purchased a poisonous substance?" Jason inquired.

Daniel thought back to the last time he'd visited a chemist with the express purpose of buying poison. It had been when they'd lived in London and Sarah had thought she'd seen a rat in the kitchen of their rented lodgings. "I bought rat poison from an apothecary in London."

"Did you have to sign a register when you purchased it?" Jason asked, tilting his head to the side as if considering something.

Daniel thought back to the day he'd purchased the arsenic. It was more than three years ago now, and the memory was hazy at best. "I can't recall."

"There's no chemist in the village, so the nearest place to buy poison would be in Brentwood. Are there many chemists in Brentwood?" Jason asked.

"There are several. I suppose I'll have to speak to them all in due course. But before I do, I need to figure out why someone would wish to kill Elizabeth Barrett," Daniel said. "What would they have to gain by her death?"

Jason took a sip of wine. "Were the Barretts happily married?" he asked.

"I wouldn't know. Why do you ask? Do you think Jonathan Barrett had something to do with it?"

"I have absolutely no basis for making such an accusation, but killing an unsatisfactory wife is a lot cheaper and less public than divorcing her."

"The man appeared to be genuinely shattered. I know nothing of their marriage, but I didn't get the impression he thought of Elizabeth as unsatisfactory."

"Do they have any children?" Jason asked.

"No, they do not."

"How long have they been married?"

"I don't know for certain, but if I had to guess, I'd say about seven years. I recall seeing them together before Sarah and I left for London." Daniel paused to consider what Jason was insinuating. "Are you suggesting she was barren? Would that be a motive for murder?" he muttered under his breath. A man might be driven to get rid of a wife who couldn't provide him with an heir, but Elizabeth Barrett had been only twenty-six. Surely there was still time for her to conceive, unless her husband knew for certain that she never would.

"She wasn't barren," Jason said, interrupting Daniel's reverie.

"How can you be certain?"

"She was with child. About four months along, I'd say."

"Have I missed lunch?" Micah Donovan burst into the room, interrupting Daniel's exclamation of surprise. "I'm starving."

"Have you washed your hands?" Jason asked calmly. Any English parent or guardian would have instantly banished the boy from the dining room, but Jason didn't seem too annoyed by Micah's lack of manners.

"Of course, I have. I washed my face too," Micah replied, smiling smugly.

"Ask Fanny for a clean plate," Jason said.

Micah bounded over to the bell pull and yanked it with all the determination of a professional bell ringer. Daniel thought the narrow strip of damask might come right off in his hand, but it withstood the assault. A moment later, Fanny bustled into the room, a place setting balanced on her tray.

"Fanny, I need a plate," Micah announced.

"I know, Master Micah. I heard ye come in," Fanny said affectionately. "Got it all 'ere for ye." She set a place for Micah. "Would you like some consommé? I can heat some up."

"Neh. I'm all right with the chicken," Micah replied, already reaching for the platter and spearing a leg with his fork. He helped himself to some potatoes and peas and snatched a roll from the breadbasket.

Jason poured him a glass of water. "Drink. Your lips are chapped, which means you are not drinking enough," Jason admonished the boy. Micah gulped down some water and began to eat.

"I'm sorry, but our discussion will have to wait," Jason said. To speak of Elizabeth Barrett's fertility in front of the boy would have been highly inappropriate, even if the boy in question behaved like a little savage. Perhaps Daniel's mother-in-law had been correct when she'd mentioned only last night that the child needed to be taken in hand.

"Tell us about your trip to Scotland. I was very pleased to receive your letter," Jason said. "It cleared up the question of Alexander McDougal's true parentage once and for all."

"Yes. Too bad the proof came too late for poor Alexander. Had he tried to stake his claim through legitimate means, he might still be alive today."

"There's nothing you could have done, Daniel. Alexander's fate was sealed long before you or I ever heard of him," Jason replied.

"I hear the Chadwicks have decamped to London," Daniel said as he resumed eating.

"Yes. It will do them all good to be away from here after what happened."

"Can we go to London?" Micah asked suddenly. "I'd like to see the British Museum and the zoo." He'd finished his meal in record time and was eyeing a bowl of fruit positioned at the center of the table.

"I don't see why not," Jason said, smiling at Micah indulgently.

"Can I invite Tom?"

"If his parents have no objection, we can take Tom along," Jason replied.

Micah clapped his hands in glee. "Oh, it will be grand. I can't wait to tell him."

"Don't tell him anything until I ask his father for permission," Jason said. "Now, if you're finished with your meal, go and read for an hour."

Micah made a face of distaste but didn't argue. He snatched a pear from the fruit bowl and left the room after bidding the adults a good day.

"I must find him a tutor," Jason said. "I've been teaching him myself, but it's not working out too well. He needs a firmer hand."

"Have you considered sending him away to school?" Daniel asked carefully.

Jason shook his head. "Micah has suffered enough loss to last him a lifetime. He deserves to be in a place where he feels safe and happy, and I can't imagine he'd feel comfortable among highborn English boys who'll forever see him as the son of an Irish farmer. Besides, he's not ready to be on his own, and to be perfectly frank, I'm not ready to part with him."

"I quite understand," Daniel said. He pushed away his plate with a small sigh of satisfaction. "I'd best go now if I hope to catch the magistrate at home."

Jason nodded. "Daniel, there's something else. I didn't get an opportunity to mention it before Micah came in, but when I examined Mrs. Barrett, I noticed signs of recent intercourse."

"How in the world could you tell if she—? Never mind. I really don't need to know," Daniel said, feeling surprisingly embarrassed to learn this fact about the deceased and to be discussing something so private openly.

"Do you think she was raped?"

Jason shook his head. "There's nothing to suggest she was forced. Her clothes weren't in disarray, nor was there any bruising or tearing. Likewise, her arms and wrists showed no evidence of being pinned down."

"Nothing untoward in a woman having relations with her husband, then," Daniel said.

"Who's to say it was with her husband?" Jason asked, a smile of amusement tugging at the corners of his mouth.

Daniel tried to cover his discomfort with a cough. "Is there any indication that it wasn't?"

"That I couldn't tell you. You'd have to ask him that."

"Are you mad? How could I ask Jonathan Barrett if he's had relations with his wife? That would be impertinent at best, deeply offensive at worst."

"Whom she had relations with might be at the root of her murder," Jason said, completely unimpressed by Daniel's dilemma. "Were she having an affair, her husband would be the obvious suspect in her death, more so because the paternity of the child would be called into question."

Daniel sighed heavily, suddenly wishing he were still in Scotland. "Yes, of course. I will question Jonathan Barrett again, but first, I must speak to Squire Talbot. As the magistrate, he'll have to be made aware of the situation. I just hope this time he allows me—us—enough time to investigate the crime properly," Daniel said, watching for Jason's reaction. Would he wish to get involved with another murder case? Would he be as eager to help as he had been the last time? Daniel didn't think he could solve this case without the captain's help.

"We did all right last time," Jason said with a smile. "We got Alexander McDougal the justice he deserved. How shall we proceed?" he asked.

Relief washed over Daniel, and he smiled at the captain. "I will begin by questioning both Jonathan Barrett and Deborah Silver, Elizabeth Barrett's sister, again."

"And I will speak to Davy Brody," Jason said.

"Why? What can he possibly add?" Daniel asked.

"He can tell me when he came upon Mrs. Barrett's body. That will narrow down the window of time during which she was poisoned. It's always helpful to have a timeline of events."

"Yes, of course," Daniel agreed. Deborah Silver had said that Elizabeth had left shortly before dawn. Davy Brody's testimony would give them the approximate time of the murder. That was something, he supposed, given that at the moment they had nothing to go on at all.

"Captain, I nearly forgot. Did you happen to notice if Elizabeth Barrett was wearing a sapphire ring with diamonds?"

"She wasn't. I looked at her hands quite closely to check if her nails might have been broken during a struggle or if there might be blood beneath the fingernails if she'd happened to scratch her attacker."

"And was there blood?" Daniel asked.

"Nothing but traces of blue paint."

"So, there must have been someone there with her," Daniel said. "She had been wearing the ring when she left the house, but she was no longer wearing it by the time we arrived on the scene."

"Might Davy Brody have taken it?" Jason asked. "He was the only person to have seen the body before we did."

Daniel considered the question. "I wouldn't put anything past Davy Brody—he's always been a shifty character—but if he were going to rob a corpse, why leave the locket and the wedding band?"

"Perhaps he didn't think them valuable enough," Jason suggested.

"Both were made of solid gold. How could they not have been worth stealing? They would have fetched a tidy sum, were he to fence them to one of his London mates."

"Would you like me to ask him, or would you prefer to put that question to him yourself?" Jason asked.

Daniel was about to tell the captain not to ask about the ring but quickly changed his mind. He and Davy Brody had been friendly once, a long time ago, but relations had been strained since Daniel had reported Brody to the excise men for his smuggling activities, a charge that had resulted in a hefty fine and the loss of a substantial income for Davy, who'd used the cellar at the Red Stag to store the contraband. Daniel had only been doing his job, but he wouldn't expect Davy to understand that or forgive what he saw as the ultimate betrayal. Even if Davy had pertinent information to share about the death of Elizabeth Barrett, he wouldn't share it with Daniel out of sheer spite.

"Go on and ask him," Daniel said. "He'll never admit to taking the ring, even if he had taken it off her finger, but you're a good judge of character. You'll be able to see if he's lying."

Jason nodded. "All right. I'll let you know what I discover."

Chapter 4

Having seen Daniel to the door, Jason went to check on Micah. He found the boy in the library, curled up in his favorite chair, reading *The History of Tom Jones, A Foundling*.

He looked up when Jason came in. "Did you want something, Captain?"

"Not really," Jason said, and experienced a pang of guilt. Micah probably thought he was checking up on him. Micah wasn't an overly eager pupil, especially when it came to mathematics and languages, but he did enjoy reading and did it willingly. He often came to Jason with a list of words he needed explained, and Jason had him write out the definition of the word, then use it in a sentence. The practice helped Micah fully understand the meaning and retain it for future use. "Just wanted to make sure you were all right."

"Why wouldn't I be?" Micah's anxious gaze told a different story. "Have you had any letters from New York?"

"No," Jason replied softly, wishing he could have given Micah a different answer. Micah was still hoping, even after all this time, that not all was lost.

Following their liberation from Andersonville Confederate Prison at the end of the Civil War, Jason had intended to return Micah to his home in Maryland, where his older sister, Mary, was meant to be awaiting his return. Micah had lost his father and brother to starvation and disease at the prison camp, and his mother had died shortly before the outbreak of the war. Had she lived, she'd never have allowed Liam Donovan to take the boy to war and have him serve as a drummer boy, but for some reason known only to himself, Liam had thought Micah would be safer with him. Weakened by hunger and shattered after the deaths of his father and brother, Micah had been anxious to be reunited with Mary, but when they'd arrived at the family farm in Maryland, they'd found nothing but charred timbers and neglected fields. Everything was gone, including Mary.

Jason had taken Micah back to his own home in New York and had engaged an inquiry agent to find Mary, but the young woman seemed to have fallen off the face of the earth. The inquiry agent, who'd come highly recommended and had an excellent track record, had been unable to discover even the most basic facts about Mary's disappearance.

Jason didn't believe Mary Donovan was still alive but couldn't bring himself to share his suspicions with Micah or abort the search, so he kept the agent on retainer and had instructed him to keep looking until he had something concrete to share with Micah.

"Are you going to send me away to school?" Micah asked. He tried to sound nonchalant, but Jason knew him well enough to sense his apprehension.

"Would you like to go to school?"

"I want to stay here with you," Micah cried vehemently.

"Micah, I won't send you away to school, but I've placed an advertisement in *The London Times*. It's time you had a proper tutor."

"I don't want a proper tutor," Micah whined. "I like the way you teach me."

"I'm not a teacher, Micah; I'm a surgeon. You need someone who has experience teaching boys your age."

"Promise me you won't engage some miserable old dullard."

Jason laughed and placed his hand over his heart. "You have my solemn promise."

Micah suddenly smiled, his blue eyes dancing with amusement. "You must be beside yourself with glee."

"Why would you say that?"

"Your friend is back, and there's a dead body that's turned up at the old ruins. That must have made your day." Micah's impish smile was like a stab to the heart.

"Micah, a beautiful young woman is dead. If you think I rejoice in that—"

"I didn't mean it that way, Captain," Micah instantly backtracked. "I only meant that you'll feel useful again. I know you've been a bit down in the mouth lately."

"Have I?"

Micah raised one eyebrow, his face taking on a comical expression. "You really ought to spend more time on that—what did you call it? —introspection. You've been moping around the house for weeks. Or is that because Miss Talbot has been away visiting her ailing aunt? Well, I hear she's back as well. Happy day for Captain Redmond."

Jason's cheeks suffused with heat. He often forgot just how observant an eleven-year-old boy could be. "Get back to your reading," Jason said with more irritation that he'd intended. "You still have an hour left."

"Don't mind if I do, *your lordship*," Micah said with an exaggerated upper-class drawl that instantly teased Jason out of his pique. "This story is most diverting," he continued in the same nasal tone.

"Well, then it should be no hardship to read an extra ten pages."

Micah stuck out his tongue at Jason, who shook his head in mock despair and left Micah to it.

Jason asked Dodson for his coat and hat and left the house, walking toward the village at a brisk pace. It was a lovely afternoon, and normally, he would have enjoyed the walk, but thoughts of Elizabeth Barrett occupied his mind. He was a trained surgeon, a man who'd seen countless dead bodies, not only on slabs but also on the battlefield and later at the prison, where dozens of men had died every day. He had no fear of death, but untimely death always made him sad. Elizabeth Barrett had been young and beautiful. He knew her looks should make no difference to how he viewed her demise, but somehow the loss of beauty was always more poignant.

He'd felt an unaccustomed sense of discomfort when he'd examined her, mentally apologizing to her for probing her most intimate places. No woman, no matter her age or social status, would wish to be undressed by a stranger and violated in ways that would make her cringe with shame were she still alive. Jason wished he could have offered Mrs. Barrett her privacy in death, but that was not to be if they hoped to identify her killer. And she had been murdered; of that he was sure. Even if she had intended to take her own life, the circumstances of her death didn't point to suicide. Someone had wanted her dead, and given their choice of murder weapon, that someone was very cunning.

Jason pushed open the door to the Red Stag and immediately came face to face with Moll, who managed to carry six tankards of ale at one time.

"Why, as I live and breathe, 'tis 'is lordship," she purred, smiling up at him. "And 'ere I thought this was going to be a most disagreeable day, what with the murder and all. Seems the whole village is 'ere," Moll complained as her gaze swept over the all-male clientele who seemed to be watching her interrupted progress from the bar with obvious displeasure. "All they want to know is whether she were—ye know," Moll said, smiling at him coyly. "Was she?" she asked, lowering her voice to a whisper. "Violated?" Moll said that last word as if it were her fondest dream to be violated herself, and given the way she parted her lips and drew back her shoulders to draw Jason's attention to her bosom, the implication was that he was her violator of choice.

Jason still hadn't figured out if Moll was truly interested in him or if she was this coy with every man who came into the Red Stag, but he had no intention of finding out. He wasn't the type of man who sought casual sex, and if he had a mind to find that type of companionship, he wouldn't do it so close to home. Moll was winsome, but her charms weren't enough to entice him. Instead, he focused on the one word that had stood out in her little speech.

"How do you know it was murder?" he asked.

"Oh, everyone knows by now," Moll said with a toss of her dark curls. "What else could it be? People don't just drop where they stand, not without a 'elping 'and, so to speak. I reckon it were the 'usband as done for 'er."

"Why would you make that assumption?"

Moll rolled her eyes dramatically. "Well, who else would want a woman dead if not 'er man? 'E's got the most to gain, 'asn't 'e?"

"Like what?"

"Like freedom, my lord," she replied matter-of-factly. "Freedom to marry someone more beautiful, or someone as got a more beautiful fortune."

"Moll, quit dilly-dallying," Davy hollered from behind the bar. "Ye've got customers waitin'."

"I'll see ye later," Moll said, giving Jason a look that would arouse a eunuch.

Jason made his way to the bar but filed Moll's comments away for future reference. According to Daniel, Jonathan Barrett had seemed genuinely shocked and heartbroken by the death of his wife, but his grief might have been nothing more than an act for the benefit of the constable. If Barrett's finances were not as stable as they should be, then perhaps Moll's insinuation that he was desperate for an infusion of cash had merit.

Davy Brody was occupied with refilling the tankards of the patrons who'd chosen to congregate by the bar. There were at least a dozen men, all animatedly discussing the morning's events. Davy directed a sour look at Jason.

"What can I do ye for, my lord?"

"I'd like a word, if you don't mind. In private."

"I'm a bit busy at the moment," Davy replied, smiling insolently. "Seems everyone is thirsty today."

"I won't take too much of your time." Jason extracted a coin from his pocket and held it between two fingers, letting it be known that he was willing to pay for Davy's time.

"Moll, mind the bar for a tic," Davy called to his niece, who was threading her way back to the bar, several empty tankards pressed to her ample breasts.

"Come on, then," Davy growled, and left his post. Jason followed the man into the back room, which was stacked nearly floor to ceiling with crates of spirits.

"Tell me what happened this morning," Jason said. There was no point wasting time on pleasantries. Davy always wore a snarl, which went well with his defensive stance. For just a moment, Jason thought he saw fear in the publican's eyes, then the expression changed to one of belligerence once more.

"I were on my way back from Brentwood with this lot." He pointed toward the crates. "I saw 'er when I rounded the bend by the abbey. She were just lying there. Peaceful as ye please. I thought she were sleeping at first."

"Why did you approach her, then?"

Davy shrugged. "A woman like 'er wouldn't be lying on the grass. Mindful of their gowns, they are, and 'er gown were very fine."

"How would you know?" Jason asked, surprised by Davy's observation.

"I've an eye for the finer things in life, yer lordship," Davy replied with scorn. "The boots were good too. New."

"So, what did you do when you reached her?"

"I knelt down and took 'er wrist to see if I could find a pulse. There was none. 'Er skin was still warm, and soft," Davy said, his expression turning dreamy. "She were so lovely, just lying there with 'er golden curls spread about 'er face."

"Did you see anyone leaving the scene when you rounded the bend?" Jason asked.

"No. I saw no one. It weren't human what killed her," Davy said.

"How do you mean?"

"That place is cursed. Always 'as been. When I were a lad, we used to go there on a dare. Nearly soiled my britches, I did, when it were my turn to touch the altar. There's a presence there. A malevolence."

Jason was taken aback by Davy's vehemence and his description. Did people really believe such nonsense? He knew better than to ask. Superstition was alive and well, and not only in Birch Hill. People liked spooky stories and attributed all kinds of characteristics to places they chose to avoid. Jason had passed the ruins several times and had thought them beautiful and melancholy, but he hadn't been brought up on stories of goblins and ghosts. His parents had been almost too matter-of-fact, never indulging in anything they couldn't prove themselves or find in a book. Perhaps it had been that very attitude that had fostered his love of science and set him on a path to medicine.

"You think she was killed by a vengeful spirit?" Jason asked, trying to hide his exasperation.

Davy shrugged. "Ye have a better explanation, yer lordship?" he asked spitefully.

"So, would it be this vengeful spirit that took her sapphire ring?"

Jason watched Davy closely, attuned to the most minute of facial reactions, but all he saw was surprise.

"Sapphire ring, ye say? She were wearing no such ring. I'd 'ave seen it," Davy replied.

"I've no doubt you would have. It would fetch a good price if you were to sell it in London, say, where no one would make the connection between the ring and the murdered woman. Or even if they did, they wouldn't care."

Davy's eyes opened wide, his bronzed face paling at the implication. "I am a businessman, yer lordship. I believe in turning a profit, and I support free trade, but I do not steal from the dead. There are things a man don't want on 'is conscience."

Jason nodded. "All right. I believe you." He tossed the coin to Davy, but the publican made no move to catch it, allowing it to fall to the floor.

"I don't want yer money," Davy spat out. "Now, if ye don't mind." He jutted his chin toward the door, making his meaning clear.

Jason picked up the coin, put it back in his pocket, and walked out, pleased by Davy Brody's reaction, which he believed to be genuine. Davy Brody was not above involving himself in dodgy business dealings, but he was just superstitious enough to believe that his soul would be in peril if he robbed a corpse, especially in a place he obviously feared.

"Don't ye want a drink, yer lordship?" Moll called to him from behind the bar, her voice pouty with disappointment.

"Not just now. Good day."

Chapter 5

Squire Talbot looked up from the ledger he'd been perusing when Daniel was shown into his study. "Good day to you, Constable. I hope you had a pleasant holiday. I trust Mrs. Haze is well?"

He seemed in a jovial mood, which Daniel was about to thoroughly ruin. Daniel had been in good standing with his employer since the murder of Alexander McDougal had been favorably resolved, at least as far as the squire was concerned, but another suspicious death only a few months later wasn't going to endear Daniel to the other man, even though Daniel was no more to blame for it than the squire himself.

"Eh, thank you, Squire. Yes, we had a very enjoyable holiday, and Mrs. Haze is very well. Thank you for asking," Daniel said. He was surprised the squire hadn't heard the news yet, but if he had been closeted in his study since early morning, as he was wont to do, no one would have dared to disturb him, especially with news he wouldn't wish to hear.

Despite the friendly tone, Squire Talbot hadn't invited Daniel to sit down, a deliberate omission to underline the difference in their stations and remind Daniel that his time was valuable.

"So, what brings you here, Constable?" the squire asked, a trifle impatiently.

"Elizabeth Barrett's body was discovered by the abbey ruins this morning," Daniel said.

Squire Talbot looked blank. "Who's Elizabeth Barrett?"

"She is the wife of Jonathan Barrett of Rose Cottage."

"Oh, yes. Yes. Now I recall. They don't worship at St. Catherine's, so I have little occasion to cross paths with them. Her body was found, did you say? Whatever happened to her? Was there an accident of some sort?"

"I'm afraid not. She appears to have been poisoned."

"Sure of that, are you?" Squire Talbot demanded, his face taking on a belligerent expression.

"Lord Redmond believes…"

"Ah. I should have known. We've had nothing but murder and mayhem here since he arrived," the squire announced, somewhat unfairly.

"I assure you, Squire, Lord Redmond had nothing to do with Mrs. Barrett's death. He was called upon to examine the body, which he did with the utmost respect for the victim."

Squire Talbot made a rude noise, then laced his fingers across his considerable paunch. "I want this matter settled quickly, Haze. We can't be seen to develop a reputation for being some sort of 'murder village.' This is the second violent death in as many months."

"Alexander McDougal was murdered in June, Squire," Daniel reminded him.

"All right, three months. That hardly makes a difference. I expect you to handle this with the utmost discretion. Better yet, I suggest you ask your questions in Brentwood. That's where the Barretts reside for the duration of the year, so that's where the answer must lie. No one in Birch Hill would have any reason to kill the poor woman. No one at all. I charge you with proving that. The inquest will be held next Friday. Ten o'clock."

"But that's only a week away," Daniel protested. "That's hardly enough time to conduct a thorough investigation."

"I'm not interested in a thorough investigation, Constable Haze; I'm interested in a speedy resolution. We don't need people fearing for their lives and thinking they're going to be murdered in their beds. Find out who did it and close the case with all possible haste. Better yet, turn it over to the Brentwood constabulary if you find no connection to Birch Hill. There; you have your instructions. Bingham will see you out. Good day to you."

"Good day," Daniel replied, and walked out of the study. Bingham, who'd been hovering nearby, handed Daniel his hat and walking stick, and escorted him to the door.

"Good day to you, sir," Bingham said as he practically slammed the door behind Daniel.

Daniel sighed and started down the drive. He couldn't say he was overly surprised. Squire Talbot, who was also the local magistrate, wasn't interested in dispensing justice. He simply wanted to get on with it, as he liked to say. Whether the right person was hanged for the crime was of no concern to him, so it was up to Daniel to make sure that a miscarriage of justice didn't occur on his watch.

He picked up the pace as he neared the wrought-iron gates. He needed to question Jonathan Barrett and Deborah Silver again, but he dreaded the task. Was there anything more intrusive than badgering the recently bereaved with indelicate questions? Probably not. But he had no obvious clues and no ready suspects, which meant he had to start at the beginning, and the beginning was always the immediate family. Daniel squared his shoulders and marched down the lane, wishing he had a dogcart at his disposal. All this walking was wearing him out and he'd kill for a cup of tea, he thought wistfully, as the first drops of rain plopped on the brim of his bowler. Daniel cursed himself for not taking his umbrella that morning and soldiered on. His only hope was that it would be a passing shower rather than a prolonged downpour. His hopes were disappointed.

By the time Daniel arrived at Rose Cottage for the second time that day, he was drenched and none too happy to be denied admittance. Dulcie, who'd let him in earlier, now informed him that the family wasn't at home to visitors, and if he wished to speak to either Mr. Barrett or Mrs. Silver, he could see them at their Brentwood residence on Monday.

"I'm here on official police business," Daniel said stubbornly, but the servant remained unmoved.

"I'm sorry, Constable, but I have my orders," she said apologetically.

Daniel watched the door close in his face, the black crepe bow that had been affixed to the front as a sign of mourning brushing against his nose. He turned on his heel and walked off.

He'd go home, change into dry clothes, have a cup of tea, and work on formulating a plan.

Chapter 6

Jason congratulated himself on returning home just before the heavens opened up, since he'd forgotten to take his umbrella yet again. He still wasn't used to English weather, always assuming that because the sun was shining brightly when he left the house it would still be doing so by the time he returned.

"Would you like some tea, sir?" Dodson asked as he took Jason's walking stick and hat.

"Yes. And some of those lovely jam tarts, if there are any left over."

"Mrs. Dodson made a fresh batch just this morning, but I'm afraid Master Micah has been helping himself," Dodson said with a smile. "She made sure to set aside a few tarts for you," he added.

"She is a gem," Jason replied. "Please ask her to bring the tea. There's something I'd like to ask her."

"Is something not to your satisfaction, Captain?" Dodson asked, instantly alarmed. Dodson wasn't overly pleased with their unorthodox household, but Jason had refused to allow him to engage more servants. With just him and Micah, he had no need of a full staff and saw no need for footmen, upstairs and downstairs maids, and a full kitchen staff.

"No, no," Jason rushed to reassure him. "I wanted to speak to her about Mrs. Barrett."

"I see. I will pass on the message, sir," Dodson said, and walked toward the green baize door that separated the rest of the house from the servants' quarters.

Jason stopped into the library to fetch the book on poisons he'd been reading when Constable Haze arrived that morning and took it into the drawing room, hoping to find something of use, but the chapter on cyanide was woefully short and he didn't manage to learn anything new. He set it aside when Mrs. Dodson entered, carrying the tea tray. Jason was always tempted to ask her to join him but had to remind himself that even though his mother had been known to share a cup of coffee with the housekeeper, that wasn't the way things were done in England, and Mrs. Dodson would never join him unless he intruded on her domain and had his tea in the kitchen, preferably at two o'clock in the morning when they both couldn't sleep.

"There you are, sir," she crooned as she set the tray on a low table. "Shall I pour?"

"Yes, please."

Mrs. Dodson poured him a cup of tea, added a teaspoon of sugar, and passed him the cup. When he'd first arrived at Redmond Hall, she'd kept trying to add milk to his tea, but he simply couldn't get used to the taste of the weak, milky brew.

"You wanted to ask me something, sir?"

"Yes. Do you know the Barretts at all?"

Mrs. Dodson knew everyone in the village, having lived in Birch Hill her whole life, and even though she prided herself on her discretion, she was something of a gossip, an affliction Jason found handy when he needed to learn something on the sly.

"No, not personally," Mrs. Dodson said, shaking her head. "Lovely woman, she was, Elizabeth Barrett. Such a shame."

"And Mr. Barrett?"

"I don't know nothing 'bout him."

Jason was about to thank Mrs. Dodson for her assistance and allow her to return to the kitchen when a slow smile spread across her face, an idea clearly taking root. "Mrs. Dodson?" he prompted.

"You should speak to Dulcie," she said, her cheeks growing rosy with excitement. "Yes, she'll know what's what."

"And who might Dulcie be?" Jason asked, amused by Mrs. Dodson's enthusiasm.

"Dulcie Wells is the Barretts' maid. Her mother and I go back a long way—all the way, you might say." She giggled like a young girl, making Jason smile. "My ma used to suckle Patty when she were a babe. Her own mother's milk had gone sour, probably on account of that oaf of a husband, who was drunk more often than not. Still is. Spends most of his time at the Stag, drinking with Roddy Styles, another waste of space on God's green earth, if you ask me," she prattled on, her voice trailing off into uncomfortable silence once she realized she'd gone completely off topic and had veered into what some might view as gross impropriety.

"Anyway, I'll have a word, shall I?" Mrs. Dodson suggested demurely. "Dulcie has her afternoon off tomorrow, and she'll come to see her mum. She always does. She might have had other plans, had she a young man courting her, but she's rather a plain girl. Not likely to catch a husband unless she resorts to something a sight more clever than staring at her feet in church," she added, shaking her head at Dulcie's obvious lack of ingenuity in hooking a man.

"I would very much appreciate your help," Jason said. "And thank you for saving me some tarts."

"Oh, no need to thank me, sir. I know how you like my tarts. Why, Master Micah nearly finished off the lot, that little rascal. And then he fell asleep right there at the table. I had Roger—I mean, Henley—carry him up to his room. If you've no objection, sir, I can ask Henley to run a message to Patty Wells. She can bring Dulcie here tomorrow afternoon, so you can have a chat while Patty and I catch up over a cup of tea."

"No objection at all," Jason said. He had little use for his valet, since he preferred to dress and shave himself, but he couldn't bring himself to dismiss the man. Roger Henley was Dodson's nephew, and despite being a skilled valet, he'd had some difficulty holding on to a job on account of his drinking problem. He was an earnest young man who seemed to genuinely want to give up the drink but was unable to stop imbibing once he'd started. Being a doctor, Jason couldn't just leave the man to his fate. He was convinced that drinking to excess was a form of addiction and hoped that with time he could help Henley overcome the problem. In the meantime, he tried to keep him occupied with looking after Micah's wardrobe, which was constantly in disarray and his clothes in need of cleaning, and sent him on minor errands, believing that fresh air and exercise would help him overcome his affliction.

Mrs. Dodson bustled from the room, leaving Jason to enjoy his jam tarts in peace. Perhaps he'd send word to Daniel, asking him to join him when Miss Wells came to call. If Jason knew anything of servants, Dulcie would be full of information about her masters, but only if she were willing to talk.

Jason glanced at the carriage clock on the mantel. It was half past four. He wondered what Katherine Talbot was doing, and if she was indeed back from visiting her aunt. He'd missed her company and wished he could simply call on her at the vicarage, but Katherine had asked him not to call on her openly. Her father was a stern man who saw Katherine more as a housekeeper than a daughter and discouraged all social pursuits. Any father would be pleased to have a man of Jason's position show an interest in his daughter, but Reverend Talbot wasn't like other men. He was selfish and self-absorbed, a man whose needs came before those of anyone else, and his daughter, who'd suffered the loss of both her mother and sister, willingly allowed herself to be subjugated by her tyrant of a father, her sense of duty stronger than her need for personal fulfillment.

Jason felt a deep sympathy for Katherine and wished she'd stand up to her father, but if he hoped to further their acquaintance, he'd have to tread carefully. The one time he'd expressed outrage at her father's selfish demands, Katherine had smiled up at Jason, her eyes twinkling behind the lenses of her spectacles, an amused smile tugging at her lips. "My dear Captain, I'm not an American. Rebellion doesn't come as easily to me as it does to you. Please, let us part as friends," she'd said, effectively cutting off what he'd been about to say. And then the following week she was gone, off to visit her aunt, probably to the great chagrin of her father.

Well, I am an American, Jason thought, *and I'm nothing if not persistent and rebellious.* Many a friendship had blossomed into romance, and he'd respect Miss Talbot's wishes and be her friend. For now.

Jason finished his tea, set down the cup, and left the drawing room, heading toward the library once again. He'd received a shipment of books he'd ordered from London only last week, and among them were several issues of Charles Dickens' periodical *All the Year Round,* featuring a new serialized novel by Willkie Collins called *The Moonstone.* Jason had been reading the installments and was enthralled, eagerly looking forward to future chapters of the riveting mystery. Jason grabbed the first three issues of the periodical and sprinted outside, hoping to catch Henley before he left with his aunt's message to Mrs. Wells.

He found Henley by the servants' entrance, just about to set off. "Did you need something, sir?" Henley asked, looking at Jason in alarm.

"Can you stop off at the vicarage on your way to the Wells' house?"

"Yes, sir."

Jason handed the man the periodicals. He should have written a note to go with them, but there hadn't been time. "Please give these to Miss Talbot with my compliments. Tell her that I quite enjoyed the installments of *The Moonstone* and think she'll find the story diverting." He sounded like a bumbling fool, but Henley didn't seem to notice. He nodded gravely, as if Jason were charging him with a life-and-death mission.

"I will deliver the message, sir. You can count on me."

"Good man," Jason replied for lack of anything better to say. "If she's not there, do not leave them with Reverend Talbot."

"Understood, sir."

Jason returned to the drawing room, eager to pass the time until dinner in the company of Willkie Collins's richly drawn characters. He'd managed to read only about two paragraphs when Micah appeared in the doorway, green-faced and clutching his stomach.

"I don't feel good," he moaned.

Jason set aside the periodical and sprang to his feet. "That's what happens when you eat half a dozen jam tarts. Come on," he said, taking Micah by the shoulder. "Looks like you and I are in for a fun-filled evening."

Chapter 7

Having luxuriated in the bath for a half hour, Daniel finally surrendered its cooling embrace and dressed for dinner. It was his and Sarah's first dinner back, and Sarah's mother, Harriet, was eager to hear all their news, having been on her own the entire time they'd been in Scotland. Unlike most men, Daniel liked and respected his mother-in-law and looked forward to seeing her. He inhaled the appetizing smell of roast beef—no doubt prepared specially to celebrate their return—and entered the drawing room, where Sarah and Harriet were waiting for him to go in to dinner, Harriet enjoying a small sherry.

"There you are," Sarah said reproachfully. "You were gone by the time I woke up this morning, and I haven't seen hide nor hair of you all day."

"I'm sorry, my dear," Daniel said, smiling into her eyes. Despite her annoyance with him, Sarah looked happy, answering his smile with one of her own. "There's been a suspicious death." He'd almost said 'murder' but had no wish to upset the ladies. They'd find out soon enough, and he didn't want Sarah to associate their homecoming with a gruesome death.

"Dinner is served," Tilda announced as she appeared in the doorway.

"Dreadful news about poor Mrs. Barrett," Harriet said once they settled in their usual seats in the dining room.

"How do you know it was Mrs. Barrett?" Daniel asked. As far as he knew, neither Sarah nor Harriet had gone into the village, happy to spend the day in each other's company after being parted for a month. Sarah was close to her mother, and Harriet would have been desperate to spend a few uninterrupted hours with her only child after communicating only by letter.

"Tilda heard it from the fruit and vegetable man, who heard it from Dickie Locke, who had it from his son Matty, who had it from Davy Brody," Sarah said.

"Of course," Daniel said, shaking his head. "I should have known better than to ask."

"Daniel, what happened?" Sarah asked, her dark eyes filled with compassion. "She was such a lovely woman, and so talented. And to die in that place…" She let the sentence trail off, but he knew what she meant. If one were to die, one would want to die at home, in one's own bed, surrounded by loved ones, not all alone in an eerie glade where others had died violently, if the stories were to be believed.

"Did you know her?" Daniel asked. Sarah had never mentioned Elizabeth Barrett, but she'd spoken about her in a way one would of an acquaintance, not a complete stranger.

"I didn't know her, exactly, but Mama and I have run into her several times while out walking. Do you remember?" she asked Harriet. "We saw her by the river not long before Daniel and I left for Scotland. She was painting the bridge. It was a clever spot to set up since she had a clear view of St. Catherine's and the graveyard, and she'd incorporated them into her painting, almost as if she meant to remind us that in the midst of life we are in death, just like it says in the Book of Common Prayer."

"Yes, of course I remember," Harriet replied. "I do think you're being fanciful, Sarah. She simply liked the way the church looked from that angle. She never gave the impression of being morbid. She was quite a gifted artist but had that annoying tendency to romanticize her subjects rather than painting them as they appeared in real life. That seems to be the trend in art these days, doesn't it?" she said. "I just don't understand it. It's so—what's the word I'm looking for? Radical, I suppose."

"Did you speak to her?" Daniel asked, ignoring Harriet's commentary on modern art and the pitfalls of giving in to romantic radicalism that she seemed about to regale them with. He barely noticed when Tilda served him vermicelli soup.

"Yes, but only for a few minutes," Sarah replied. "She showed us her painting and said she was glad to be back in Birch Hill for the summer."

"She said she loved Rose Cottage," Harriet chimed in. "They didn't have much of a garden at their Brentwood house."

"Was that all? How did she seem?" Daniel persisted, his soup untouched.

"She seemed happy. Didn't she, Mama?" Sarah asked.

"Yes. She said she was looking forward to her sister's visit," Harriet added. "I can't recall her name. Mrs. Singer, or something like it."

"Silver," Daniel corrected her. "I met her this morning. Is that all you can tell me about Elizabeth Barrett?"

"I'm afraid so," Sarah said. "The Barretts didn't mix with the villagers, not even with the Chadwicks or the Talbots, who are of their social class. They had their own circle of acquaintance in Brentwood, I suppose."

"Do you know what Mr. Barrett does for a living?" Daniel asked no one in particular. He'd only spoken to Jonathan Barrett once, that morning, but even during a time of great stress, there was something about the man that struck Daniel as controlled and businesslike despite the display of emotion. "Is he a man of business?"

"He and his younger brother are partners in a thriving law practice," Harriet said. "They have an office at Lincoln's Inn in London as well as in Brentwood," she added.

"And you have this on good authority?" Daniel asked, wondering where Harriet got her information.

"The Barretts were mentioned the last time I played bridge with Mrs. Paulson and the Misses August a fortnight ago."

"In what context?" Daniel asked.

"Daniel, your soup is getting cold," Sarah reminded him gently.

"Thank you, my dear," Daniel said, mechanically lifting the spoon to his mouth.

"Now, let me see. I think it had something to do with a contested will."

"Whose will?" Daniel asked.

"I can't recall. What does it matter, Daniel?" Harriet asked irritably. "Surely it has no bearing on Mrs. Barrett's death."

"No, I don't suppose it does, but I was wondering what sort of clientele they deal with," Daniel replied.

"The wealthy and well-connected kind," Harriet replied, turning her attention to the soup.

Daniel nodded. So, the Barretts were wealthy and probably well connected themselves. It figured. He'd found during his time as a peeler in London that there were quite a few murders committed by the rich against the rich. The poor people didn't need to bother with plotting to kill each other. All they had to do was wait long enough and their enemies might get carried off by hunger or disease, since the death rate was shockingly high in the poverty-stricken areas of London. When the poor did stoop to murder, the execution was usually bloody and brutal, the weapon whatever the perpetrator had to hand, like a knife between the ribs or a hammer to the back of the head. Well-thought-out murders were for the rich, who had the time and the means to get creative and find ways to avoid immediate detection, knowing from the newspapers that if a suspect wasn't apprehended within the first few days, most likely the murder would go unsolved.

The murder of Elizabeth Barrett certainly fell into the latter category and would take dogged police work to solve, if it were to be solved at all, since this clearly wasn't a crime of passion. This crime had been well planned and carefully executed, the killer not only cunning but obviously very patient.

"I want to hear all about Scotland," Harriet said, deftly changing the subject. "I've waited all day to get you both in the same room."

Sarah began to recount an incident that had happened early on in their holiday when the wheel of their carriage had come off in the barren wilderness of the Highlands and they'd had to wait nearly four hours for someone to pass that way and offer assistance. Daniel smiled fondly at the memory. They had huddled together for warmth and told spooky stories around the campfire they'd built. It had been a gray and misty day and the mountains of Glencoe that surrounded the gorge they were in made them feel completely cut off from the rest of the world. Had it not been for the presence of the coachman, the mood might have taken a more romantic turn, but it had been an adventure, nonetheless, and they'd made up for the lack of privacy once they finally got to their hotel and warmed up by the roaring fire, enjoying the complimentary bottle of whisky the hotel manager had sent up. Daniel's gaze caressed Sarah's face as she told the story, and she blushed and averted her eyes, her reaction not lost on her mother, who tried to hide her smile of joy behind her napkin.

After dinner, once both Sarah and Harriet had gone up to bed, Daniel retired to the drawing room to enjoy a brandy and further consider the case. A message had arrived from Captain Redmond while he was in the bath, informing him that the Barretts' maid would be at Redmond Hall tomorrow at teatime. Daniel grinned to himself. Captain Redmond possessed better detective skills than many of the higher-ups he'd met in London, who prided themselves on their record for solving crimes and treated their subordinates with cold disdain. Jason was not only clever, observant, and brave, but he was also proactive and resourceful, two qualities that were necessary in a good detective. Daniel was grateful to him for facilitating the interview with Dulcie Wells, a meeting Jonathan Barrett probably wouldn't sanction were he to get wind of it.

Daniel took a sip of brandy and considered his immediate options. Dulcie wouldn't arrive at Redmond Hall until teatime. Regardless of what she revealed, if anything at all, he could hardly afford to waste the day in the hope that she'd provide viable leads. He had to identify leads of his own and follow them until they either yielded results or proved to be a dead end.

Having decided on a course of action, Daniel finished his drink and headed upstairs. He was tired, and he'd have to be up early tomorrow if he were to catch one of the farmers on the road going up to the market in Brentwood and get a lift into town.

Chapter 8

Saturday, September 8

Having arrived in Brentwood by seven o'clock, Daniel decided to pass the time by having some breakfast. Situated approximately twenty miles from London, Brentwood had always been a coaching stop and boasted numerous inns and public houses, the landlords eager to accommodate passing travelers and relieve them of their coin. The arrival of the railroad had drastically reduced the number of coaches passing through the town, but the establishments had remained, and Daniel had his pick of eateries to choose from.

He found an inn close to the center of town and ordered himself a hearty breakfast accompanied by a pot of strong tea. A man couldn't be expected to think clearly on an empty stomach, he reasoned as he tucked into fried eggs, beans, sausages, and buttered toast. The dining room of the inn was nearly empty, and the young girl who served him looked as if she were asleep on her feet, so he didn't bother asking her any questions. He had a plan and he would stick to it.

Sated, Daniel settled his bill and left the inn, hailing a passing hansom cab. It drew to a stop, and Daniel climbed in.

"Where to, guv?"

"To the chemist," Daniel announced.

"Which one?"

Daniel did his best to look confused. "Why? How many are there?"

"Three that I can think of," the cabbie replied.

"Hmm. My wife has ordered something from one of them and charged me with collecting the parcel, but I can't recall the name of the establishment," Daniel said, shaking his head in mock dismay.

"Well, there's Gentry's, Linnet's, and Munk's. Any of those three ring a bell?"

"No. I suppose we'll have to visit them all. Have you the time?"

"I'm a cabbie, guv. All I's got is time," the man replied. "If ye're paying, I'm driving."

"Excellent. Let's start with the closest one, then," Daniel replied, and leaned back against the seat. Three chemists wasn't so bad. He thought there might be more, given that Brentwood had expanded considerably, especially since the railroad had made the town more accessible.

As the hansom drove down the high street, Daniel wondered why Jonathan Barrett had chosen Brentwood as his place of residence. Surely a wealthy man with a thriving law practice would prefer a place like London, or even Chelmsford or Colchester, but perhaps this was where Jonathan Barrett had been born and raised and felt an affection for the place. Or maybe there were fewer well-established law firms in Brentwood and Barrett had a steady supply of clients, whereas in London or Chelmsford, he'd have to compete with other practices.

"'Ere we are, sir. Munk's," the cabbie announced as they drew up to a shabby-looking storefront a few streets from the railway station. At first glance, it looked like the kind of place no self-respecting patron would frequent, but then again, that might make it the perfect place to purchase something that might be considered suspect.

"Wait here," Daniel instructed the driver, and climbed out of the cab. Daniel approached the shop. The paint on the dark-green door had seen better days and was peeling in places, and the doorknob shone with grease, making Daniel grimace with disgust. He pushed open the door without touching the glistening knob and entered the shop, which was as grim inside as it had appeared from the outside. The bottles that lined the shelves were dusty and contained substances that looked murky, the labels faded to near illegibility. The front window was covered with a layer of grime, and the wooden counter was scratched and could use a coat of polish.

An old man stood behind the counter, his waistcoat stained with brown spots that may have been dried blood. "Good morning, sir. How can I help?" he asked. "We have just received a new shipment of Smedley's Chillie Paste," he announced, pointing toward several yellow boxes displayed on the counter. "Smedley's will surely cure whatever ails you."

Daniel looked at the packages with distaste. Smedley's was billed as the 'King of Cures,' and there were those who swore by it, but Daniel didn't believe their endorsement for a moment. Any remedy that claimed to cure everything from a sore throat to gout was bound to be a confidence trick, and only someone utterly gullible would trust in its promises.

"Thank you, but I'm quite well," Daniel said. "I'm in need of rat poison."

Last night, Daniel had decided that buying arsenic for himself would afford him the best chance of seeing the ledgers. Since he wasn't attached to the Brentwood Constabulary, the chemists were under no obligation to show him their confidential records, but if he purchased a poisonous substance, they would unwittingly allow him to see the ledger, even study it, while he pretended to take his time filling out the required information.

"Ah, I see. Why didn't you just say so?" the old man demanded, seemingly offended by Daniel's refusal to consider investing in Smedley's.

"I just did."

"How much do you require?"

"A small amount will do. I only have the one room," Daniel said, giving the impression that he resided in some lodging house. "Would cyanide be more effective in getting rid of the nasty buggers?" he asked casually.

"Arsenic is what you need."

"Do you sell cyanide?" Daniel persisted, curious to see the man's reaction to his inquiry. It was immediate. The man's brows knitted above eyes narrowed in suspicion, his hands splaying on the counter as he leaned forward, the posture just aggressive enough to discourage further questions.

"We do have it in stock, but unless you're hoping to send someone other than rats to an early grave, I don't recommend purchasing it. It is rats you're looking to get rid of, isn't it?"

"Yes, of course."

The man relaxed marginally and took down a container made of dark brown glass. He measured out about two teaspoons of arsenic into a small envelope. "Here you are, then. Be careful," the man said. "It can easily be mistaken for sugar."

"I won't be adding it to my tea," Daniel said. He paid and made to leave, but the man called him back.

"Not so fast, sir. You must sign for it." Mr. Munk, for Daniel presumed he was the proprietor, pushed a ledger toward him and opened it to the correct page. Daniel made to peer at the page, as if unsure what was required of him, and made a mental note of the last few entries.

"Name, date of purchase, name of substance, and address, sir. Nowadays, we must be vigilant."

"Of course," Daniel said. He signed his name as D. Hale and provided a phony address.

"Thank you, sir. And good luck with the rats," Mr. Munk said as Daniel closed the ledger and pushed it toward the chemist.

"Good morning," Daniel said, and left the shop.

He alighted the hansom, pulled out a small notepad he'd brought with him, and jotted down the names he'd seen. Given his own perfidy in the shop, he had no way of knowing if the names and addresses were legitimate, but none of the four people who'd purchased poison since June first had purchased cyanide.

"Was this the one?" the cabbie asked.

"No. Let's try the next one."

"As ye say, sir." The hansom pulled away from the curb and merged with other traffic.

Daniel repeated the charade at the other two chemists. "That was the one," he said after emerging from Linnet's, which was by far the nicest shop of the three, and certainly the cleanest. He could see someone like Elizabeth Barrett frequenting Linnet's to buy scented soap or lavender oil for her bath, but would her killer have risked such a well-run establishment to purchase the poison? He had no answer to that question, or any of the others that were teeming in his brain.

"Take me back to the station," Daniel said to the driver irritably.

"Right, guv."

Daniel paid the cabbie once they reached the Brentwood railway station, then walked the short distance to the market square. He had no trouble finding Jacob Hurley, who'd given him a ride into Brentwood that morning. Jacob was doing a brisk trade.

"I'm nearly done 'ere," Jacob said, indicating his dwindling pile of vegetables. "If ye'll wait a spell, I'll take ye back."

"Thank you, Jacob," Daniel said. "I'll wait in your wagon, if that's all right."

"Suit yerself. 'Tis just over yonder," Jacob said, waving toward the row of wagons that lined the street.

Daniel found Jacob's wagon and climbed onto the bench, grateful to be away from the unpleasant smell of the market. He liked fish and vegetables as much as the next man, but not after they had been left lying in the sun for several hours, their aroma growing more pungent by the minute as flies circled around the squashed fruit and vegetables like vultures sensing a fresh kill. Daniel took one of the packets of arsenic from his pocket and peered inside. It looked so innocent. It didn't even have a strong smell to warn an unsuspecting victim, which was the reason so many died by arsenic poisoning.

Many times, it really was an accident. A cook mistook arsenic for sugar or flour in her haste or because of inadequate lighting, or a family decided to paper their house with dark green wallpaper, not realizing their décor of choice contained lethal amounts of arsenic that permeated the air with poison, killing the inhabitants within weeks. And then there were the intentional deaths. Arsenic was mixed into food or even into the dye used on fabric. Daniel had recently read an article about 'arsenical cardigans'—garments poisoned by women with the intent of killing their unsatisfactory husbands. It had become something of a trend.

Quite a few got away with the crime since they had the patience and cunning to administer the poison in small doses, making their loved one's death look like the natural outcome of a prolonged illness, but others opted for a quick result and ended up swinging for murder. Arsenic was everywhere; cyanide was an unusual choice, and a clever one. Every doctor who performed a postmortem on a victim of a suspicious death was trained to look for traces of arsenic, but few would be able to identify cyanide. Captain Redmond had said that had he not bent to look inside Elizabeth Barrett's mouth, he might never have smelled the telltale odor, which likely would have faded within a few hours after death. This would have been the perfect weapon, had a trained man not been to hand. Everyone would have assumed that Elizabeth had suffered from heart failure brought about by a terrible fright, or some congenital issue her family hadn't been aware of. Given that Jonathan Barrett had forbidden an autopsy, a decision the killer might have anticipated, the cause of death would never be known, leaving the murderer free to get on with their life.

Daniel sighed with frustration and returned the packet to his pocket. The morning's work had served no purpose since he was now aware not only that someone could have used a false name and address, but also that they might have procured the poison somewhere other than Brentwood. The packets were small enough to conceal in a pocket and carry around until needed. The cyanide might have been obtained in London or any other big city, where the number of chemist shops would preclude even the most determined policeman from visiting them all or obtaining the correct information.

Jacob returned to the wagon about a half hour later. He loaded the empty sacks and barrels in the back, then heaved himself onto the bench and reached for the reins. Daniel was more than ready to return home. To find the killer, he had to focus on those close to Elizabeth, not the source of the poison.

I still need to find the source of the poison, he thought bitterly. *The poison in someone's soul.*

Chapter 9

It was nearly four o'clock by the time Daniel presented himself at Redmond Hall. He'd used the time after luncheon to prepare a list of questions that he intended to put to Dulcie and hoped she'd be able to answer at least some of them. He expected to find Patricia and Dulcie Wells in the drawing room, taking tea with the captain, but the captain was quite alone, a delicate cup in his hand as he stared into the flames leaping in the fireplace.

"Ah, there you are," Jason said, clearly pleased to see him. "Tea?"

"Please," Daniel replied as he settled across from the captain.

Jason poured the tea with the skill of a practiced hostess, added two cubes of sugar and a splash of milk, having remembered how Daniel took his tea, and passed the cup to him. "Have some cake. It's delicious."

Only one slice was missing from the heavenly smelling sponge. "Is Micah out again?" Daniel asked as he helped himself to a thick slice.

"Micah is upstairs, nursing an upset stomach," Jason replied. "He overdid it with the jam tarts yesterday."

"Is he allowed to eat whatever he likes?" Daniel asked, recalling how strict his nanny and later his parents had been about mealtimes and the amount of food served to the children.

"Micah came close to starvation at Andersonville," Jason said, his eyes taking on a faraway look. "I can't find it in myself to deny him food. He'll learn to self-moderate in time, but for now, he must eat whenever he's hungry."

Daniel nodded in understanding. Knowing what Jason and Micah had endured while at the prison afforded him a unique understanding of Jason's predicament when it came to raising Micah.

"Has Dulcie changed her mind about speaking to us?" Daniel asked before he took a bite of cake and savored the delicate flavor, almost feeling sorry for Micah that he was missing out.

"Dulcie and her mother are having tea in the kitchen with Mrs. Dodson."

"Is Mrs. Dodson conducting an investigation of her own?" Daniel asked, smiling as the image of buxom, middle-aged Mrs. Dodson in a peeler uniform popped into his mind.

"Very likely, which is why I made no objection to her speaking to Dulcie first. I'm sure she will be much more forthcoming with a member of her own class whom she's known her whole life. And Mrs. Dodson is not to be underestimated when it comes to gathering intelligence."

"Don't I know it!" Daniel said with a chuckle. "Middle-aged women are highly underrated as military assets. My mother-in-law could infiltrate any polite gathering and glean information that could win wars and alter the course of history."

"I doubt Mrs. Dodson is as skilled as that, but if there's something to ferret out about the life of Elizabeth Barrett, I've no doubt she's up to the task."

Daniel and Jason were finished with their tea by the time Dulcie Wells was ushered into the drawing room. She had the look of someone going to the gallows and stole glances at her mother, who'd probably arranged this meeting without asking for Dulcie's consent.

"Please, take a seat," Jason invited the ladies. "It's so kind of you to take time out to speak to us."

Patricia Wells preened at the compliment, but Dulcie looked even more mortified, if such a thing were possible, bright spots of color appearing on her pale cheeks when she recognized Daniel.

"I don't feel right talking 'bout my mistress," she choked out.

"Your loyalty does you credit," Jason interjected smoothly. "You needn't tell us anything you consider too private. Just the facts. Surely you'd like Mrs. Barrett's murderer to face justice."

"Are ye sure she were murdered?" Dulcie asked, her voice rising in panic as she looked from Daniel to Jason.

"Yes, I'm sure. She was poisoned," Jason replied. "She would have died quickly, but very painfully."

"But who would do such a thing? She were lovely, she was. A real lady."

"We don't know, Dulcie, which is why we need your help," Daniel said, taking control of the interview. "Would you say the Barretts were happily married?"

Dulcie nodded vigorously. "The master adored Mrs. Barrett. Never a harsh word spoken between them, just 'yes, my dear,' 'whatever you wish, my dear,'" Dulcie mimicked.

"Is he a jealous man?" Daniel asked.

Dulcie shrugged. "No more than most. 'E wouldn't like it if some man became overly familiar, say, but 'e's not the type to fly into a rage if someone 'ad paid 'is wife a compliment or asked 'er to dance. 'E liked to show 'er off. It pleased 'im that other men found 'er attractive."

"And what about Mrs. Barrett? Was she the type of woman to invite over-familiarity?" Daniel asked.

Dulcie looked at Daniel in horror. "Lord, no. She loved Mr. Barrett. It were obvious to anyone who cared to look."

"Dulcie, do you work for the Barretts only at Rose Cottage, or do you also serve them at their home in Brentwood?"

"I work for them all year round."

"And did Mrs. Barrett have a lady's maid?" Daniel asked. A lady's maid knew more than anyone about her mistress's private life, whether she cared to or not, and would be an excellent source of information.

"Mrs. Barrett has...*had* a lady's maid in town, but she never brought her to Birch Hill. She thought of the village as a place to be free. She didn't entertain during the summer months."

"Surely there were some visitors to the house," Daniel suggested.

"Well, Mrs. Silver 'ad come to stay. First week of April, that were, and she'd accompanied the master and mistress to Birch Hill. She were widowed last autumn, but it'd taken 'er till April to sort out 'er husband's affairs. She weren't really a visitor, as such."

Daniel cast his mind back to his visit to Rose Cottage. Deborah Silver had not been wearing mourning colors when he'd met her yesterday. In fact, she'd worn a fashionable gown in a soft shade of peach that brought out her youthful complexion and complemented her fair hair. She was a few years older than her sister had been, at least thirty, in his estimation, but she was still an attractive woman who might wish to remarry should an opportunity present itself.

"Were they close, Mrs. Barrett and Mrs. Silver?" Jason asked.

"Oh, yes. Mrs. Barrett was very pleased to have 'er sister come to stay. And Olly too."

"Sorry, who's Olly?" Daniel asked.

"Mrs. Silver's son. 'E just went off to school last week. 'E's a sweet lad. Quiet," Dulcie added. "Likes to sit in the garden and watch the birds."

"Was there anyone else who'd spent time at the house?" Daniel asked. "Friends, perhaps?"

Dulcie looked thoughtful, her round face pink with concentration. She no longer seemed nervous, only eager to be of help. "Well, there was Mr. Arthur Barrett, Mr. Barrett's brother. 'E came down once or twice, but 'e's not fond of the country. 'E's always saying so. And Mr. Sullivan, of course."

"And who is he?" Jason asked.

"Mrs. Barrett's art teacher. She started out painting for pleasure, as many young ladies do, but she had ass-parations. She wanted to see her work displayed alongside the greats of the age," Dulcie said, clearly repeating a phrase she'd heard from her mistress.

"Tell us about Mr. Sullivan. What's he like?" Daniel prompted.

"'E's nice, I s'pose. Young. Shy," Dulcie added with a smile. "I think 'e fancied Mrs. Barrett something awful."

"Really?" Daniel and Jason asked in unison.

"Oh, yes. She thought it charming. She told Mrs. Silver to be kind to 'im and not to eh…belittle 'is feelings."

"So, Mrs. Barrett knew the young man cared for her?" Jason asked.

"She knew. I think she enjoyed 'is attentions, but she never encouraged 'im, mind. She always behaved with the utmost propriety," Dulcie said, once again mimicking someone else, possibly Deborah Silver.

"How do you know nothing untoward happened when they were alone together?" Daniel asked.

"I know because Mrs. Barrett always left the door open when Mr. Sullivan were there, and I often brought them refreshments when they took a break from painting and spoke of art and the like."

"Is there anyone else you can think of? Did Mrs. Barrett have any female friends?" Daniel asked.

"Some ladies came to call, but they weren't particular friends of Mrs. Barrett's. They was the wives of Mr. Barrett's associates, so Mrs. Barrett had to receive them. She were always happy when they left. She said they bored 'er senseless."

"Dulcie, can you think of anyone who'd wish to harm your mistress?" Jason asked.

Dulcie shook her head. "No, I can't," she said, and promptly burst into tears, effectively ending the interview.

After the Wells women had gone, Fanny cleared away the tea things and added coal to the fire. It had grown considerably colder outside, a fact Jason remarked on with disbelief.

"September is still summer in New York," he said as he moved his chair closer to the fire. "But then again, what passes for summer here is nothing like what I'm used to. It's cold and damp and dreary."

"Was summer so much more pleasant in New York?" Daniel asked, wondering, not for the first time, what America was like.

Jason laughed. "No. It was hot, humid, and sticky. Anyone who could afford it went north for the summer months."

"Did you go north? Before the war, I mean?" Daniel asked.

"Yes. My fiancée's father owned a summer cottage in Rhode Island. We had some wonderful times there," he added wistfully.

Jason had never spoken of his fiancée before, and Daniel was tempted to ask what had happened to end the engagement but decided not to pry. Clearly, things hadn't worked out, or Jason wouldn't be here on his own.

"Cecilia married my best friend while I was in prison," Jason suddenly said. "She and Mark were expecting their first child by the time I returned home." Daniel could see the hurt in his eyes. The betrayal still stung. "Anyway, what are your thoughts regarding this murder?" Jason asked, abruptly changing the subject.

"The art teacher sounds promising. If he was in love with Elizabeth Barrett and she rejected him, he might have retaliated by murdering her."

"Yes, that's certainly a possibility. Unless she returned his feelings," Jason pointed out.

"Might the child have been his?" Daniel speculated.

"We'll never know for certain, but it's entirely possible that Jonathan Barrett thought so. He might have killed her to prevent her from foisting her lover's child on him."

Daniel sighed. "It would have been a fortuitous coincidence if I'd seen his name in one of the ledgers at the chemists' shops I visited this morning, but alas, no such luck. Of course, he could have easily used an alias, as I did when purchasing arsenic at three different shops."

"You used a fake name?" Jason asked, clearly amused.

"No point in bringing attention to myself," Daniel replied. "There are so many arsenic-related deaths that noticing the same name, on the same date, in three separate ledgers would virtually guarantee I'd hang for something."

"Very clever of you," Jason said, still grinning. "Did you use the same name three times, or did you invent a new identity for each shop?"

Daniel felt heat rising in his cheeks. "I made up a new name at each establishment. I'm not proud of myself, being a former policeman, mind you."

"You did the wrong thing for the right reason. What did you do with the arsenic?"

"I labeled it and stowed it on a hard-to-reach shelf in the potting shed."

"Good man. So, how do you intend to proceed?" Jason asked. He stretched out his legs, bringing the heels of his boots dangerously close to the fire.

"Tomorrow, I will go in search of Mr. Sullivan. I wish I knew his Christian name, but how many Sullivans can there be in Brentwood?"

"What makes you so sure he lives in Brentwood? He may have traveled here from London."

"Yes, that's a valid point," Daniel conceded. "I may have to hold off until I speak to Jonathan Barrett again. I was told not to call again until Monday."

"But I wasn't," Jason said. "I will pay a condolence call tomorrow afternoon and endeavor to speak to Mrs. Silver. She might be more forthcoming than the husband, especially if she was close to her sister. She'll know the name of the tutor, as well as where he can be located."

"You are a very useful man, Captain," Daniel said, rising to his feet. He was expected home for dinner.

"I'll keep you abreast of what I discover," Jason replied, a trifle sadly.

"Has this case upset you?" Daniel asked, wondering what was troubling his friend.

"As a surgeon, I'm accustomed to death. It's life that's sometimes difficult to deal with. I manage to keep busy during the day, but at night, once the servants retire and Micah goes to bed, the house gets very quiet and lonely. I never enter most of the rooms, haven't done since I first arrived. I have no need of them, and they're eerie in their silence, the furniture and paintings relics of a time when my grandfather was a young man. The rooms are teeming with memories and are filled with shrouded antiques, but they're not my memories, nor my possessions."

"Perhaps it's time you redecorated," Daniel suggested. "It's your house now."

"I know, but sometimes I feel like an impostor, someone who's here by an accident of birth."

"Jason, all of us are where we are in life because of an accident of birth. I might have been born to a prostitute in Seven Dials and grown up to be a thief who loathes the police, and you might have been born to a plantation owner and would have fought for the South instead of the North and valued an entirely different set of principles. Embrace your good fortune," Daniel suggested as they walked toward the door. "And perhaps find a good woman to keep you company."

Jason chuckled at the suggestion. "Perhaps I will, but for the moment, I will have to content myself with the company of Mrs. Dodson."

Chapter 10

Once Daniel departed, Jason crossed the foyer to the green baize door that would take him to Mrs. Dodson's subterranean domain. It was nice and toasty in the cavernous kitchen and smelled of freshly baked sponge cake and cloves. Jason sat at the scrubbed pine table, making sure he wasn't in the way of dinner preparations. Mrs. Dodson gave him a deeply suspicious look as she continued to peel potatoes, the knife moving over the spuds with practiced ease.

"Master Micah says he's hungry," she finally said.

"He can have a boiled egg, dry toast, and sweet tea for dinner," Jason replied. "I'll know if you have snuck him something you shouldn't have, Mrs. D."

"But he's feeling so much better, the poor lamb," she protested.

"And I'd like to keep it that way. One day of bland food will not harm him."

"If you say so," she muttered under her breath. "I hope you plan on eating. I'm making chops and mash."

"Sounds delightful," Jason said, even though he wasn't the least bit hungry. "The sponge was delicious."

Mrs. Dodson's cheeks grew rosy with pleasure. "Glad you liked it."

"Did you make an extra cake for your own guests?" Jason asked, wondering what the ever-resourceful Mrs. D had used to loosen Dulcie's tongue.

"I may have."

"Come now," Jason said, giving her his most winsome smile. "Don't make me beg. You know why I'm here."

Mrs. Dodson let out a throaty laugh and nodded sagely. "Oh, aye, I know why you're here, Captain."

"Well, then. Did you learn anything useful from Dulcie?"

"Depends on what you consider useful. The poor girl's terrified of losing her position should Mr. Barrett get wind she's been fraternizing, so to speak. No one wants a servant they can't rely on for discretion."

Jason thought that if most employers valued discretion above all else, they'd have to fend for themselves, since few servants ever refrained from belowstairs gossip. They tended to know more of what went on within a family than the family members themselves.

"Now, I know what you're thinking," Mrs. Dodson said, skewering him with her knowing gaze. "Servants will gossip. Aye, that's true. But there's a world of difference between talking to other servants and giving information to the police. That's a breach of confidence, you might say," she said gravely. "Punishable by sacking without a character. Dulcie took a great risk in speaking to you tonight."

Jason nodded, feeling appropriately chastised. Mrs. Dodson was right; Jonathan Barrett could hardly dismiss Dulcie for having tea with her mother's oldest friend, but he could and would dismiss her if he found out that Dulcie had willingly spoken to the constable, and would most likely refuse to provide her with a character reference that would allow her to find another position.

"I will offer Dulcie a place here if she loses her job," Jason said. "I won't allow her to suffer because of me."

"Oh, is that so? I thought you didn't need any more staff," Mrs. Dodson said archly.

That was the first time she'd made a reference to Jason's reluctance to hire proper staff, something that Dodson had moaned about from the beginning. Jason sighed. Did two people really need a staff of ten to look after them? He studied Mrs. Dodson's plump face, not quite sure what had brought on her pique. She'd been the one to suggest inviting Patricia and Dulcie Wells for tea with the express purpose of learning something that might be of help in solving the case, but now she was carrying on as if he'd somehow pressured Dulcie into coming and in the process had exposed Mrs. Dodson to ridicule because she didn't have a kitchen staff to order around.

"Mrs. Dodson, if you feel you need help in the kitchen, then, by all means, find someone you think is suitable," Jason replied in a conciliatory manner.

Mrs. Dodson made a low noise in her throat. "Well, I could use a scullion," she finally said, tearing her gaze away from the potatoes at last. "It's a lot to be getting on with." She made an expansive gesture using the knife as a pointer. "I'm getting on in years."

Jason wasn't quite sure what a scullion was, but he assumed it was someone who helped in the kitchen, and he was more than happy to provide Mrs. Dodson with one. It was a small price to pay for keeping her happy. His mother had always said that the kitchen was the heart of the house, and at Redmond Hall, Mrs. Dodson was the heart of the kitchen.

"All right. Now that the question of the scullion has been settled, can we return to the subject at hand?" he asked, catching a small smile tugging at Mrs. Dodson's lips. "Elizabeth Barrett has been dead for nearly two days and we have no leads to speak of. By all accounts, she was a lovely woman who was liked by everyone, adored by her husband, admired by her art tutor, and cared for deeply by her sister. Why would anyone kill such a paragon of virtue?"

Mrs. Dodson shrugged. "I'm afraid there isn't much I can tell you that you don't already know. According to Dulcie, the Barretts were happily married, not that she'd know a happy marriage if she fell over one. Her parents are happiest when they're at the opposite ends of the village, as are her brother and his wife."

"Did she mention the art teacher?" Jason asked. "Was there more to that relationship?"

"Not really. Dulcie said Mrs. Barrett loved to paint and was pleased with the man's tutelage."

"Surely there must be someone she didn't get on with."

"Not that I know of."

"What about the husband? Did he have enemies? Debts?" Jason asked. He knew he was getting a bit desperate, but surely the Barretts had some problems in their life. Most people did.

"Do you think she's clairvoyant?" Mrs. Dodson asked reproachfully.

"Did she say anything about the sister?" Jason persisted.

Mrs. Dodson immediately brightened. "That she did. Said Mr. Silver passed suddenly last September, just after Mrs. Silver had returned home to Oxford from visiting her sister. Must have been quite a shock."

"Did Dulcie say how he died?"

"No, she didn't. She'd never met the man, so wasn't too interested, I reckon," Mrs. Dodson said. She had quartered the potatoes and dropped them into a pot of boiling water before turning her attention to the chops.

"And Mrs. Silver? Does she still reside in Oxford?" Jason inquired.

"No. Had to get away from her shame, didn't she?" Mrs. Dodson replied spitefully.

"What shame? Did she have an affair? Did he?" Jason prompted.

"No, nothing like that," Mrs. Dodson replied, flicking a plump hand to punctuate the statement. "Some men gamble or spend money on whores; well, this one fancied himself a medieval scholar. Liked to collect ancient manuscripts. Mrs. Silver thought she'd be comfortably off in her widowhood, but the reality proved to be quite different. Her husband had spent everything they had and then borrowed money to acquire some illuminated manuscript from the twelfth century. Imagine that, wasting your son's inheritance on some moldy old book. When they came, the bailiffs took everything, and the house had to be sold to cover the debts. The poor woman hid some of her jewelry to keep it from being taken off her. Came to Rose Cottage with little more than the clothes on her back."

"What about the manuscripts? Did their sale not offset the debt?" Jason asked, intrigued by the story.

Mrs. Dodson scoffed. "The daft sot left the manuscripts to some library in Oxford. His life's work, he called it in his will."

"The Bodleian library?" Jason asked.

"How should I know? All I know is that he left his family in dire straits."

"And how does Dulcie know all this?" Jason asked.

"Overheard it while serving tea to Mrs. Barrett and Mrs. Silver, didn't she? Mrs. Silver were crying her heart out, Dulcie said. Ashamed to throw herself on her brother-in-law's mercy. Of course, once Mr. Barrett heard of her predicament, he offered her a home and even settled an allowance on her, so she wouldn't feel so dependent on him."

"That's kind."

"He's a kind man, by all accounts, and generous. Gave Dulcie a silver brooch for Boxing Day last year and gave the cook a fortnight's worth of wages and time off so she could go visit her dying mother in Colchester."

"Mrs. Dodson, that is not helpful," Jason said, rising to his feet and sighing with disappointment.

"No, I don't suppose it is, but I won't go making things up. The poor man has just lost his wife. He's got enough to contend with at the moment. I won't go blackening his character."

Jason nodded. "Do you think you can save those chops for tomorrow?"

"What? Why?"

"I have no appetite for dinner," Jason replied.

"Suit yourself, but know you'll be having them for luncheon tomorrow."

"I'll look forward to it. Thank you, Mrs. D."

Jason left the kitchen and returned to the main part of the house. He was glad Mrs. Dodson felt comfortable talking to him. Unlike her husband, who always stood on ceremony, she'd taken on the role of surrogate mother to both Jason and Micah and spoiled them at every opportunity. She probably found it a little strange that the lord of the manor came down to the kitchen for friendly chats, but never seemed to mind, talking to Jason as if they were equals rather than servant and master. She instinctively understood that was what he needed. He missed his own mother, whom he had always been able to talk to and ask for advice, but she was gone, buried next to his father at the Trinity Church graveyard in New York. In some ways, he was as alone in the world as Micah was.

Instead of returning to the drawing room, Jason headed up the stairs and quietly entered Micah's room. The light from the gas lamp cast a golden glow on Micah's freckled face. He was fast asleep, his red hair tousled from tossing and turning. Jason gently touched his cheek, then turned off the lamp and retired to his own room, where he pulled open the curtains that Fanny kept insisting on drawing as soon as it grew dark. He liked to see the nighttime sky when he woke during the night, which he did nearly every night.

The nightmares had abated somewhat since his arrival in England, but from time to time, he still dreamed of the prison and woke in a cold sweat, his stomach contracting with imaginary hunger, a sense of untold dread weighing down his soul. He could still see the sightless eyes of the men he'd failed to save and smell the ever-present stench of death that had permeated the camp. Never before had he seen such depth of human despair, and he prayed that he wouldn't see it ever again. He hoped, in time, that Micah would be able to forget the horrors he'd witnessed and truly get on with his life, but he still woke crying in the night and sometimes crawled into Jason's bed in the small hours, pressing himself to Jason's body for comfort and warmth. Jason usually carried Micah back to his own bed before dawn to spare him embarrassment come morning, but he understood only too well and was glad he could help at least one person.

It was too early to go to sleep, so he lay on the bed and reached for the periodical he'd left on the bedside table, eager to read the next chapter of *The Moonstone*. He briefly wondered if Katherine was reading it as well and wished she'd have sent him a reply with Henley. He'd endeavor to see her tomorrow. It'd been way too long.

Chapter 11

Sunday, September 9

Sunday morning dawned gray and wet. An impenetrable mist enveloped the grounds, the trees at the edge of the lawn nothing more than menacing shadows. Jason reached for his watch and flipped it open. Nearly eight o'clock. It was time to get going. He got out of bed, pulled on his dressing gown, ignored the slippers that Fanny kept leaving by the bed, and went through to Micah's room, his bare feet silent on the polished wood floor. Micah was awake, but he lay huddled under the covers that were pulled up to his chin.

"Are you all right?" Jason asked, concerned. He sat on the side of the bed and laid his palm on Micah's forehead. He wasn't fevered, and the room wasn't that cold.

"Can we skip Mass today?" Micah asked in a small voice.

Despite being a Protestant himself, Jason took Micah to a Catholic Mass in Brentwood every Sunday, believing that Micah's need was greater than his own. He'd given up on God a long time ago, but kept his opinions to himself, especially around the boy, who seemed to find peace in the familiar rhythm of the Latin prayers and the presence of a statue of the Virgin that he always stopped in front of before leaving the church.

"Are you still feeling ill? If your stomach still hurts, then maybe it's not just an upset," Jason said, cursing himself inwardly for not examining Micah more thoroughly. He hoped he hadn't missed signs of appendicitis.

"I'm all right," Micah replied. "My stomach doesn't hurt anymore."

"So, why don't you want to go to Mass?"

Micah's eyes filled with tears. "I've been praying and praying, asking God to restore Mary to me, but she's gone, isn't she? She's dead, just like the rest of them, and I'm all alone. God doesn't care what happens to me, just like he didn't care about all those men that died in prison and on the battlefields. They prayed too. I heard them. They prayed as they lay dying. Well, I'm through praying. Whatever happens is going to happen anyway."

"That's rather a grim view, but I won't force you to do anything you don't want to do. When you feel like going to church, you tell me."

Micah's eyes brightened. "You won't make me do anything I don't want to do?"

"No."

"Then I don't want a tutor."

"Yes, you do. You just don't know it yet," Jason replied with a smile.

"How do you figure?"

"You like learning; I know you do. You just need someone who'll make it more interesting than I do."

"I don't mind learning about history and stuff, but I hate doing sums."

"I know, but you need to learn some mathematics."

"Why?" Micah whined.

"Because you must be able to figure out how far your money will go, or if someone has given you the correct change, or is charging you a fair price. You'll be an adult one day, and you'll have to learn how to fend for yourself."

"Won't you be there anymore?" Micah asked, his gaze growing fearful once again.

"I will always be there for you, but I don't think you'll want me managing your affairs when you're a grown man."

"I'll still want your advice."

"And you'll have it. Always."

Micah seemed to relax a little. "I think you should go to church by yourself."

"I don't want to leave you alone."

"I'm not alone. I have Mrs. Dodson, and Fanny," Micah added with a dreamy smile. "She's pretty."

"Yes, I suppose she is."

"Miss Talbot is pretty too, in a bookish sort of way. You'll see her if you go to church. I know you want to."

"All right. I will. But first, we'll have breakfast together. Are you up to some eggs and sausages?"

"Yes!" Micah exclaimed. "I'm starving. I promise not to gorge myself on tarts again," he added, his expression contrite.

"I hope you've learned your lesson."

"I have," Micah promised.

"Good. Now wash up, get dressed, and I'll meet you downstairs in fifteen minutes," Jason said, thinking he needed to shave if he were to attend the service, and he meant to do it himself. He didn't trust Henley with a cutthroat razor, not if the man had indulged in drink the night before.

Micah bounced out of bed as soon as Jason stood, racing toward the water closet they shared. "Beat you to it," he called out as he slammed the door. Jason chuckled softly and returned to his room, where he rang for Henley.

"Good morning, sir," Henley said cheerfully as he entered the room.

Jason studied the man, wondering if he was trying to cover up a hangover, but Henley looked bright-eyed and energetic.

"I'm going to church. Please lay out my clothes while I shave."

"I'd be happy to shave you, sir."

"I can manage. Just the clothes, please."

Henley nodded and sprang into action, yanking open the doors to the wardrobe with single-minded determination.

The sermon was mind-numbingly dull, but Jason would expect nothing less from Reverend Talbot. The man had been offered the parish thanks to the goodwill of his cousin, Squire Talbot, in whose gift it was to offer it to a relative. Reverend Talbot droned on and on, nearly putting even the most zealous churchgoers to sleep. Katherine Talbot sat in the third pew near the aisle, her head turned toward the pulpit as she listened attentively. Jason wished he could catch a glimpse of her face, but her wide-brimmed bonnet hid it from view. Katherine hadn't noticed him since he'd come in just in time for the service and taken a seat toward the back. His gaze strayed to her frequently, caressing the slender neck that was just visible above the modest lace collar and the slender shoulders that drooped with either boredom or fatigue.

Once the service was finally over, Reverend Talbot left the lectern and walked toward the door, where he would speak to the parishioners as they departed. Members of the congregation filed out of the church, eager to get home and enjoy their Sunday dinner, but Jason stayed behind, hoping to catch Katherine alone. She straightened the altar cloth, collected her father's notes from the lectern, and righted an arrangement of flowers that had tilted to one side; only then did she turn around and see him. Her reaction sent Jason's heart aflutter. At first, her face lit up with a joyous smile, then she blushed furiously and looked down at the floor, clearly needing a moment to compose herself. When she looked back up, the smile was demure, the blush fading, but the look in her eyes told him everything he needed to know. She was happy to see him, nervous to be in his presence, and pleased that he'd waited for her.

"Captain Redmond," she said, holding out her hand.

Jason took it and brought it to his lips. "Miss Talbot. I trust your aunt is well?"

"She's well. Thank you. To be honest, it was all a bit of a ruse," Katherine confessed as they stood together in the empty nave.

"A ruse? How so?"

"My aunt gets *ill* from time to time, simply to give me an excuse to visit. Were she simply to invite me, father would never let me go, citing my duty to him and his parishioners, but he can hardly refuse the summons of a sick relative. Aunt Vera is my mother's sister, you see, so she's—"

"Nothing like your father," Jason finished for her.

Katherine nodded, blushing again. "We have a most diverting time together. Father doesn't know this, of course, but we went to Brighton for a few days. Oh, it was lovely. We walked by the sea every day," Katherine said dreamily.

"I'm glad you enjoyed yourself. You deserve a holiday."

"That's what Aunt Vera says. She always manages to become unwell during the summer, so we can enjoy an adventure while the weather is pleasant. And how have you been, Captain? And Micah?"

"We are both well. A bit bored rattling around that empty mansion."

"Yes, it can get lonely when there's no one to talk to," Katherine agreed. "I find reading to be such a comfort." She looked up at him, her eyes sparkling with mischief. "Thank you for the periodicals. I stayed up half the night yesterday. My goodness, what a story! Do you have the rest?"

"I'm in possession of two new issues."

"When you're done with them, perhaps you can send them on to me," Katherine said shyly.

"I'll do better than that. I will bring them in person. Will you be visiting the sick on Tuesday and Thursday, as before?"

"Yes," Katherine said softly. "I'll be paying a call on Mrs. Galen on Tuesday. She's been poorly."

"Shall I come see her, in my professional capacity?"

"There's no need, I don't think. She's just lonely after her husband passed and needs a bit of cheering up. And after that, I'll stop in at the Caulfields'. Mrs. Caulfield is due any day now and could use a hand with the twins. They're only two, and absolute terrors. I should be finished by three o'clock."

"Then I will meet you in the lane at three," Jason said, smiling down at her.

"Three o'clock," Katherine whispered just as Revered Talbot reentered the church, having seen everyone off.

"Katherine, I need you back at the vicarage," he said rather loudly. "It's time for luncheon."

"Yes, Father. Good day, Captain."

"Good day, Miss Talbot. It was a pleasure to run into you," Jason said, loudly enough for the Reverend to hear and assume they'd met by accident rather than by design.

He watched as Katherine followed her father down the nave and toward the vestry, her head held high, her shoulders tense. She might not be American, but he'd make a rebel of her yet.

Chapter 12

After lunch with Micah, Jason headed out to pay the condolence call. He wasn't sure what the proper protocol was for such matters in England, but he didn't think he'd be turned away at the door. He may have been had he still been plain Mr. Redmond, but now that he was Lord Redmond, doors opened for him before he even bothered to knock. Jason had never asked for his title. The only title he'd ever wished for had been that of Dr. Redmond, and he had been happy with that until he'd joined the army at the onset of the Civil War and eventually become Captain Redmond.

He'd never expected to be anything more since his father had turned his back on his own father and the Redmond estate when he'd fallen in love with an American and followed her to New York nearly thirty years before. He would have been the one to inherit the title when Giles Redmond finally gave up the ghost, but Geoffrey Redmond and his wife had died in a railway accident three years before, leaving Jason saddled with his grandfather's sizable estate. Jason's initial plan had been to sell the lot and return home, but he found that he was enjoying his stay in England and saw no reason to hurry back. No, he'd remain in England a little while longer, especially if he found a way to openly court the charming Miss Talbot.

Jason glanced out the window of the elegant brougham, glad he was safe from the pouring rain. It rained way too often in this country. That was probably what made it so green and lush, he mused, as the brougham pulled up to Rose Cottage. He walked the short distance to the door, glad he'd remembered to bring his umbrella this time. The black crepe bow was limp with rain, the lovely roses nodding their heads and dripping as if crying for the loss of their mistress. Jason knocked on the door and hoped it would be answered by someone other than Dulcie, but luck was not on his side.

"Good afternoon," he said when an abashed Dulcie opened the door. "I'd like to offer my condolences to Mr. Barrett and Mrs. Silver." Dulcie looked as if she were going to be sick.

"I won't mention that we spoke," Jason said under his breath. "We've never met, you and I, not before today."

Dulcie nodded and finally allowed him in out of the rain, leaving him to wait in the foyer while she went to announce him. Less than a minute later, Dulcie invited him to follow her to the parlor, where Jonathan Barrett and Deborah Silver stood poised to meet him.

"Lord Redmond," Mr. Barrett said solemnly. "You honor us."

"Lord Redmond," Mrs. Silver said demurely. "Please, won't you have a seat. Will you take a dish of tea?"

"Thank you, yes."

While Mrs. Silver rang for tea, Jason surveyed the room and observed his hosts. The house was already rigged out for mourning, the drapes closed against whatever feeble light managed to penetrate the gloom on this dreary day. A heavy gilded mirror was covered with a length of black crepe, as was a framed photograph that stood on the mantel. Jason had no doubt that black-bordered death announcements had already been ordered and would be in the mail as soon as they were delivered by the printer. Both Mr. Barrett and Mrs. Silver were decked out in unrelieved black, the drab color doing little to dull their good looks.

Since Jason hadn't met Jonathan Barrett when he'd come to collect his wife's body, he was eager to make the man's acquaintance and take his measure. He was a handsome man, and surprisingly fit for someone who spent his days sitting behind a desk. His shoulders were slightly stooped with grief, and he looked somewhat bewildered, either by the death of his wife or by Jason's visit. Perhaps a bit of both.

Mrs. Silver was attractive as well, despite the red-rimmed eyes and haunted gaze of the newly bereaved, her good looks not in the least diminished by the high-necked black silk gown she wore. The overall impression Jason got was that of soft femininity and charm.

"I know we haven't had the pleasure of meeting in the past, but I wished to offer my deepest sympathies on the death of Mrs. Barrett," Jason said. "Having been called to examine her remains, I feel a particular connection with the victim."

Jonathan Barrett winced at Jason's choice of words, but quickly schooled his features into an expression of bland civility. "Thank you, my lord. Very kind of you. My wife would have been grateful that her privacy has been respected."

Dulcie brought in the tea and Mrs. Silver poured, her hand shaking ever so slightly in her distress. "Milk and sugar?" Mrs. Silver asked Jason.

"Just sugar," Jason replied, and accepted the cup she passed him. "The real reason for my call," he began, "is that I'm assisting Constable Haze in the investigation and was hoping you might permit a few questions."

Had Jason not been titled, he was sure Jonathan Barrett would have thrown him out then and there, but the man did an admirable job of controlling his temper. "Of course. Whatever we can do to help," he said, his voice tight with suppressed irritation.

Jason nodded his thanks. "Is there anyone who would profit from your wife's death?"

"Profit? She was set upon by some passing ruffian and robbed. Her sapphire ring was taken," Jonathan Barrett sputtered angrily. "I'm sure the rogue will profit by selling it, if that's what you mean."

"Mr. Barrett, your wife was poisoned. I hardly think it was a random attack. Whoever wished her dead was well known to her."

"And who might that be?" Jonathan Barrett exclaimed, his voice rising by an octave.

"That's what I mean to find out. Did she have any enemies?"

"God, no," Mrs. Silver chimed in. "Elizabeth was the kindest, most caring person I've ever known."

"You have a brother, do you not, Mr. Barrett?" Jason asked, clearly surprising the man with his question.

"Yes. Why do you ask?"

"Younger or older?"

"Younger."

"Might your younger brother have been threatened by the prospect of an heir?"

Jonathan Barrett's face went slack, as if he'd just suffered a stroke. "An heir?" he choked out. "Are you suggesting that Elizabeth was with child?" He seemed to be struggling for breath and pulled at his collar as if it were choking him.

"I'm sorry, Mr. Barrett," Jason said, genuinely contrite. "Did you not know?"

Tears filled Jonathan Barrett's eyes and he looked helplessly at Deborah, whose face had turned ashen. She held out a hand and he grasped it, squeezing her fingers tightly.

"I did not know," he croaked. "How long?"

"She was about four months along," Jason replied softly, wishing he hadn't blundered so.

"You... You examined her?" Barrett stammered. "You had no right."

"I needed to determine the cause of death and check whether she had been violated by the murderer. Had she been found in Brentwood, she would have been examined by a police surgeon, who would have performed a postmortem despite your objections."

"Are you suggesting I should be grateful you didn't cut her up before I got there?" Jonathan Barrett asked, barely controlling his temper.

"Mr. Barrett, I only performed the most basic of examinations to try to determine what led to your wife's death. She was a healthy young woman who had died suddenly. I assumed,

86

mistakenly perhaps, that you'd wish to know what killed her," Jason said, trying to coax Jonathan Barrett out of his anger.

"Did she suffer?" he asked, the fight going out of him.

"Very briefly. She would have felt confused and nauseated, and possibly experienced a terrible headache and a pain in her abdomen. This particular poison acts quickly, so she wouldn't have had time to feel truly scared."

"She was all alone in that dreadful place," Deborah Silver whispered. "My poor Lizzie."

"Elizabeth thought the ruins were beautiful," Jonathan Barrett said wistfully. "She died on what would have been consecrated ground."

Jason made a mental note of that remark. The abbey had been a Catholic institution, which suggested that the Barretts were Catholic. That would explain why they didn't worship at St. Catherine's when in Birch Hill and traveled to Brentwood instead. He cast his mind over the times he'd taken Micah to the Catholic Mass, trying to recall if he'd seen them. He may have, but he hadn't been paying attention. He tended to bring a book and read discreetly during the service, since he had little interest in listening to it.

Jonathan Barrett set down his cup and stood. "If you will excuse me, Lord Redmond. I'm afraid I feel unwell."

Jason stood too. "Again, I'm sorry for your loss." Jonathan Barrett inclined his head in acknowledgement and left the room.

"May I ask you a few questions, Mrs. Silver?" Jason resumed his seat.

"Of course. Whatever I can do to help find whoever did this," Deborah Silver exclaimed. She leaned forward in her seat, her expression eager. Jason noticed a hint of distinctly feminine interest in her eyes. As an unmarried man of position and wealth, he was becoming accustomed to being sized up as potential husband material.

87

"Did your sister associate with anyone regularly? Did she have any particular friends?" he asked, hoping the tutor would come up.

Deborah shook her head. "Elizabeth often entertained Jonathan's friends. Their wives and daughters came to call, and she called on them as well, but she didn't enjoy their company. She said they were too stodgy, too closed off to new ideas. Lizzie was a free spirit. She hated feeling hemmed in." Deborah smiled wryly. "Quite a predicament in a society that does its best to control every aspect of a woman's life from the moment she's born."

"Yes," Jason agreed. "She must have found it frustrating."

"She did. She did have one friend she could commiserate with. Jane Dawlish. A born spinster, if I ever saw one. Lizzie sometimes had Jane to tea. They liked to discuss art, but I suspect they spoke of other things when Lizzie went to visit Jane in her lodgings."

"Is Jane Dawlish an artist as well?"

"More an admirer of art than an artist. She is quite a gifted musician, though. Pianoforte. She played for us once. I found her performance quite moving."

"Would Jane have had any reason to want to see Elizabeth dead? Would Elizabeth have stopped spending time with her once she became a mother?"

"I don't think so. Lizzie wasn't like that. She was devoted to the people she cared about, and Jane was someone she could be completely herself with."

"Could she not be herself with you?" Jason asked.

Deborah's eyes misted with tears. "Older sisters can be as demanding as mothers at times, and having lost our mother when Lizzie was just twelve, I think she always viewed me as a sort of amalgam of the two, since it was up to me to guide her through some of the most confusing and difficult years of her life."

"Was she often unhappy?"

"Not at all. She loved Jonathan, and he adored her. As you can see, he gave her free rein. She came and went as she pleased, without having to account to her husband, as most married women do. Jonathan even supported her artistic endeavors and engaged a tutor for her. Rather a tender-hearted young man."

"Can you provide me with his name and address?"

"Shawn Sullivan. I don't have his address, but Lizzie said he lived in Clerkenwell, I believe. He came to the house in Brentwood every Saturday by train."

"Did he ever come to Birch Hill?"

"Yes, he's been here several times."

"Would you say there was anything more than a pupil/tutor relationship between him and your sister?" Jason asked carefully.

"Shawn was in love with her. That was clear to anyone who cared to look. Even Jonathan knew it."

"Was he jealous? He seems to have a temper."

"He's grieving for his wife, Lord Redmond. Can you blame him for becoming overly emotional when asked such personal questions?"

"No, I suppose not, but you haven't answered my question," Jason reminded her.

"No, he wasn't jealous. He found Mr. Sullivan's devotion to Lizzie amusing. She liked Shawn and was kind to him, but it was the painting she was interested in, not the man."

"Could he have killed her because she'd rejected him?"

Deborah looked thoughtful. "I hadn't considered that. I guess we'll never know what someone will do when driven beyond the point of endurance. I suppose someone as emotional as Shawn Sullivan could be capable of anything, even taking the ring off her finger and selling it."

Or keeping it as a souvenir, Jason thought. "Mrs. Silver, did you know your sister was pregnant?" he asked, watching Deborah intently.

She smiled wistfully. "Yes, I did. She told me a week ago."

"Why hadn't she told her husband?"

"I normally wouldn't share such private information, but as you're a doctor, I suppose it can do no harm. Lizzie married Jonathan when she was just seventeen. It took her nearly four years to conceive the first time, and she miscarried soon after. The second pregnancy lasted a little longer but ended in disappointment. This was the third time Lizzie had become pregnant. She didn't want to break Jonathan's heart should this one end the same as the others. She wished to wait and swore me to secrecy. She was going to tell him once we'd returned to Brentwood and she had seen her physician."

"I see. So, Mr. Barrett's brother wouldn't have known of it?"

"No."

"Did he come to the house often?" Jason asked.

"Who, Arthur? Yes, I suppose he did. He and Jonathan would talk business and then he'd stay for dinner."

"Is Arthur Barrett married?"

"No, he isn't. A confirmed bachelor, that one."

"What was his relationship with Elizabeth like?"

Deborah wagged her finger at him playfully. "Now, your lordship, you're trying to trick me into speaking ill of my sister, and I won't."

Jason cocked his head to the side, taken aback by Deborah's answer. Was she suggesting that Elizabeth Barrett had been carrying on with her brother-in-law, or was she simply offended by the intrusive nature of his questions? He was fishing for information; that was true, but since Deborah was on to him, Jason didn't think she'd clarify, so he let the matter drop.

"Well, I've taken up enough of your time. Thank you for speaking with me, Mrs. Silver."

"I would be happy to speak with you anytime, your lordship," Deborah replied coyly. "If you're ever in Brentwood, do call on us."

"Will you continue to reside with your brother-in-law?" Jason asked as he stood to leave.

"Unfortunately, I have no place to go. My husband left me destitute, so it will be some time before I might be independent."

Jason waited for her to clarify. If she remarried, she certainly wouldn't be independent, and if what Mrs. Dodson had said was accurate, there was no money left from Mr. Silver's estate.

"I have an elderly aunt, you see," Deborah said, lowering her voice as if telling him a secret. "She's quite well off, and I'm her favorite niece, so I have some hope, faint as it is, of getting on my feet."

"I wish you well, then," Jason said, and stood to leave. He didn't think he'd discover anything more from Deborah Silver.

Chapter 13

Once back at home, Jason retired to the drawing room, poured himself a brandy, and settled before the fire to consider what he had learned. Jonathan Barrett had seemed genuinely shocked when he'd heard about the pregnancy, so it wasn't likely that he'd killed his wife because he doubted the paternity of her child. Despite his outrage, which was natural given the circumstances and suddenness of her death, Jason didn't think the man had killed his wife. He seemed shattered by his loss, but it was also possible that he could be grieving the woman he'd fallen in love with and married and not the woman Elizabeth Barrett had become.

Then again, killing, even government-sponsored killing, did strange things to men. Jason wouldn't have thought so before the war, but time and again, he'd seen how easily some soldiers managed to disassociate themselves from the atrocities they committed in the name of their cause and allowed their crimes to spill onto the civilian population, especially the womenfolk, who had every reason to fear when detachments of enemy soldiers were nearby. Despite his obvious distress, Jonathan Barrett couldn't be completely ruled out, but Jason's gut instinct told him Barrett wasn't their man.

Who, then? There was the tutor, who came to the house at least once a week and may have been rejected by Elizabeth Barrett. Both Dulcie and Deborah Silver had mentioned that Shawn Sullivan had been in love with Elizabeth and thought him an emotional young man. Emotional could be synonymous with volatile. And then there was the brother-in-law, about whom Deborah Silver had been surprisingly tight-lipped.

Might Elizabeth have had feelings for Arthur Barrett? He was the younger brother, therefore automatically less desirable than Jonathan Barrett, who would have inherited the family estate when his father passed. Elizabeth's father might have pressured her into marrying the older brother against her wishes, but that was neither here nor there. Jason had no proof that Elizabeth had loved, or even liked, her brother-in-law. Perhaps he'd been in love with her and had made things difficult by refusing to accept her loyalty to Jonathan. Again, mere speculation based on one careless comment.

Deborah Silver seemed genuinely devoted to her sister and probably had no wish to tarnish her memory. Some people hungered for justice, while others only wanted to protect the dead from posthumous scandal and get on with their lives as soon as their loved ones were decently buried. Given that Deborah was widowed and still of marriageable and childbearing age, she wouldn't want her family tainted by scandal, not when she might have hopes of attracting the attention of an eligible bachelor. Perhaps Jonathan Barrett had friends or business associates who were either still unmarried or widowed and who might pass on someone as charming and attractive as Deborah Silver if unsavory details about her sister's life came to light.

And then there was the friend—Jane Dawlish. Would she have had any reason to kill Elizabeth Barrett? Could she have come to Birch Hill on Friday morning, killed Elizabeth, and returned to Brentwood before anyone realized she'd been there? People paid little attention to women, especially plain ones, and Deborah Silver's description of Jane Dawlish hadn't painted her in a flattering light. A born spinster, she'd called her. Jason immediately imagined some homely, whey-faced miss who had no wit or personality to speak of.

At any rate, there were now three new leads: Jane Dawlish, Shawn Sullivan, and Arthur Barrett. As much as he wished he could question them, Jason would have to pass the information on to Daniel Haze. After all, he was the parish constable, and this was his jurisdiction. It was up to him to conduct the official investigation.

I might have made a half-decent detective had I not chosen medicine, Jason thought as he downed his brandy. He enjoyed the mental challenge of an investigation. It was like a puzzle that needed to be solved, a riddle that had few clues. If only he could solve the disappearance of Mary Donovan. Perhaps he should have searched for her himself rather than delegating the task to an inquiry agent. Mr. Hartley had come with good references and had a high rate of success, according to the people Jason had consulted, but he'd made no headway into his investigation into the disappearance of Mary.

Jason would lose Micah for good if Mary ever turned up, but he was willing to bear the pain of the separation for the sake of the boy. He loved him and wanted more than anything for him to be happy. To be reunited with his sister was his fondest dream.

"Where are you, Mary?" Jason asked the silent room. Unsurprisingly, the room didn't answer.

Chapter 14

Monday, September 10

Daniel was surprised to discover that Sarah was already up and had breakfasted by the time he came down on Monday morning. He was usually up first. Sarah liked to sleep in.

"What's your plan for the day?" Daniel asked when Sarah came into the dining room to greet him and have a cup of tea to keep him company while he ate.

"Cook and I are making apple jam."

"Lovely," Daniel said. "I hope you'll let me have some before you store it all for the winter."

"Of course, you can have some. I got a bit overexcited and ordered an entire bushel of apples from John Caulfield when I saw him after church yesterday. Tilda took the delivery this morning. There are a number of sacks currently cluttering up the larder."

"Any chance of an apple and blackberry tart for tonight's pudding?" Daniel asked.

"A very good chance, I should think," Sarah replied playfully. "And what are your plans for today?"

"I fervently hope Captain Redmond was able to discover something of interest when he visited Rose Cottage yesterday. I'm afraid I have no leads to speak of."

Sarah smiled at him. "The captain is a very resourceful man. I wager he's full of news this morning."

"No doubt he would appreciate your faith in him, but there's only so much one can learn from grieving relatives," Daniel said, knowing from experience how reticent people could be when someone close to them died unexpectedly.

"I suppose you'll have to go over there and find out for yourself," Sarah said. Her cheeks were rosy, and Daniel was relieved to notice that the pain that had been in her eyes for so long seemed to have vanished sometime during their trip. Scotland had done her good. It'd done them both good. They'd never forget Felix or stop loving him, but it was time to move on, maybe even have another child. The thought of a baby tugged at Daniel's heartstrings. He longed to be a father again, but he hadn't brought up the subject with Sarah. He had to tread carefully and hope that she wasn't secretly taking precautions against another pregnancy.

"Well, I'm off," Daniel said as he pushed away his plate. "Looks to be a fine day."

"Thank God the rain has let up," Sarah said, glancing toward the window. "I'm always amazed by what a difference weather makes to one's mood."

Had it rained on Friday, Elizabeth Barrett might still be alive, Daniel thought. Or maybe not. Perhaps her killer would have found a different way of getting to her.

Daniel grabbed his umbrella from the stand by the door, just in case the weather turned, put on his hat, and headed out. He'd walk to Redmond Hall and see if Captain Redmond had been able to glean anything from the family. If not, he'd have to scramble to find some fresh leads. As of now, all he had was the art tutor.

Dodson didn't seem overly surprised when Daniel called at such an early hour. He showed him into the drawing room, which was becoming as familiar to Daniel as the one in his own house, and informed him that the captain would be with him presently. Captain Redmond arrived a few minutes later, looking a bit agitated.

"Are you all right, Jason?" Daniel asked.

"If you've ever tried to do sums with a pigheaded eleven-year-old, you wouldn't be asking me that."

Daniel chuckled. "That's what tutors are for."

"I've placed an advertisement but haven't come across anyone suitable yet."

"Dare I ask why? Surely there are countless candidates out there."

"I want someone who'll make learning fun," Jason said as he sank into a wingchair.

"Fun?" Daniel asked, failing to hide his incredulity.

"Fun is highly underrated in this country," Jason replied.

"If you say so. Were you able to learn anything useful yesterday?" Daniel asked, leaning forward in his eagerness.

"I have. The tutor's name is Shawn Sullivan, and he resides somewhere around Clerkenwell, if that means anything to you. Deborah Silver described him as an emotional and tenderhearted young man."

"In other words, someone who'd be likely to commit a crime of passion."

"I wouldn't say that poisoning someone is a crime of passion, but someone of such a sensitive nature could certainly have a volatile reaction to being rejected."

"Or to finding out that the woman you love is carrying someone else's child," Daniel chimed in.

"Or *your* child. If Mr. Sullivan and Mrs. Barrett had been having an affair, how would he feel about his child being brought up by Jonathan Barrett, his own involvement minimal at best, nonexistent at worst?"

"I seriously doubt that Jonathan Barrett would allow this man any involvement if he learned the truth. He'd have him horsewhipped sooner than let him see his child," Daniel mused.

"But if he never suspected, Shawn Sullivan might have continued as Mrs. Barrett's tutor and seen the child from time to time, something that might have been very painful for him."

"Yes, you have a point there," Daniel conceded. "I'm curious to meet this man and see for myself what we're dealing with. Anything else?"

"Elizabeth Barrett was close friends with a woman called Jane Dawlish, who might give us greater insight into Elizabeth's daily life. And there's a brother-in-law, Arthur Barrett, who might have been involved with the victim in some way. Also—and this is important—Jonathan Barrett had no idea his wife was pregnant, but Deborah Silver had been told."

Daniel nodded, impressed with the captain's interviewing abilities. "So, what you're saying is that Jonathan Barrett would have had no reason to question the paternity of the child."

"Which is not to say that he didn't kill her out of jealousy. But that theory doesn't feel right somehow," Jason said, looking thoughtful.

"Why do you think that?" Daniel asked. It sounded plausible to him.

"Whoever killed Elizabeth Barrett had planned it all in advance. They went through the trouble of buying or making cyanide. Had Jonathan Barrett been our man, it'd most likely have been a crime of passion, unplanned and brutal. He might have strangled her or bludgeoned her to death, but I don't see him using a rare poison and patiently awaiting his chance."

"Yes, that makes sense," Daniel admitted grudgingly. "I suppose the best course of action is to question Jane Dawlish and Arthur Barrett today. Tomorrow, I will travel to London and search for Shawn Sullivan."

"May I join you? I have some business in London that I've been putting off."

"Of course."

"Excellent. I'll come for you at ten, if that's convenient," Jason said.

"I'll see you then. Best of luck with your pupil," Daniel said as he tried to hide his smile.

"Thank you. I need it. Do you need a ride to Brentwood?" Jason asked as he walked Daniel to the door.

"Don't trouble yourself."

"It's no trouble, and the horses could use the exercise. I don't use them nearly enough."

"In that case, I would be most grateful."

Jason accompanied Daniel to the stables, where Joe was brushing down a beautiful chestnut mare and speaking to it as if it were a woman, his voice low and seductive.

"Joe, please take Constable Haze to Brentwood and wait for him to complete his business."

"There's really no need for Joe to wait," Daniel protested.

"There's every need. My carriage is at your disposal for the day," Jason said. "Good luck with your inquiries."

"Thank you, Jason," Daniel said with feeling. He couldn't afford a carriage of his own, not on a parish constable's salary, and the dogcart wasn't the best means of transportation when going into town, since he would have to leave the horse and buggy somewhere while he interviewed the suspects and either pay a fee at a nearby livery or risk it not being there when he returned. Having Joe mind the carriage gave him the freedom to pursue his inquiries without worrying about his property.

"Where to, Constable?" Joe asked once they were ready to depart.

"Are you familiar with Barrett and Barrett law firm, by chance?"

"Aye. I know where it is."

Joe held the door open for Daniel and waited for him to get in before closing the door and climbing onto the box. Soon, they were on the move. Daniel leaned back against the padded seat and gazed out the window, enjoying the luxury of the sleek brougham. He'd never be able to afford such a conveyance, and really had no need of one, but it would have been nice to be able to take Sarah out in style from time to time. She asked for so little when it came to material possessions—a new gown twice a year, a pair of boots, but only when hers were nearly worn through, and occasionally a new bonnet. It pained him that he couldn't give her more. He would have loved to present her with some expensive trinket on her birthday, which was coming up in a few weeks, but simply couldn't allow such an expense, not after their long-delayed trip to Scotland. Frugality was the order of the day since Squire Talbot was not about to loosen his purse strings and give Daniel a pay increase.

Daniel pushed aside his financial worries as the carriage entered the outskirts of Brentwood and made its stately way toward the center of town. Brentwood was busy on this Monday morning, drays and carriages fighting for space as they trundled down the high street, street vendors already on their street corners, jealously guarding their territory, and crossing sweeps darting out into the street with their twig brooms to clear away the steaming piles of horseshit in the hope of earning a few pennies for their dinner. Pedestrians walked close to the buildings for fear of being run over.

A burly man shoved a girl of about twelve, who stood near an intersection selling bunches of posies, nearly making her lose her balance. She was thin and pale, her eyes darting from one person to another as she held out her posies, desperate to sell her stock before it began to wilt. Daniel was accustomed to poverty; he'd seen enough human misery to last him several lifetimes, but it was always the children who tugged at his heart and made him wish he could somehow help ease their plight. He smiled when a smartly dressed matron stopped and purchased two bunches of posies, the girl's face lighting up with such joy that he almost wished he could ask Joe to stop the carriage so he could purchase the rest of her stock. But he had a job to do, and the posies would wilt by the time he returned home. He couldn't permit the waste.

The carriage drew up before a red-brick building overlooking the high street. Its tall bay windows, double doors, and high-peaked gables were modern and attractive, the brass plate next to the door carefully polished but discreet. The solid and elegant appearance of the building served to silently reassure any potential client that Barrett and Barrett was a successful law firm, the partners men of means and useful connections.

"Thank you. I shan't be long," Daniel said once he alighted from the carriage.

"Take as long as you need, Constable," Joe replied respectfully.

Daniel walked up the wide stone steps and opened the door, which led into a spacious waiting room tastefully paneled in dark wood.

"Can I help you, sir?" a youngish clerk with impressive muttonchops asked as soon as Daniel walked in. The clerk sat behind a desk that faced several unoccupied leather chairs. There were three doors leading off the waiting area, all closed at present.

"Good morning. My name is Daniel Haze, and I would like to speak with Arthur Barrett," Daniel said.

The man looked confused for a moment. "Do you have an appointment?" he asked as he quickly leafed through an appointment book, searching for Daniel's name.

"I don't. I'm the parish constable for Birch Hill, and I'm investigating the death of Mrs. Jonathan Barrett."

The clerk's mouth opened in obvious shock. "I'm sorry. I h-had no idea. Mr. Barrett—Mr. Jonathan Barrett, that is—sent a note asking me to cancel his appointments for this week but offered no reason for the request. I thought he might be ill."

"And Arthur Barrett?"

"He's not here at the moment. He stepped out to see a client." Daniel's face must have shown surprise because the clerk prattled on. "Mr. Crowe is bedbound, you see, so Mr. Barrett goes to him when summoned. It's very kind of him, to be sure," he added, unnecessarily praising his employer.

"When do you expect him back?"

"Oh, not for an hour or two. Mr. Crowe is rather fussy. Likes to go over everything again and again, since he's hard of hearing. I expect Mr. Barrett back after luncheon."

"Very well. Please inform him that I will return at one o'clock."

"Yes, sir. He'll be back by then, I should think."

"Are you by any chance acquainted with Miss Jane Dawlish?" Daniel asked.

The clerk blanched and stared at his hands, which were splayed on the appointment book as if he were keeping it from blowing off his desk by an unexpected gust of wind.

"Miss Dawlish is a client of this firm," he said at last, "but I'm not at liberty to divulge any further information."

"I only need her address. I must speak with her," Daniel said sternly. The clerk remained mute, his jaw stubbornly set.

"Or should I involve the Brentwood Constabulary?" He felt a trifle guilty for bullying the poor man; he was only doing his job, but Daniel needed the woman's address, and this was the easiest way to obtain it, especially since he had several hours to kill before Arthur Barrett returned to the office. "Where might I find her?" Daniel asked again, noting with some satisfaction that the clerk's stubbornness seemed to have been replaced with indecision.

"She lives in a lodging house on Green Lane. Mrs. Martle's," the clerk finally replied, having evidently concluded that giving out a client's address would be less damaging than having police officers descend on the office in his employers' absence.

"Thank you. Much obliged," Daniel said, and left the office.

Green Lane wasn't far from the office and was too narrow for the brougham to remain blocking it for any length of time, so Daniel instructed Joe to wait at the bottom of the street and walked. Mrs. Martle's establishment was the fourth house from the corner and looked clean and respectable. The front step was neatly swept, the lace curtains at the window looked crisp and white, and the black door appeared to have been freshly painted. Daniel knocked. The servant who answered the door stared at him in surprise, but quickly gathered her wits about her and asked the purpose of his visit. Daniel suspected there weren't too many men calling at the lodging house.

"Is Miss Dawlish at home? I'm Constable Haze from Birch Hill, and I would appreciate a few moments of her time."

"Wait here, sir. I must consult Mrs. Martle," the maid said, after allowing him to enter the foyer. Daniel heard a muttered conversation coming from what must be the parlor, and then the proprietress herself came out, followed by the maid. Mrs. Martle was a plump woman in her fifties who wore an old-fashioned lace cap over her graying bun and a delicate cameo brooch pinned to her bodice. She must have been a handsome woman in her day, and clearly still took great pride in her appearance. Her gaze swept over Daniel, probably missing very little. She nodded to the maid, who hurried up the stairs, presumably to inform Miss Dawlish that she had a visitor.

"Constable, we don't allow gentlemen callers in the rooms. You may speak to Miss Dawlish in the parlor. I will make sure you're not disturbed. Would you care for some tea?"

"Thank you, no. This won't take long."

Mrs. Martle inclined her head and gestured toward the parlor. "Very well, then. Make yourself comfortable."

Daniel entered the room and took up a position by the fireplace, his gaze fixed on the door. He liked to see a person coming toward him; it gave him a few extra moments to form an opinion before explaining the purpose of his visit.

Based on Mrs. Silver's description of Miss Dawlish, Daniel had expected a crusty old spinster, but the woman who entered the room looked anything but. She wore a modest but well-cut gown of burgundy silk, the lace fichu at her throat and the lace-trimmed cuffs a deep black. A mourning armband encircled her arm. Her dark hair was parted in the middle with artful curls framing the face, and her enormous black eyes studied him openly as a shadow of a smile hovered about her full lips. She was lovely, and judging by the look in her eyes, she was well aware of it.

"Good morning, Constable," Jane Dawlish said. "Please, sit down." She settled on a floral-patterned settee and looked at him expectantly.

Daniel sat across from her and crossed his legs, hoping he appeared more at ease than he felt. Jane Dawlish was an unknown quantity, and he wasn't at all sure how to proceed. She beat him to it.

"I suppose you're here to talk about Beth."

"If you mean Elizabeth Barrett, then yes," Daniel answered.

"She preferred to be called Beth, but that sister of hers always called her Lizzie. It annoyed her to no end."

"Why?"

"Because it made her feel like a child. It does have a condescending ring to it. Don't you agree?"

Daniel smiled. His father had called him Danny when he was angry with him and had wanted to make him feel small, so he could relate. "Yes, I suppose I do," he finally said, his gaze never leaving Miss Dawlish's face. She appeared amused and a little angry all at once, not a demeanor he came across often. "You don't seem overly upset by Beth's death, if you don't mind me saying so," Daniel pointed out.

"I will miss Beth more than you'll ever know. She was a rare friend, the kind that comes along once in a lifetime, but I won't grieve for her because now she is finally free."

"Miss Dawlish, Elizabeth Barrett was murdered in cold blood. I hardly consider what happened to her to be a freeing experience."

Jane Dawlish shook her head. "I'm sorry. I expressed myself badly."

"What did you mean, then?"

The woman took a deep breath as she glanced toward the lace-covered window. A look of defiance passed over her face, her mouth compressing into a thin line. "I don't expect you to understand, Constable, but Beth hated the restrictions placed on her by society. What people saw was a young woman who was happily married, comfortably off, with nothing to worry about except ordering new gowns and planning the next dinner party, but Beth wasn't what she seemed."

"Oh? What was she?" Daniel asked, suddenly realizing that he was holding his breath in anticipation of her answer.

"She was trapped. By convention. By society. By her position as the wife of a successful solicitor. Beth's father and Deborah had pressured her into marrying Jonathan Barrett when she was very young. She liked him well enough, but she wasn't ready to be a wife, or a mother. I suppose they had their reasons. Jonathan was already established in his career. He was handsome and charming and proclaimed to be head over heels in love with Beth. He was the ideal husband, and they didn't want her to miss her chance of marrying a man who adored her, but Jonathan wanted a traditional wife. He wanted children, a family. When Beth failed to produce an heir, he grew increasingly frustrated and redoubled his efforts. Beth resented his dogged approach."

Daniel might have expected another woman to blush when discussing such intimate details of her friend's life, but Jane Dawlish looked angry rather than embarrassed.

"He wouldn't leave her alone. He wanted a son."

"What did Beth want?"

"She wanted to be a painter. She was quite good. Very good, in fact. But her father had refused to engage a tutor, thinking her little hobby would lose its appeal once she married and had wifely responsibilities to occupy her. Jonathan indulged Beth's desire to paint because it made her happy, but not because he respected her as an artist, or even a person in her own right. He never accompanied her to any exhibitions or even asked to see her work. Beth wanted the space to be herself; she told me so quite often."

"You mean she envied your unmarried state?" Daniel asked carefully.

"She did. Society looks down on unmarried women, but I've had plenty of opportunities to wed and I've passed them up. I don't want to be some man's chattel. I want to make my own decisions and manage my own money. Oh, yes, Constable, I have my own money," she said in response to his obvious surprise. "My parents left me quite well off. I could rent a house and hire a staff, but I would much rather travel and see the world. I don't need the trappings of a lifestyle valued by others. Beth often spoke of how much she'd have liked to come with me, to Paris or Rome, or Geneva. She asked endless questions because she knew Jonathan would never take her to any of those places. He had no interest in travel, saw it as a waste of time and money. He was born in Brentwood, and in Brentwood he will die. Despite his good looks and valuable connections, he's nothing but a glorified merchant."

"You don't paint a very flattering picture."

"He's not a man worthy of flattery," Jane Dawlish replied with a shrug.

"But is he a violent one? Would he have killed his wife had she expressed a desire to leave him?"

"No. Jonathan doesn't have a violent bone in his body. Being small-minded is not a crime, Constable, only a handicap."

"Miss Dawlish, did you know that Beth was with child?"

Jane Dawlish pursed her lips and nodded. "She told me as soon as she suspected."

"Was she pleased?"

"She was pleased for Jonathan. She wanted to give him a son. She did care for him, Constable. But she didn't want the child for herself. She felt no maternal stirrings, she said, and would have been happy never to be a mother."

"Did her sister know how she felt?" Daniel asked, curious whether Jane Dawlish had been the only one to see that side of Elizabeth Barrett.

"No. Beth loved her sister. They'd been close since childhood, but Deborah is a very different woman. Whereas Beth was artistic, passionate, and curious about the world around her, Deborah has always been exactly what society demands: subservient and pragmatic, a blank slate for her husband to write on. She married a suitable man, gave him a son, and dedicated her life to being the perfect wife."

"Does Mrs. Silver enjoy being a mother?" Daniel asked. The question had nothing to do with the investigation, but given what Miss Dawlish had said about Elizabeth Barret, he was curious.

"She enjoys the knowledge that she's fulfilled the role society has cast her in, but I don't believe she's particularly close to the boy. She sent him off to boarding school as soon as he was old enough to be enrolled, but made sure it was a prestigious institution, one that would pave his way into society and expose him to the scions of some of the wealthiest families in Britain."

"Pardon me, Miss Dawlish, but I was given to understand that Mrs. Silver is practically destitute," Daniel said, wondering if Mrs. Dodson had exaggerated Deborah Silver's financial hardships.

"She is. Her husband left her high and dry, so to speak. Jonathan is paying the tuition. I never said he wasn't a kind man," Jane said, her tone softening. "Had I been of a mind to get married, I'd have snapped up someone like him."

"And suffer his dullness?" Daniel asked, a bit spitefully. He couldn't help wondering if Sarah found him dull.

"There are worse things than a husband who doesn't stimulate one's mind."

He could almost guess the rest. *Like a husband who doesn't stimulate one's body.*

Miss Dawlish was a spinster, admittedly by choice, but had she had lovers? It wasn't relevant to the case, but the woman fascinated him. He'd never met anyone like her before, and she attracted and repelled him in equal parts. He thought Jason would like her. He wouldn't feel threatened by her refusal to adhere to convention. He'd respect her rebellious spirit and applaud her resolve to stand up for what she believed in. It rather surprised Daniel that Jason's opinion mattered to him so much, but he found that Jason Redmond was the type of man he'd want by his side in a crisis. He wasn't some sniveling British aristocrat; he was a product of another society and different set of values— values which were perhaps more modern and risqué than Daniel's own. He had much to learn from Jason Redmond, if he were willing to set his own well-cemented opinions aside. Perhaps a woman like Jane Dawlish would have something to teach him as well, and for a moment, he was sorry he'd likely never see her again.

"Was indulging in a liaison with her tutor a way for Elizabeth Barrett to break her bonds?" Daniel asked rudely and watched Jane Dawlish's face for a reaction. He'd expected outrage and immediate denial, but the woman just laughed, the throaty sound filling the parlor with surprising lightness.

"You're missing the point entirely, Constable Haze. Beth didn't want a man. She already had one. She wanted the freedom to be herself, to pursue her own dreams. Shawn Sullivan helped her to improve on something she loved doing, but she had no romantic interest in him whatsoever. He was a friend, someone who shared her passion for art and talked to her about the things that interested her above all."

"Sometimes a shared passion can lead to other forms of sharing," Daniel said slyly.

"Yes, it certainly can, but that wasn't the case with Beth and Shawn. They were just friends."

"You seem awfully sure."

"I know Shawn. I was the one who'd recommended him to Beth. He's not at all what you think he is," Jane Dawlish replied cryptically.

"Do you have his address, Miss Dawlish? I will need to speak to him."

"Yes, his lodgings are in Britton Street, Clerkenwell. Number seventeen."

"Thank you. Will you be attending the funeral?" Daniel asked. "Given that you don't think your friend's death was a tragedy."

"Her life was a tragedy, a very common one in the world we inhabit," Jane Dawlish countered. "But yes, I will attend the funeral because I mourn Beth's squandered potential, and I miss my friend." For the first time, he saw genuine sorrow in her eyes and felt gratified somehow. Sorrow he could understand; a complete rejection of society's mores he could not.

"Thank you for speaking to me," Daniel said. "May I call on you if I have any further questions?"

"Of course. I'm at home most mornings."

Daniel thanked Mrs. Martle, who'd been hovering outside, and stepped out into the overcast morning. He felt melancholy and confused. He wasn't sure why Miss Dawlish had unsettled him so, but he'd found her viewpoint startling, possibly because he'd never imagined that women might have desires outside of home and hearth. He took it for granted that every young woman wanted to get married and have children. To imagine that they might not, that they might have aspirations and dreams of their own, was eye opening and strangely unnerving.

Did Sarah have dreams of a future that didn't involve him? Did she want to have another child, or was there something else she'd rather do, like travel, or write, like Jane Austen or George Sand? Sarah was a devotee of George Sand, whom Daniel had thought was a man until Sarah had enlightened him. Was it really necessary for a woman to pose as a man to be taken seriously? He hadn't asked her what she wanted, not in a long time, assuming she wanted what all women wanted—a family. Perhaps it was time he spoke to her as he would to an equal and not just a wife.

"You all right, Constable?" Joe asked as Daniel approached the carriage, his mind still on the puzzling Miss Dawlish, her outlandish ideas, and his possible inadequacy as a husband.

"Yes. We have some time before Arthur Barrett gets back. What do you say you and I have some lunch?" Daniel offered. "My treat, of course."

Joe seemed surprised by the invitation, but instantly accepted. "Don't mind if I do. Thank you, Constable."

"I breakfasted at the Rose and Crown the other day and thought the fare was rather good."

"Whatever you choose is fine with me," Joe said. "I'm not a finicky eater."

Daniel climbed into the carriage and they drove to the tavern, where Joe surrendered the carriage to a waiting stable boy.

"Feed and water the horses," Joe said, tossing the boy a coin.

"Yes, sir."

They entered the pub, found a table by the window, and took a seat. Daniel ordered a steak and ale pie and a half pint. Joe did the same.

"Were you able to learn anything useful?" Joe asked as they waited for their food.

"I was, but I'm not sure how it fits into the investigation," Daniel replied truthfully. "Miss Dawlish is a remarkable woman."

"In what way?" Joe asked.

"In every way," Daniel replied, but wisely chose not to elaborate. He owed Miss Dawlish the respect of keeping what she'd shared with him private. "Ah, here's our lunch," Daniel said with forced enthusiasm. He wasn't even that hungry, his desire for food overshadowed by his impatience to speak to Arthur Barrett and get his take on his sister-in-law. "Elizabeth, Lizzie, or Beth?" he muttered under his breath. Who had she been to Arthur?

"You say something, Constable?" Joe asked.

"No. Nothing."

Chapter 15

Jason and Micah had just about finished with Micah's lessons for the day when Dodson came into the schoolroom. He had the kind of disapproving look on his face that usually announced a visit from one of the villagers who required medical assistance. Dodson, being the snob that he was, didn't think a nobleman should be stitching cuts and setting bones, especially free of charge, but Jason was always glad to be of help.

"What is it, Dodson?"

"There's a lad from the Red Stag here. It seems Matty Locke took a tumble and broke his leg. He's asking you to come," Dodson added disdainfully.

"Please tell him I'll be there shortly," Jason replied, pushing the slate he used for Micah's math problems aside with ill-concealed relief.

"Can I come with you?" Micah pleaded. "I can help."

"All right. Let's go," Jason said, earning another look of reproach from Dodson. Most of the time, Jason appreciated Dodson's help in navigating the myriad rules of British society, but sometimes, he secretly thought it would do Leslie Dodson a world of good to remove the stick from his pompous ass.

By the time they came downstairs, Fanny was already holding out Jason's medical bag. "I added some clean cloths, sir, and strips of linen, should you need bandages. Mrs. Dodson has also replenished the brandy in the flask, sir."

"Thank you, Fanny. You always know just what I need."

"I make it my business to know what you need, sir," Fanny replied as she blushed with pleasure. "And you too, Master Micah," she added when she saw Micah's crestfallen look.

Jason strongly suspected that Micah had something of a crush on Fanny, who was young, pretty, and approachable. But what really endeared Fanny to the boy was that she treated him like a young gentleman rather than a wayward child. Micah didn't mind it so much from Mrs. Dodson, who clucked over him like a mother hen and spoiled him rotten, but Dodson's haughty disapproval grated on him, and he went out of his way to annoy the older man, something Jason turned a blind eye to since he could hardly expect a boy from a farm in Maryland to suddenly transform into an English lordling.

Jason and Micah donned their coats and hats and headed toward the village on foot, since Joe was still in Brentwood with Constable Haze. It wasn't a long walk, and before long they were by the Stag. Davy Brody was outside, pacing like a man whose beloved wife was in labor.

"I knew this were going to 'appen," he sputtered as soon as he saw Jason.

"What would happen?"

"It's that place. I've been to that cursed place, the ruins, and now Matty's gone and broken 'is leg."

Jason didn't see what one thing had to do with the other but didn't bother to argue. Talking people out of their superstitions was about as effective as trying to turn a wolf into a vegetarian. Jason walked into the stable, where Matty lay on a pile of straw in one of the stalls, moaning pitifully. Micah sniggered and Jason gave him a look that instantly wiped the smirk off his face. Micah had seen much worse suffering than a broken bone, but that didn't mean Matty didn't deserve sympathy. Pain was pain, no matter what shape it took.

"Hello, Matty," Jason said as he removed his coat and hung it on a nail protruding from one of the beams and tossed his hat onto a bale of hay. He squatted next to the boy. "Tell me what happened."

"I tripped and fell out of the loft," Matty said. He was pale and his forehead glistened with sweat. "I'm hurting bad, yer lordship," he moaned. "Right 'ere." He pointed to his shin.

"Well, let's take a look."

Matty looked frightened but didn't object. Jason carefully examined the leg, starting at the ankle and moving toward the knee.

"Is it bad?" Matty whispered.

"No, not bad at all. You've broken your fibula," Jason said calmly.

"My what?" Matty cried. "Am I going to be a cripple?"

"It's the thinner of the two calf bones. You are going to be just fine. I'm going to set the bone and then I will splint it. You will have to stay off your leg for about six weeks."

"But how will I get 'round?" Matty asked. He looked as if he were about to cry.

"I'll ask Mr. Roberts to fashion you a crutch, but you're to use it only when absolutely necessary, like getting yourself to the privy. You must stay in bed for a month at least if you want your bone to heal properly. Do you understand?"

"Yes."

"Micah, run across the green to Mr. Roberts' workshop and ask for two thin planks, about this long." Jason moved his hands apart to indicate the length of the wood, then turned to Davy, who was hovering in the doorway. "Mr. Brody, I need a cup of water."

"Right away, sir."

While Davy went to fetch the water, Jason tried to distract Matty with conversation. "Did you know the murdered woman, Matty?"

"I seen 'er 'round a few times. She were pretty," Matty said through gritted teeth.

"Yes, she was," Jason agreed. "Talented too."

"Yeh, she liked to paint the ruins."

"How do you know?"

"Seen her there a couple o' times."

"Was she always alone?" Jason asked.

113

"Not always. I seen that lady with her, Mrs. Silver, 'er name is. They was chatting and laughing. And they had a picnic with 'em. And cake," Matty added dreamily.

"Did you ever see anyone else?"

"Like who?"

"Like Mrs. Barrett's husband, or any other man," Jason replied.

"No."

"What about here, at the Stag? You see every person who comes and goes, don't you, Matty?"

"I surely do. Nuffin' much gets by me," Matty said proudly.

"Did you see any strangers around on Thursday or Friday morning?"

Matty shook his head, his pain momentarily forgotten. "I seen no one, yer lordship. Just all the regulars."

Moll appeared in the doorway, putting an end to the conversation. She handed Jason a cup of water and eyed Matty with distaste. "Ye clumsy oaf," she said with feeling.

"I tripped," Matty exclaimed, clearly wounded by the insult.

"If ye didn't 'ave two left feet, ye wouldn't 'ave tripped," Moll taunted him.

"Moll, that's really not helpful," Jason said.

"I'm sorry, yer lordship," Moll said, her demeanor instantly changing to one of contrite femininity.

"Here, hold the cup for me." Jason extracted a small vial of laudanum and added three drops before taking the cup from Moll. "Drink this, Matty. It will ease the pain."

Matty gulped the water down as if it were the elixir of life and handed the cup back to Moll.

"I feel better already," he said with a sigh of relief.

The laudanum hadn't taken effect yet, but Jason didn't bother to point that out. Setting the bone would be painful, so the more relaxed Matty was, the better.

Micah returned a few minutes later with the planks. "Will these do?"

"Yes. Well done."

Matty screamed loud enough to be heard on the other side of the green, but Jason paid no attention to him and swiftly set the bone. He then instructed Micah to hold the splints on either side of Matty's calf as he bandaged the wood firmly into place. By the time he was finished, Matty was out, his mouth open as his head lolled to the side.

"Pathetic weasel," Moll hissed.

"Moll, I need to speak to your uncle."

Moll looked mutinous at being dismissed but left the stable and went to fetch Davy. When Davy appeared a few minutes later, Jason was already brushing the straw off his trousers and reaching for his coat.

"Mr. Brody, I take it Matty sleeps in the loft?"

"He does."

"Well, as I'm sure you can see, he'll be unable to climb the ladder. He must have complete bed rest for a month. I'll leave it to you to find him a place to bed down, preferably one where he won't need to navigate stairs. Once you do, he'll have to be moved very carefully. I'll come back to check on him tomorrow."

"I'll get one of the other lads to take him home to his father. 'E's no use to me if 'e can't work."

Davy reached into his waistcoat pocket for a coin, but Jason waved him away. "You needn't pay me, Mr. Brody."

"Thank ye, sir," Davy said. "Very kind of ye to see to poor Matty 'ere."

"Tell his father to send for me should there be any problems."

115

Jason walked out of the stable, followed by Micah. "He really is a clumsy oaf," Micah said under his breath. "Who falls out of a loft?"

"Accidents happen. Don't be unkind."

"Sorry," Micah mumbled. "Can I go visit Tom after lunch?"

"May I."

"Well, may I?"

"You may," Jason said, trying to hide his smile as Micah skipped next to him happily.

Chapter 16

By the time Daniel returned to the offices of Barrett and Barrett, Arthur Barrett had not only returned but was expecting Daniel's visit. He came out to greet him and ushered him into a well-appointed office dominated by a massive walnut desk.

"Please, have a seat, Constable. Can I offer you a drink? The sun is over the yardarm," he said with a conspiratorial wink.

"No, thank you," Daniel declined politely, although, in truth, he wouldn't have minded. But he was here in his official capacity and not for a social call, so accepting a drink wouldn't be appropriate.

"Suit yourself. I hope you don't mind if I help myself."

"Not at all."

Daniel took the opportunity to study the man while he poured himself a drink. The resemblance to his older brother was pronounced, but whereas Jonathan Barrett was attractive, Arthur Barrett was handsome in the true sense of the word. The hair was thicker and fairer, the eyes bluer, and the cheekbones sharper, his profile reminiscent of a Greek statue. He was also a bit taller and broader in the shoulders, possibly a consequence of hours spent at a boxing gymnasium. His clothes were understated but well cut and of the finest cloth. Even his hands were beautiful. The fingers were slender and graceful, the nails clean and manicured. This was a man who devoted time to his appearance, and the results were well worth it.

Arthur Barrett sat behind the desk, took a sip of his Scotch, and set aside the glass, his expression one of mild curiosity.

"Mr. Barrett, I'd like to ask you some questions about your sister-in-law. I have reason to believe Mrs. Barrett was murdered," he added, in case Jonathan Barrett had decided to keep that information to himself for fear of damaging the reputation of the firm.

Arthur nodded, his eyes filling with sadness. "Yes, Jonathan told me. I can't believe she's gone. Elizabeth was always so full of life."

"Can you think of anyone who might have wished Mrs. Barrett harm?" Daniel asked.

Arthur Barrett leaned back in his chair and shook his head, his gaze thoughtful. "No, I honestly can't. Are you certain she was murdered? Surely her death could have been an accident, or the result of a fright. Perhaps something startled her. That place gives me the creeps, I'm not ashamed to admit. It's beautiful, to be sure, but there's an atmosphere there—for lack of a better word—a presence. It's like someone is watching you. Perhaps the monks have never truly left," he said with a nervous laugh.

"Unless a ghost monk plied Mrs. Barrett with cyanide, it was murder, and it was carried out by someone she knew."

Arthur Barrett looked startled. "Someone she knew, you say? Who on earth would wish to kill her? And more to the point, how would they get her to take cyanide?"

"That is precisely what I'm trying to find out," Daniel replied, wondering exactly how much Jonathan Barrett had shared with his brother.

"Elizabeth knew some artsy types, but I doubt they could poison a rat, much less a woman they know. If they wished someone dead, they'd paint them on their deathbed with a cup of hemlock in their hand and consider the deed done."

"Mr. Barrett, this is no laughing matter," Daniel said sternly.

"I'm sorry, Constable. I didn't mean to sound flippant. I'm simply trying to understand. Deborah said Elizabeth's ring was taken. Surely, if anyone killed her, it was the person who robbed her."

"So, you do believe there was someone there with her other than a ghostly presence," Daniel said. He hadn't meant to sound sarcastic, but Arthur Barrett was beginning to annoy him, since

Daniel was sure he was downplaying the seriousness of the crime intentionally. "Have you ever visited the ruins with Mrs. Barrett?"

"No, never."

"Did you see Elizabeth Barrett often?"

"I live in London, Mr. Haze. In Maida Vale. I spend most of my time there, since there isn't much to tempt a bachelor in Brentwood, but I come here quite often since my brother and I are partners. I dined with Jonathan and Elizabeth at least twice a week before they decamped to their summer home, and I have visited them in Birch Hill several times this summer. Charming village," he added airily. "I enjoyed the peace and quiet. For about five minutes."

"Where were you Thursday night?" Daniel asked.

"I was in London. I dined at my club and then joined a few friends for an after-dinner brandy. I didn't return home until eleven. On Friday morning, I was scheduled to appear in court at nine. There are countless people who can verify this information."

"May I have the name and address of your club as well as your home address in Maida Vale?"

Arthur Barrett scribbled both addresses on a piece of notepaper and passed it to Daniel. "Knock yourself out, Constable."

"Can you tell me something about Elizabeth Barrett? What was she like?" Daniel asked in the hope that some spark of personal interest would make itself known. Arthur seemed saddened by Elizabeth's death, but Daniel hadn't noticed any evidence of personal loss or guilt.

Arthur shrugged. "She was beautiful, charming, and utterly selfish."

"Selfish?" Daniel asked, shocked by the choice of adjective and the casualness with which it had been used to describe a young woman who'd been murdered only a few days before.

"I know women, Constable. I've had many, from all different walks of life. I have a fondness for chorus girls; I freely admit that, and believe me, in London, there's an endless supply of beauties treading the boards and dreaming of stardom. I've also had relationships with several married women of my own class and even one or two affairs with women of rank. Fascinating creatures, women; so changeable, and so tragically underestimated by men, who think themselves superior when it comes to intelligence."

"I'm not sure I follow," Daniel said, wishing the man would stop the verbal fencing and get to the point.

"No, I don't expect you do. Are you married, Constable?" he asked, even though Daniel's wedding ring was clearly on display.

"Yes, I am, but it's not my wife we're talking about, is it?"

"I certainly hope no one finds cause to poison your wife," Arthur Barrett quipped, setting Daniel's teeth on edge. "I'm sorry. I digress. It's a professional hazard, I'm afraid. I often have to talk circles around the jury in order to dilute the significance of the opposing counselor's evidence and make them doubt their own judgement."

"Is that what you're trying to do with me?" Daniel asked, not bothering to hide his frustration. "Why did you refer to Elizabeth Barrett as selfish, Mr. Barrett? And please, just answer the question."

Arthur Barrett fixed him with a direct stare, his earlier glibness replaced with something malign. "Very well, then. At first glance, Elizabeth was the perfect wife: loving, respectful, and easily managed. I envied Jonathan at first and thought he'd found something I'd never have—true love—but it was all an act, at least on Elizabeth's side. She always had her own agenda, and it had little to do with my brother's feelings or needs."

"How do you mean?" Daniel asked as casually as he could to disguise his excitement. Now they were getting somewhere.

Arthur Barrett leaned forward in his chair, his gaze burning with the intensity of his feelings. "In our business, appearances matter. Reputation matters. We don't find new clients by advertising our services in *The Times*. We rely on referrals from individuals who were pleased with the way we'd handled their cases. As the wife of a solicitor, Elizabeth should have been dedicated to furthering her husband's interests. A supper party, a musical evening, a fancy-dress ball; those types of events help nudge a professional relationship toward becoming a personal one, binding our clients to us socially and securing a more permanent business arrangement in the process. And loyal clients refer their associates and friends to lawyers they trust and consider to be their friends," he explained.

"Elizabeth couldn't be bothered. Oh, she never said no outright; she just convinced Jonathan that there was no need to do anything and all he had to do was trade on his reputation as a successful lawyer. She hated playing the hostess and hated his associates even more. She barely managed to sit through tea with some of their wives without fainting with boredom."

"How do you know this, Mr. Barrett?" Daniel asked. "Were you present when these ladies called on your sister-in-law?"

"No, I wasn't, but Elizabeth told me so herself," Arthur Barrett replied smugly. "She said she couldn't bear the mind-numbing banality of conversations that revolved around unfounded gossip and mean-spirited innuendo. The complete lack of imagination or desire for anything other than material possessions and social status disgusted her. She said she envied me my freedom and the ability to mix with the lower orders. She longed to spend time with artists and poets, and even chorus girls, not the middle-aged matrons Jonathan foisted on her. Deborah would have made Jonathan a much more suitable wife, and I told him so."

"Deborah Silver?" Daniel asked, surprised by the comment.

"Yes. Jonathan had been courting Deborah for months and had planned to propose to her when he met her little sister. Elizabeth was fifteen at the time. For Jonathan, it was love at first sight, so he told Deborah the truth. Said he couldn't possibly be a loving husband to her when the woman he loved was always there but out of his reach."

"And how did Deborah take this?"

"Not as badly as one would expect. She was never in love with Jonathan. She was enamored of his prospects and the life he could give her. Shortly after Jonathan ended their relationship, she accepted Anthony Silver's proposal and was married by the time Elizabeth turned sixteen. She was instrumental in convincing Elizabeth to accept Jonathan. She thought they were made for each other and assured her sister that she bore her no ill will and would never blame Jonathan for turning his back on her. She quite understood and wished them well."

"And there was never any resentment between them?" Daniel asked, not quite sure which 'them' he was referring to. Deborah had every reason to resent not only her sister, but the man who'd turned his back on her and had possibly tarnished her reputation by doing so. She was lucky to have found another suitor so quickly, but things could have turned out very differently had she been left single for long. As it was, things hadn't worked out too well in the long run, since Deborah had been ruined by her husband and now had to rely on her brother-in-law's generosity and support in her hour of need.

"Not at all. Deborah and Elizabeth remained close, and Jonathan did everything he could for Deborah after Anthony died and left her in a precarious situation. Jonathan insisted on paying Oliver's school fees and invited Deborah to move in with him and Elizabeth. He cares for Deborah and her son and genuinely wants to help. There's no rancor between them."

Some part of Daniel wanted to doubt Arthur Barrett's words, since prior events could always be counted on to provide a motive for murder, but he'd witnessed genuine affection between Jonathan Barrett and Deborah Silver, and they had both appeared shocked and united in their grief. Jonathan had thrown over Deborah more than ten years ago. Whatever anger and hurt she may have felt were clearly water under the bridge. With his wife gone, Jonathan Barrett was under no obligation to support his sister-in-law and nephew, which, in Daniel's opinion, was much more important to Deborah Silver than a decade-old disappointment. He briefly wondered if Deborah Silver had been content in her marriage before finding out about the debts but decided not to ask Arthur Barrett. What could he know of the marriage? Few people were aware of what went on between a man and wife, especially if both parties were good at hiding their true feelings.

"And what of Elizabeth's tutor? Do you know him?" Daniel asked.

Arthur scoffed. "We've met. Not someone I would hire to teach my wife, if I had one."

"Why not?"

"Not the right sort. Jonathan had his reservations, but Elizabeth was adamant. He's an acquaintance of Jane Dawlish, so Jonathan relented. Shawn Sullivan and Elizabeth were awfully chummy. Always blathering about this painting and that mural. It bored the rest of us to tears, but Jonathan treated him like one of the family."

"Do you think there was anything romantic between them?" Daniel asked carefully.

Arthur Barrett rolled his eyes. "If you think my brother killed his wife because he was jealous of some affected fop, you're very much mistaken. Jonathan only wanted to make her happy. He refused to see her for what she was, and Elizabeth, God rest her soul, played him like a violin. She knew his every weakness, his every desire. All she had to do was smile at him and tell him she wished for something, and Jonathan would set aside his every need in order to please her. She played at being in love with him, and she did it so effectively, she sometimes deceived even me."

"How do you know she was playing? Perhaps she really did love him."

"I know because there was a reserve there, an aloofness. When a woman loves you, you can see it in her eyes, feel it in her every gesture. Her love permeates her soul and informs her every decision. Elizabeth did and said all the right things, but her soul was very much her own. To tell you the truth, I secretly admired her for that. She was not a woman who allowed herself to be defined by her love for a man or her matrimonial status. She had a free spirit and a single-minded desire to follow her dreams. Now, if there's nothing else, Constable, I'm afraid I have an appointment."

Arthur Barrett drained the rest of the Scotch in one gulp, set the empty glass on the table, and pushed to his feet, leaving Daniel no choice but to do the same.

"Thank you for your time, Mr. Barrett. You were most helpful."

"Was I?" Arthur Barrett asked. He seemed genuinely surprised. "Glad to help. I hope you catch whoever did this, Haze. If she was indeed murdered and this is not some silly mistake made by your colonial surgeon." He said the last bit with a sneer, as if no one from America could possibly rival the knowledge or the practical experience of an English-trained surgeon.

Daniel didn't think Jason Redmond's verdict was a silly mistake, but he was beginning to think this case was a riddle he wouldn't be able to solve. Elizabeth Barrett might have been different things to different people, but he couldn't see why anyone would wish to kill her. Her husband had been besotted with her and would have been thrilled to learn she was pregnant. Her sister had loved her despite losing her suitor to her in the past and was currently supported by Elizabeth's husband, not an arrangement she'd wish to jeopardize, given her situation. And Arthur Barrett had held her in grudging esteem, even if he didn't quite understand her brand of femininity. Before meeting Arthur Barrett, Daniel had thought Elizabeth Barrett might have been carrying on an affair with her brother-in-law, but nothing in Arthur's demeanor had supported that supposition. He didn't seem particularly affected by her death, and Daniel hadn't noticed any signs of nervousness or evasiveness once Arthur had started talking. He also claimed to have a solid alibi, something Daniel would have to verify before eliminating Arthur from the investigation.

To date, Daniel didn't have any viable suspects, nor did he have any idea how the poison had been administered. Since there was no sign of a struggle, Elizabeth must have ingested it willingly, which meant that she'd trusted whoever had given it to her—unless she had ingested the poison before leaving the house, but Captain Redmond said cyanide worked quickly. Had she been given the fatal dose at home, she wouldn't have made it to the ruins, nor had an opportunity to paint. The paint on the canvas had still been wet when Daniel had arrived at the scene.

Sighing with frustration, Daniel climbed into the coach, leaned back against the seat, and closed his eyes. In the months before Felix's death, he'd dreamed of becoming an inspector, of being in charge of an investigation and dazzling his superiors with his quick and brilliant police work, but conducting a real investigation was a lot more difficult than a fantasy one. Leads didn't fortuitously present themselves, and the suspects were not as easily identifiable. Nor was he about to make some serendipitous discovery that would make everything clear. His only hope was that the tutor would prove to be the culprit and he could lay Elizabeth Barrett's murder to rest.

Chapter 17

Daniel returned home close to teatime. The weather had turned, and a gusty wind was blowing, dark clouds blanketing the sky. Daniel handed his umbrella, coat, gloves, and hat to Tilda and walked into the drawing room, taking his favorite seat by the hearth.

Sarah had been reading by the window, but came to join him, her eyes searching his face for clues. "How did it go? Did you learn anything?" she asked.

"Sarah, do you think me dull?" Daniel blurted out and instantly regretted his outburst.

Sarah's eyebrows lifted in surprise. "What a question! Why would you ask me that?" she asked, watching him intently.

"Well, do you?"

"No, I don't think you dull," Sarah replied. Daniel thought he saw a hint of a smile tugging at her lips.

"Do you think I'm oblivious to your needs?" he asked, plunging deeper into the awkward and potentially dangerous subject.

"Daniel, what in the world?" Sarah exclaimed, arching her eyebrow in the way she did when she was puzzled.

"Please, Sarah. I need to know."

Sarah sighed, a look of resignation passing over her lovely features. "Sometimes, but I think you're equally oblivious to your own needs."

"I am?"

Sarah nodded. "Daniel, I know I forced you to give up your dreams when I insisted that we move back to Birch Hill after Felix…" Her voice trailed off for a moment, but she collected herself and continued. "I was distraught and couldn't bear to remain in a place where he…where we had lost him. Perhaps I was being selfish, but I needed to hide from the world for a while in order to heal. But you never felt that same need; you had to act, to keep busy, to turn your mind to other things. You ignored your own needs in favor of mine. You allowed me to mourn in a way I needed to in order to find the strength to go on."

"I'm not sure I understand what you're saying, Sarah," Daniel said softly.

"You're wasted here. You were a good policeman, and you would have had a future with the Metropolitan Police had we remained in London."

"But we didn't."

"No," Sarah said, watching him. "But I think it's time for you to see to your own desires."

Daniel shook his head in confusion. He'd intended to ask Sarah about her needs, to make certain she didn't feel frustrated or ignored, but somehow, they'd ended up talking about what was best for him. No wonder men never really knew what their wives were thinking; the confounding creatures always managed to turn the conversation in the direction they wanted it to go.

"Everything I desire is right here," Daniel said softly, watching her. "I would like us to have another child. Is that something you might want as well?"

Sarah smiled. "Yes, I would like us to have a child, Danny."

She rarely called him that, and his heart melted when she did because it was a sign of emotion, of deep affection. "And I hope we will. But having a child won't satisfy you. You have a keen mind and a lot of ambition. I've always admired that about you. You must find work that will allow you to use both."

"Are you suggesting we return to London?" Daniel asked, utterly shocked by the turn the conversation had taken.

Sarah shook her head. "I don't want to move back to London. I like it here, and I like being close to my mother, but we're so very close to Brentwood, and Brentwood has its own constabulary."

"Sarah, I'm too old to be a bobby, nor do I wish to be one."

"That's not what I was suggesting. Danny, you have what it takes to become a detective, but you must start somewhere. You've already been a beat cop, and you've been a parish constable these three years. Perhaps you can approach the head of the Brentwood constabulary and offer your services. Surely, they can find a position for you. A detective in training, if there is such a thing."

Daniel considered Sarah's suggestion. He had to admit that it had merit, and the idea of working in a police station again held great appeal. But what did he have to recommend him other than his time on the Metropolitan Police Service? He'd conducted one murder investigation to date, and even though he and Captain Redmond had been able to discover who'd killed Alexander McDougal and bring about a sort of justice, he had nothing to show for it. The murderer had never gone to trial or been sentenced for his crime. The notes from the inquest would do nothing to support Daniel's claim that he and the captain had solved the crime. On the other hand, the police force in Brentwood was in its infancy, and they might need good men. Perhaps Sarah was right, and it was time he took a chance. He'd be no worse off if his application was denied.

"Do it," Sarah said. "I want you to. I want to see you happy, Danny."

"And I you."

"I am at peace now," Sarah replied. "I don't think I will ever be completely happy, but I'm content. You were right; it's time to move forward."

She held out her hand and Daniel took it, squeezing her fingers gently. Sarah's cheeks turned a lovely shade of rose, and it wasn't from her proximity to the fire.

"Shall we go upstairs?" she asked shyly. "I feel rather tired," she added as Tilda came in to ask if they'd like tea.

"Yes, I think a lie-down is in order," Daniel said, rising to his feet. He tried to look dignified, but inside, his heart was singing.

Chapter 18

Tuesday, September 11

The railway car swayed gently as it sped through the countryside, a misty haze hovering over the golden haystacks and Tudor farmhouses in the distance, but neither Daniel nor Jason paid much attention to the scenery. They were alone in the compartment, a happy coincidence that allowed them to exchange information and go over the case.

"So, what you are telling me is that we have no motive, no suspects, no idea where the poison might have been obtained, or how it was administered," Jason said, summarizing what they knew to date.

"Precisely. And I received a note from Jonathan Barrett yesterday evening, asking me to come to his Brentwood residence today to give him an update on the investigation. What am I to tell him?" Daniel asked, his voice cracking with desperation.

"The truth, I suppose," Jason replied. "You can't produce a suspect out of thin air. If you are to find out who murdered Elizabeth Barrett, Jonathan Barrett has to give you something more than 'she was the perfect wife.'"

"But what if she was, in his eyes?" Daniel added. "I certainly haven't heard anything that would make me believe Elizabeth Barrett had an enemy in the world. Sweet, loving, free-spirited, talented, and a bit selfish at times. Those are not the characteristics of a person who makes enemies. She was human, no more, no less."

"Yes, and humans tend to provoke jealousy, hatred, obsession, and all those other volatile emotions that so often lead to murder."

"This wasn't a crime of passion, Jason. Someone had planned this, thought this through, and prepared thoroughly. They made sure she was alone at the ruins on a morning when the ground was too dry to leave any footprints. They had the poison ready and either tricked or forced her into taking it, and then left the scene of the crime leaving not a trace of their presence. They also chose a location where it would take time for someone to come across Elizabeth Barrett's body, making sure she was good and dead by the time she was found. Had Davy Brody not gone to Brentwood so early Friday morning, by the time Elizabeth had been found, there'd have been no trace of the poison."

"There would have been, but given that Jonathan Barrett refused an autopsy, it'd never have been discovered."

Daniel looked up at Jason, his brows knitting with consternation. "So, what you're saying is that the killer knew Jonathan Barrett well enough to anticipate his refusal?"

"Not necessarily. Most people view a postmortem as a violation, a crime against the dead. Chances are the family would refuse to grant permission, especially to a parish constable and an American surgeon who just happens to be on hand."

"Yes, you're right," Daniel said, nodding. "I don't have enough authority to demand they allow a postmortem."

"And let's not forget the missing ring," Jason said. "Someone took that ring off her finger. Either they meant to sell it or, more likely, keep it as a reminder of what they had done."

"You think someone wanted a keepsake?" Daniel asked, even though he knew Jason had a valid point.

"Why not? People often keep things that belonged to the dead. Perhaps the person who killed Elizabeth Barrett wanted something to remember her by."

"Or maybe they wanted something that reminds them of their audacity and cunning," Daniel suggested.

Jason nodded. "Whoever poisoned Elizabeth Barrett is exceptionally clever."

He sighed. "So, I suppose it's too much to hope that Shawn Sullivan has bottles of cyanide haphazardly strewn about his residence and that he was crazed with lust for the unfortunate Mrs. Barrett," he said, smiling dolefully.

Jason laughed. "Yes, it is too much to hope for, but don't let me stop you."

"I don't know where to look next, Jason."

"Perhaps Mr. Sullivan will offer up a new lead."

"And if he doesn't?" Daniel's shoulders slumped in defeat.

"Then we go back to the beginning, reevaluate everything we know, and try to connect the dots."

"What dots? We have no dots."

"Don't lose heart, Daniel. We still have several days before the inquest. Something will turn up."

"You're too optimistic, Captain. It's the American in you," Daniel grumbled. "The English always expect the worst. It's practically a national trait."

"Nonsense. The English are tenacious. *You* are tenacious. And you will solve this case."

As the train pulled into Charing Cross station, the men put on their hats, buttoned their coats, pulled on their gloves, and reached for their umbrellas. Daniel hailed a hansom.

"Britton Street," he informed the cabbie as they settled in for the ride.

"Yes, sir," the man replied as the hansom lurched away from the curb.

Jason looked around, noting that the area changed dramatically as they got further from the railway station. When preparing for the trip to London, Jason had expected the English capital to resemble midtown Manhattan, with towering mansions, leafy side streets, and elegant carriages traveling at a stately pace down wide, evenly paved streets. There were parts of London that fit that description, but the majority of the neighborhoods Jason had seen reminded him of the Five Points area of New York, a neighborhood known for its grinding poverty, eclectic mix of New

Yorkers and immigrants, and seedy bars and dance halls. During the day, the streets teemed with wagons, street vendors, and ragged children who were always looking for a way to make a few pennies to help their families, if they were lucky enough to have one. At night, it was inhabited by streetwalkers, gamblers, and petty thieves who often prayed on the lost souls who haunted the opium dens, losing whole days to drug-induced stupor.

Clerkenwell wasn't as filthy or as crowded as Five Points, but its grim atmosphere seemed to weigh heavily on the people who lived there. The passersby looked downtrodden and put-upon, their shoulders hunched, and their gazes fixed straight ahead, as if they were afraid to attract undue attention. Jason shuddered with apprehension as the hansom rolled past several sprawling brick buildings that were surrounded by high barbed-wire-topped walls, the barred windows looking blankly onto the nearby streets. Jason could almost feel the soul-crushing desperation that clung to the place and shuddered inwardly, recalling the last time he'd felt such misery. He didn't need to ask what he was looking at; he knew. These were prisons, and he was sure that most of the inmates only traveled beyond the walls either wrapped in sackcloth or safely stowed in plain pine boxes—unless the prisons had their own cemeteries, and those who'd entered through the gates were never allowed to depart, not even in death.

"Is this a high crime area?" Jason asked, wondering why there were several prisons in such close proximity to one another.

"Most of London is a high crime area. Poverty leads to crime, which, in turn, leads to poverty."

"How does crime lead to poverty?" Jason asked as the hansom rattled past a brewery that gave off the yeasty smell of hops. Jason found it nauseating.

"If a man commits a crime, no matter how minor, he's either sent to prison or executed, which leaves his family to fend for themselves. Few women can earn enough to support their children, so they turn to prostitution, an occupation that's not synonymous with longevity and good health. London is teeming with orphans, most of whom survive by begging, stealing, and selling anything of value they can get their hands on, including their bodies. The cycle of poverty and crime is yet to be broken."

"Is there no government assistance of any kind for these women and children?" Jason asked, horrified by Daniel's matter-of-fact recital of the facts.

"There are workhouses, but they are a last resort for most folk. Once people go in, they're not likely to come out. Many die of disease, others of despair."

"Can nothing to be done to help these people?" Jason asked.

Daniel shook his head. "As long as a small percentage of the population owns nearly all land and industry, no one will lift a finger to help the poor. They are a bad investment."

"That's an awful way of thinking," Jason snapped.

"It is, but that's how things are. At least for now. There are some who are advocating for social reform, but that could take years, decades even. Clerkenwell's not too bad. You should see the rookeries. I'm a grown man and I'm afraid to set foot in there. That place will eat you alive and spit you out, your bones picked clean."

"You make it sound like a real tourist attraction," Jason retorted.

"I'm telling it like it is. Are you suggesting there's no poverty in America? What about all those slaves you have so recently freed? What are they doing now? Are they living the high life, sleeping in mansions and eating like kings?"

Jason cringed. Daniel was right. The South was a cauldron of unrest following the war, with gangs of freed slaves roaming the countryside looking for work, dispossessed land owners trying to find a way to survive in an unfamiliar world, and countless carpetbaggers from the North lining their own pockets and cheating people who were already on the brink of desperation into buying into their schemes and investing the last of their resources. It would take decades for the Southern states to find their footing and get back to some semblance of order and prosperity.

"No, they are not," Jason conceded. "It will take years to recover from the war, and not only for the South. I can only assume Mr. Sullivan's circumstances are reduced, as you British like to say," Jason observed, eager to change the subject.

"I'll say," Daniel replied as the carriage came to a stop. Daniel examined the ground before carefully getting out, mindful of slipping on the refuse that lined the street or getting splattered as another conveyance drove by. "Watch where you step," he warned Jason.

The red-brick building might have been, if not elegant, of pleasing proportions once. Now it was run down and neglected. Many of the windowpanes were cracked or missing altogether, the remaining windows grimy and uncurtained, and the paint on the frames and door peeling, the large flakes revealing a different, darker-color paint beneath. A strong smell of waste wafted from the alley that hugged the building on the left, and the steps were smeared with muck.

"I don't expect this will take very long," Daniel muttered as he chose where he stepped carefully. "Let's hope our man is in or we will have had a wasted journey."

Chapter 19

Daniel used the scratched brass knocker to announce their presence. A young woman opened the door. A round-faced baby sat on her hip, and an older child hovered behind her, peeking out from behind her skirts. Despite the condition of the building, the woman looked clean and tidy, and the children appeared healthy and well fed.

"'Ow can I 'elp ye, gentlemen?" the woman asked.

"We're here to see Mr. Sullivan," Daniel said, his gaze straying to the baby, who was studying him with unblinking concentration. With its fair curls and baby gown, it was hard to tell if it was a boy or a girl, but it was sweet all the same.

"Top door on the right," the woman said, and stepped aside to let them by. "What'd I tell ye 'bout getting under foot, John?" she scolded the boy, who nearly fell over when she moved unexpectedly. The boy looked like he was about to cry, so she grabbed him by the hand and dragged him through an open door that must have led to her own lodgings.

Jason and Daniel walked up the rickety stairs and knocked on the door. At first, there was silence, then they heard light footsteps. The door was opened by a fair-skinned man with unruly auburn hair and wide blue eyes. His worried gaze went from Daniel to Jason and back again, his unease obvious.

"Are you the bailiffs?" he asked, his voice quivering with apprehension.

"No, Mr. Sullivan. I am Constable Haze, and this is Captain Redmond. We're investigating the death of Elizabeth Barrett," Daniel explained. "May we come in?"

The man didn't look too pleased at the prospect of letting them into his rooms but relented, obviously relieved they weren't the bailiffs after all. Looking around, Jason wondered what the bailiffs might have taken, as there was nothing of value on display. There was a threadbare settee, a scarred table and two chairs, and an easel with a half-finished painting propped on it. The painting was rather good, but Jason was no expert on art. He only knew what appealed to him. The door to the other room was closed, but he couldn't imagine that the bedroom was any more luxurious than the sitting room. The man was dirt poor and clearly terrified of losing what little he had.

"Please," Shawn Sullivan said, gesturing toward the chairs.

Daniel and Jason sat down, but Shawn Sullivan remained standing, probably poised for flight. He exuded a nervous energy that Jason would have otherwise found irritating but under the circumstances could easily forgive. Were he in Shawn Sullivan's shoes, he'd be nervous too.

"Mr. Sullivan, were you aware that Mrs. Barrett is dead?" Daniel asked.

The man nodded. "I had a letter from Miss Dawlish just yesterday. She is a mutual friend," he explained. "I can't believe Elizabeth is gone." He looked unbearably sad, his eyes swimming with tears.

"Where were you on Thursday night and then on Friday morning?" Daniel asked.

"I was here," the man said so softly, Jason could barely hear him.

"Can anyone confirm that?" Daniel asked. He seemed immune to Shawn Sullivan's distress.

"Mrs. Moore, the downstairs tenant, saw me on Thursday evening. I went out to buy an eel pie for my supper. It must have been around seven. I didn't go out Friday morning."

"When was the last time you saw Elizabeth Barrett?"

"About a fortnight ago. We went to the National Gallery. It was one of Elizabeth's favorite places. Her husband never accompanied her, so she usually asked me to come along. Afterward, she stood me lunch. She was always very generous."

"Did she come to London on her own?" Daniel asked, surprised.

"No. Deborah—that is, Mrs. Silver—came with her. They often did things together."

"Did Mrs. Silver go to the gallery and to lunch as well?" Daniel asked.

"No. She had plans to visit her modiste for a fitting. Elizabeth and Deborah met at the train station at three. They wished to get home well before dinner. I saw them off at Charing Cross." Evidently tired of standing, Shawn Sullivan sank down on the settee, but didn't attempt to get comfortable. He perched on the edge, his elegant, pale hands clasped in his lap.

"Did Mrs. Barrett come to London often?" Jason asked.

Shawn Sullivan shrugged. "Once in a while, when she needed 'a breath of air,' as she liked to say. Elizabeth found Brentwood unbearably dull."

"How long had you been her tutor?" Daniel inquired.

"For more than a year. Miss Dawlish introduced us."

Daniel cast a meaningful look about the dingy room. "Mr. Sullivan, do you have any other pupils?"

"Not at the moment. I'm in need of a new post."

"As an art tutor?"

"I don't just tutor art," he replied softly. "I'm also qualified to teach mathematics, reading, and history, and I have several languages, but I'm having a difficult time finding a position," he admitted miserably.

"I see," Daniel replied, his tone gentler now. "That must be distressing."

"It is, rather," Shawn Sullivan agreed. "With Elizabeth gone, I have no source of income at the present."

And given that he'd mistaken them for bailiffs, clearly no savings, either, Jason thought. He studied the man casually, not wishing to make him uncomfortable. He was handsome, but his features were delicate, and a trifle effeminate, making him look more youthful than he probably was. He was clean shaven and wore a silk puff tie in a vibrant shade of green that clashed violently with his untrimmed auburn locks but went well with the flower-embroidered waistcoat that boasted green leaves splashed against a pale-yellow background, putting one in mind of a spring garden.

Jason had detected a slight Irish lilt beneath the studied English accent, which only confirmed what he'd already suspected. Being Irish, probably Catholic, would make finding employment in a Protestant household difficult, more so given his fiery looks and Celtic surname. There was something else as well, but Jason didn't want to jump to conclusions based on a hunch. Not yet.

"Mr. Sullivan, were you in love with Elizabeth Barrett?" Daniel asked pointedly.

"I cared for her, but I had no reason to harm her." Shawn Sullivan sounded desperate and scared; his wide eyes fixed on Daniel as if he could convince him with the sheer strength of his will that he'd done nothing wrong.

"I've made no suggestion that you have," Daniel replied calmly.

"Isn't that why you're here? To discover if I had a motive to kill her? Well, I didn't," he cried defiantly. "Elizabeth was always kind to me. She treated me as an equal, even though I was nothing more than an employee. She spoke to me of art, and life, and her feelings. She considered me a friend and had made me her confidante. Yes, I loved her with all my heart, but I wasn't in love with her. And as you can see, I needed the income Jonathan Barrett was paying me to live, so killing her would go against my own interests."

Daniel nodded. "Can you think of anyone who might have wanted to harm her?"

Shawn Sullivan shook his head. The defiance had burned out as quickly as it had flared, and he looked sad again, his shoulders sagging with the weight of his woes and obvious grief for his friend. "Elizabeth was liked by everyone. She was a devoted wife, a loving sister, and a gifted painter, but she never boasted or made a grab for attention. She was very humble about her abilities, always eager to learn and improve, and compliment others, even though their work wasn't nearly as accomplished as hers. Had she been a man, free to pursue her art more aggressively, she'd be famous. I've no doubt of that. In truth, there was little I could teach her, but she liked having me around. I was someone she could talk to about things that mattered to her, and I could be frank with her in return."

"Could she not talk to her husband?" Daniel asked.

Shawn scoffed at the suggestion. "Jonathan loved Elizabeth; I don't doubt that, but he never saw her, not the way she wanted to be seen. He indulged her love of art because it amused him, not because he thought her good or because it was important to her. He patronized her the way one patronizes a child to keep them happy. I've no doubt he would have put an end to our lessons if Elizabeth had a child and expected her to devote herself to being a mother instead of gallivanting around the countryside in search of views that inspired her."

Daniel stiffened at the mention of a child. "Did you know she was with child, Mr. Sullivan?"

Shawn Sullivan's reaction was an answer in itself. He looked stunned, his eyes widening in disbelief. "No. No, I didn't."

"Were you ever intimate with Elizabeth Barrett?" Daniel asked, his gaze hard and probing.

Shawn Sullivan smiled wryly. "No, Constable. In fact, if you must know, I have never been intimate with a woman."

Daniel nodded, clearly satisfied. Shawn Sullivan was a man who wore his heart on his sleeve, something both Deborah Silver and Jane Dawlish had alluded to when questioned. Jason didn't think he was the type of man to meticulously plan a murder and then carry it out in cold blood. It simply wouldn't fit with his personality, unless he was a consummate actor, something Jason doubted.

"So, you can think of no reason someone would wish to poison Elizabeth Barrett?" Daniel asked, his shoulders sagging with the futility of the interview.

"None whatsoever," Shawn Sullivan replied. "Elizabeth chafed at the constraints placed on her, but in reality, she was one of the luckiest people I have ever met."

"How so?" Jason asked, curious about this man's perception of her life. He'd certainly been forthcoming thus far.

"Elizabeth lacked the support and encouragement she craved in her artistic pursuits, but she'd never known loneliness or despair or real hardship," Shawn said, his Adam's apple bobbing as he swallowed hard, his eyes misty. "Can you imagine such a thing? Her parents had adored her, her husband worshipped the ground she walked on, and her sister wanted nothing more than to protect her from life's inevitable disappointments."

Jason wondered if Shawn Sullivan was referring to Elizabeth's miscarriages. Would a woman speak of such things to a man, or was Shawn speaking in broader terms, possibly referring to what Jane Dawlish had said about Elizabeth feeling unable to follow her dreams and forge her own path? Jason felt a pang of pity for this emotional young man. Clearly, he hadn't been loved much, possibly not at all. His lodgings were a testament to a life of poverty and loneliness, his background a cause for persecution. And given what Jason suspected, he probably didn't open up to too many people, fearful of the consequences.

"Had Elizabeth Barrett rejected you?" Daniel asked, misreading Sullivan's emotion as bitterness rather than wonder that someone could lead such a charmed life.

"She never rejected me, Constable. She was one of the few people who accepted me," Shawn said quietly, cementing Jason's suspicions.

"Mr. Sullivan, do you have character references?" Jason asked, and both men looked at him in surprise.

"Stating that I'm not a ruthless killer?" the young man said, gallows humor lighting up his eyes for the first time.

"No, references from your past employers."

"Yes, I do," the man replied, clearly confused by the turn the conversation had taken.

"May I see them?" Jason asked.

Jason saw the apprehension in the man's eyes, but he didn't deny the request. Shawn Sullivan disappeared into the bedroom and returned a few moments later with several sheets of paper, which he handed to Jason. The references were impeccable, but the signatures bore names that would put some potential employers off. Misters O'Leary, Malone, and Harrington, which could be Irish, and a diploma from Trinity College in Dublin.

"Thank you," Jason said as he handed back the sheaf of papers. "These are impressive."

Daniel looked nearly as confused as Shawn Sullivan, probably assuming Jason had some trick up his sleeve, but said nothing.

"How do my references relate to the case, Captain Redmond?"

"They don't. Mr. Sullivan, I have a young ward who's in need of a tutor. The position comes with room and board, and two afternoons off per week. Lord knows you'll need them," Jason added with a smile. "I'm offering a fair salary, which will include a pay raise after one year. Three months' probation," he added, so as not to sound too flexible. "What do you say?"

Shawn Sullivan's mouth opened in shock as his eyes searched Jason's face as though looking for any hint of subterfuge. "Are you serious, sir?"

"I am. Think it over and let me know what you decide by the end of next week. I'll give you my address."

"I don't need to think it over. I accept," Shawn said, his face splitting into a grin. "I won't let you down, sir. How old is the pupil, if I may ask?"

"He's eleven. He's had some schooling, but not much, and he's stubborn as a donkey. He's also clever, resourceful, and very kind. I think you two will get along just fine."

Daniel's mouth hung open, his eyes daring Jason to explain himself, but Jason simply handed the references back to Shawn Sullivan and stood. "If you're finished, Constable."

"Eh…yes. Thank you for your time, Mr. Sullivan. We'll see ourselves out."

Daniel didn't explode until after they had verified with Mrs. Moore that she had indeed seen Shawn Sullivan on Thursday evening around seven and had heard him moving about his rooms on Friday morning, and had reached the corner where it would be easier to hail a hansom. Not a single cab was in sight.

"What in the name of all that's holy was that? I'm questioning a suspect and you decide to offer him a job?"

"Daniel, Shawn Sullivan didn't kill Elizabeth Barrett."

"And how can you be so sure? His alibi is flimsy, at best. Just because Mrs. Moore saw him and heard someone moving about doesn't mean he couldn't have traveled to Birch Hill late on Thursday or early on Friday morning, having left someone in his rooms while he was out. Did I miss some vital clue?"

A smile tugged at the corner of Jason's mouth, but he tried to hide it from his irate companion. "I think you may have."

"Enlighten me, then, if you please. Why couldn't Shawn Sullivan have killed Elizabeth Barrett, aside from the fact that he was supposedly at home?"

"For one, he had absolutely no reason to. For another, the wage Jonathan Barrett paid him was the only thing keeping him from abject poverty. And the most important reason is the man wasn't in love with Elizabeth Barrett, so his motive would not have been romantically motivated."

"And how, pray tell, do you know that? Just because he said so? I agree that he probably didn't kill her. He's too temperamental to carry out a plan that calls for a cool head and some semblance of patience, but he could have been acting for our benefit. He's an artist, after all. They're known for the volatility of their emotions."

"I don't believe he was acting, Daniel. I think with Shawn Sullivan, what you see is what you get, except for one thing, which he must hide out of self-preservation. He's homosexual."

Daniel's mouth dropped open, his eyes growing round with disbelief. "How do you know he's a molly?"

"The high-pitched voice, the effeminate gestures, the exaggerated emotional response to your questions, not to mention the ready admission that he'd never been with a woman. He also stressed that Elizabeth Barrett had accepted him for what he was. I think he was referring to his homosexuality."

Daniel looked thoughtful. "You are sure?"

"I wouldn't stake my life on it, but yes, I think so."

"So, why would you want to hire him to teach Micah? What if he, you know—" Daniel's face was creased with puzzlement, his eyes searching Jason's face as though looking for signs of a sudden onset of insanity.

"Just because he's homosexual doesn't mean he'll force himself on a pupil any more than either of us would force ourselves on some girl simply because we prefer women," Jason replied. He couldn't blame Shawn Sullivan for being terrified of being discovered. People were ignorant and prejudiced against men like him, and homosexuality had been a hanging offense if proven in court until only a few years ago. He suspected the man's romantic feelings for Elizabeth Barrett were probably nothing more than a smokescreen, an extra layer of protection should someone begin to suspect the truth.

"So, you hired him out of pity?" Daniel asked, still trying to understand Jason's motives.

"I hired him because he has excellent references, desperately needs employment, and shares a common background with Micah that will help them bond."

"And you don't mind sharing a house with someone like him?"

"Why, do you think he'll fall desperately in love with me?" Jason asked, wiggling his eyebrows comically.

"Be serious."

"I am."

"You're a very progressive man," Daniel said, shaking his head.

"I like to think so."

"But what if Elizabeth Barrett had discovered the truth and threatened to expose him? That would be motive for murder," Daniel suggested.

Jason shook his head. "I don't see it. If she had threatened him, which I really don't think she did, then he'd have to act quickly, before she went and told someone. Do you think he'd take days or weeks to procure the poison, then wait for an opportune moment to give it to her? A man in that predicament would have to resort to whatever weapons he had to hand: a blunt object, his hands, a body of water, if one happened to be nearby," he mused.

Daniel was about to say something when a hansom pulled up, putting an end to their discussion. The men got in, and Jason gave the driver an address.

"Where are we going?" Daniel asked.

"Remember I'd mentioned that I had an errand to attend to?" Jason asked.

"Yes, of course."

"It won't take long. I have written to my grandfather's solicitor asking him to draw up a will. He needs my signature on the document and you can witness it, if you've no objection."

"Happy to be of service," Daniel replied.

Jason was glad Daniel didn't ask any prying questions. He wouldn't have minded telling him that he'd made Micah his sole heir, but this was not a topic he wished to discuss with anyone, least of all Micah. The will was just a precaution in case anything happened to Jason before he married or had children of his own.

He would see to Micah's future regardless, but if he had a family, the terms of the will would change accordingly.

Jason pulled out his pocket watch and checked the time. "Excellent, we should be back in Birch Hill with time to spare."

"Do you have a pressing engagement there as well?" Daniel asked, now smiling at Jason knowingly.

"I have plans to meet Miss Talbot."

"Ah, I see. Well, we'd best hurry back, then."

Chapter 20

Jason strolled down the lane, keeping an eye out for Miss Talbot and thanking the gods of English weather for not sending a torrential downpour to ruin their assignation. Despite the lack of progress in the investigation, he was in a remarkably good mood. Shawn Sullivan would settle his affairs in London and report for duty next week. Jason was about to see Miss Talbot, and he'd had a letter from Mr. Hartley, who thought he might have a clue to Mary Donovan's whereabouts.

The word 'whereabouts' held infinite promise, since it wasn't normally associated with a corpse. Jason was willing to pay any amount of money for Mr. Hartley to follow Mary's trail, wherever it led. He hadn't shared the news with Micah, of course. He'd only tell him if there was something concrete to impart. Micah had already lost Mary once; he didn't need to keep losing her every time he got his hopes up that she was alive and well.

Mary faded from Jason's mind as soon as he saw Miss Talbot in the distance. She wore a new bonnet, at least new to him, and looked very fetching. Katherine spotted him and a smile of such sweetness spread across her normally serious face, it took his breath away. Jason raised a hand in greeting, and she waved back as she hurried toward him.

"Miss Talbot," Jason said, tipping his hat. "Lovely afternoon."

"It is," she agreed as she fell into step beside him. "I'm glad to come outdoors at last." Now that she was so near, he could see that she looked tired and a little frazzled.

"Whom did you visit today?" Jason asked, wondering what had kept her inside all day and why she looked so worn out.

"Mrs. Caulfield. The poor woman is so heavy with child, she can barely move, and her husband is out all day, working in the orchard. The children are running her ragged, especially the twins. They're only two and as clever as two little monkeys, devising ways to torture whoever is unfortunate enough to have to mind them."

"Does she not have any family that might help?"

"She has a sister, but Mrs. Carter's got her hands full with her own family. Mrs. Carter has six boys under the age of ten. I'll go back tomorrow and the day after. It's the least I can do."

"Will you be passing this way on Thursday?" Jason asked, hoping he'd see her again soon.

"Yes, I suppose I will, unless Mrs. Caulfield goes into labor. I might have to stay and care for the children. Father won't be pleased, but if I tell him it's the Christian thing to do, he won't grumble as much."

"Perhaps once Mrs. Caulfield is safely delivered, we can have a picnic by the river," Jason suggested, hoping the weather would hold long enough for them to enjoy the outing.

Miss Talbot shook her head. "I'm afraid I can't, Captain. Father would never countenance such a plan."

"We can bring a chaperone," Jason suggested, his frustration quickly mounting. Did the woman want to spend the rest of her days looking after her despot of a father? Surely, she deserved some happiness in her life.

"Captain, please don't look so thunderous," Miss Talbot said, her dark gaze worried behind the lenses of her glasses. "I would like nothing more than to have a picnic with you, but surely you can see the impropriety of such an arrangement."

"All right, then. What kind of arrangement wouldn't be fraught with impropriety? Can I invite you to tea?"

"Father and I would be delighted," she answered sheepishly. "Father is anxious to bring you into the fold. He says it's important for members of the quality to attend church services, to inspire the lower orders."

"Then perhaps he should liven up his sermons," Jason replied, instantly wishing he'd kept his opinion to himself.

Katherine gave him a reproving look. "Sermons are not meant to be diverting, Captain. They're meant to educate and inspire, and in some instances, terrify the sinful masses into fearing the wrath of God." For a moment, Jason thought she was serious, but then he saw the mischievous look in her eyes and realized she was quoting her father. "I shouldn't poke fun at my father," Katherine said, obviously sorry to have given in to a momentary desire to criticize. "He genuinely cares about his flock. It's not his fault he's not given to pretty words and clever metaphors."

"No, of course not," Jason agreed, frustrated to be speaking of Reverend Talbot again. He wanted to talk about Katherine, about what interested her, pleased her, and made her dream. Did she ever allow herself to dream, or did she just go from day to day, doing what was expected of her and never imagining that her life could be so much more? He found himself wanting to make her happy, to surprise her into smiling widely and laughing until tears coursed down her cheeks. He wanted to kiss her.

Inwardly groaning with frustration, Jason decided to change tack. "Do you like to dance, Miss Talbot?"

That got her attention. "Yes," she replied shyly. "Although I don't get much opportunity to dance these days."

"Then how about I throw a party that will coincide with your birthday?" Jason suggested. "It's next month, isn't it? We can celebrate in style."

"No!" Katherine cried. "Please, I couldn't." Her cheeks heated with embarrassment.

"Is it the party you object to, or celebrating your birthday?" Jason asked, confused by her reaction.

Katherine shook her head. "I'm sorry. That was awfully rude of me. It's just that everyone would know why you were doing it. People are already talking. You know how these small villages are. Well, maybe you don't, coming from where you do, but please believe me, I couldn't weather the scandal if someone began to make insinuations about our relationship. Neither could father. He could lose his post."

Jason was so taken aback, he was momentarily at a loss for words. "Katherine, please forgive me. You're quite right. My suggestion was inappropriate, and I'm sorry if I placed you in an awkward position. Things are more relaxed in the United States, and we love parties."

"We love parties as well. In fact, my uncle throws a Christmas ball every year and invites the whole village. There's a buffet supper, and sometimes there's even raspberry ice. And there's dancing," she added wistfully.

"Then I will wait patiently until Squire Talbot's Christmas ball to dance with you," Jason said softly.

"So, you'll still be here then?" she asked, her voice small.

The question took Jason by surprise. Was that why she was afraid to allow him to court her openly? Did she think that he was simply toying with her and would suddenly return to New York, leaving her with her reputation in tatters? Or did her fear go deeper than that? Was she afraid he'd break her heart?

"Katherine, I'm not going anywhere for the foreseeable future. In fact, I've just hired a tutor for Micah and offered him a year-long engagement."

Katherine's eyes lit up with pleasure. "I'm glad you're not leaving, Captain. It's been so nice having you here. For the villagers, I mean. Given that you're a physician."

"Yes," Jason agreed, trying hard to appear serious. "The villagers are my number one concern."

"You're mocking me," Katherine said, trying to suppress a smile.

"I'm not. Well, not really. I do wish they would call on me when they require a doctor. I like to keep busy, and I genuinely wish to help."

"They still don't know what to make of you. You're neither fish, nor fowl, nor good red herring as far as they're concerned."

"I'm really not sure how to take that."

Katherine laughed. "I suppose that didn't sound very flattering. It's just that you're a nobleman who acts like a common man and has a profession, which is not something they're used to. And the fact that you're helping Constable Haze with his investigations puzzles them."

"I don't see why it should. I'm a surgeon. I've taken an oath to preserve life, but when I can't, I can try to understand the factors that led to the victim's death and aid the investigation with my findings."

"Do you not mind handling the dead?" Katherine asked. "Does it not scare you?"

"You mean because it reminds me of my own mortality?"

"I suppose."

"I'm not afraid of death," Jason replied truthfully.

"What are you afraid of, then?" Katherine asked, her gaze soft and vulnerable.

"I'm afraid of not living my life to the fullest. I'm afraid of not being happy or fulfilled."

"What would make you happy?"

Kissing you, Jason thought, but instantly dragged his thoughts in another direction. "Helping people, saving lives, finding a woman to love and starting a family with her. Watching my children grow up." *Dancing with you*, his mind added unhelpfully.

"You are helping, in ways you don't even realize."

"How do you mean?"

"People are talking about Mrs. Barrett's death, making up spooky stories about that place and dredging up old stories about Pagan gods and bloodthirsty druids. By finding out what happened to her, you're dispelling their fears and reaffirming their faith. Do you know who killed her?"

"No."

"Will Constable Haze be able to figure it out before the inquest? The squire just wants this to go away. I heard him speaking to my father. He'll be happy to rule Elizabeth Barrett's murder 'death by misadventure' and close the case."

"Why is he so averse to seeing justice done?" Jason asked.

"Murder is bad for business, Captain, and my uncle only cares about profit. He's not an unkind man, but he sees little point in drawing the investigation out. He's afraid the village will get a reputation, what with Alexander McDougal's murder only in June and now this."

"I can understand his concerns, but we owe it to the victims to punish their killers. They were human beings. They mattered. They can't just be written off and forgotten about."

"Are you speaking about Alexander McDougal and Elizabeth Barrett or about the men you saw die during the war?" Katherine asked softly.

"Both, I suppose. People are so quickly forgotten. It's almost as if they'd never existed."

"They live on in the hearts of those who'd loved them. They live on in your heart," Katherine said.

"Yes, they do," Jason agreed. "I wish I'd seen my parents one last time before they died. I wish I'd told them I loved them."

"I'm sure they knew," Katherine said. "Anyway, you can tell them now."

"Do you think they can hear me?"

"I talk to my mother and sister all the time. I believe they can hear me, and that comforts me when I feel sad."

"You can talk to me," Jason said. "I will always listen."

"Thank you, Captain, but sometimes it takes a woman to understand a woman's heart. I'm sorry, but I must get back. Father will be wanting his supper soon. He prefers to dine before Evensong."

"Shall I walk you back to the rectory?" Jason asked, wishing she didn't have to go.

"You may walk me part of the way," Katherine conceded.

"As you wish," Jason said, smiling down at her. "And I'll wait for you in the lane on Thursday."

"Don't wait too long," Katherine said.

"I'll wait as long as it takes," Jason replied, and meant it.

Chapter 21

As Daniel approached the Barrett residence, his stomach muscles clenched with anxiety. He'd been instructed to come at half past four, but he didn't think he'd been invited to tea. The note had been brief, the tone commanding, the summons coinciding with his own plan to interview the family again but letting him know in no uncertain terms that he would not be in charge of the interview. He knocked softly on the door that had been decked out in white-trimmed black crepe and was promptly admitted. The maidservant took his coat and hat.

"You're expected, sir. Go right in."

The room was typical of a house in mourning. The mirror had been covered, and the clock on the mantel stood still, the hands pointing to the approximate time of Elizabeth Barrett's death. Somewhere in the house, the deceased lay in state, her hair dressed, her gown one she might have favored in life. Soon, she would begin her final journey, but not before the inquest on Friday. Frequently, the body of a murder victim was displayed at the inquest, but no such degradation would befall the remains of Elizabeth Barrett. Her husband would never permit it.

Jonathan Barrett stood by the hearth, his hands clasped behind his back, while Deborah Silver and a man Daniel didn't know occupied the settees that faced each other across a low table. Tea things were arranged on the table, a platter of tea cakes nearly empty and three empty cups waiting to be collected by the maid. Daniel bowed from the neck and waited to be asked to sit, but no such invitation came. He was left standing like an errant schoolboy in front of the headmaster.

"Constable, this is Chief Inspector Coleridge of the Brentwood Constabulary," Jonathan Barrett announced. "I have asked him here today because I believe my wife's murderer will be apprehended faster if you work in tandem."

"The murder occurred in Birch Hill, Mr. Barrett," Daniel pointed out. *On my patch*, he added mentally.

"I am aware of that, Constable, but Chief Inspector Coleridge is a family friend, and I would value his input—unless, of course, you tell us you've solved the crime and have the culprit in custody."

Daniel fought a sudden urge to laugh. *In custody.* That was a very grandiose way of putting it. Birch Hill did not have any type of detention facility, not even a blind house. Such structures had sprung up throughout England over the past several hundred years and were small, circular stone buildings with just a door and a slit for a window to hold drunks until they sobered up or detain thieves or murderers until they could be brought up before a magistrate, but there wasn't one in the parish, so even if Daniel had apprehended the killer, he'd probably have to deliver the culprit to Squire Talbot, who'd be hard-pressed to figure out what to do with the accused until the inquest.

"Well, have you?" Jonathan Barrett goaded him.

"No, sir, I have not."

"And do you have any suspects?" Coleridge asked. He appeared to be in his mid-fifties and had a balding pate and wooly whiskers. The broken capillaries in his skin were a testament to unhealthy living, as was the sizable paunch that strained against his somber waistcoat. He didn't seem hostile, though, which was reassuring given that Daniel was about to get the dressing-down of his life.

"I do not. I have questioned several individuals but have not been able to establish a motive for the murder, nor who may have carried it out."

"And you are sure it was murder?" Coleridge asked.

"Yes, sir. Lord Redmond," Daniel decided to use Jason's title as a shield against Coleridge's inevitable scorn, "is a trained surgeon who practiced not only in a hospital in New York but on the battlefields of the American Civil War. He's an experienced and thorough man who was able to identify cyanide as the murder weapon."

"Were many people poisoned with cyanide on the battlefields of the American Civil War?" Coleridge mocked.

"I wouldn't think so, sir, but that doesn't mean Lord Redmond is unable to detect it. His skills are not limited to battle wounds."

"No, I suppose not," Coleridge conceded. "Our own police surgeon is one carcass short of being a butcher."

"How is it possible, Constable, that you have absolutely no leads?" Deborah Silver asked, her tone dripping with accusation. Her narrowed gaze made Daniel uncomfortable.

"Whom have you spoken to?" Jonathan Barrett demanded.

"Aside from you and Mrs. Silver, I have spoken to every chemist in Brentwood, have interviewed Miss Dawlish and Mr. Sullivan, and have followed up with Davy Brody, who found the body, and his stable boy, Matty Locke." Daniel decided not to share the fact that it was actually Jason who'd spoken to the latter two or that they'd interviewed Dulcie Wells. He had no desire to get her in trouble with her employer. He also chose not to mention that Mrs. Dodson had imparted some information about the family, since it wasn't relevant to the investigation. "If you have any notion as to who might have wished to harm Mrs. Barrett, I'm all ears," Daniel said. He hadn't meant to sound impertinent, but the family had given him very little to work with. "If there's someone you haven't told me about, now would be the time. The inquest is on Friday, and I'm running out of ideas."

"It must have been the tutor," Deborah Silver exclaimed, looking from Jonathan Barrett to Inspector Coleridge. "He's an excitable young man, prone to bouts of melancholy. Poor Lizzie must have rejected his advances, and he flew into a rage and killed her."

"Have you interviewed this tutor?" Coleridge asked.

"I have. Only this morning."

"And?" Jonathan Barrett demanded from his place by the hearth.

"And I don't believe he did it."

"You don't believe?" Mrs. Silver asked incredulously. "Of course, he killed her. Who else would have done it?"

"Deborah, please," Jonathan Barrett said softly, and she instantly altered her demeanor, deferring to him as the master of the house.

"If, as you suggest, Mrs. Silver, Mr. Sullivan had been rejected and had flown into a rage, I doubt he would have waited to procure a deadly poison, then bided his time until the opportunity to administer it presented itself. He would have killed Mrs. Barrett then and there, using whatever means he had to hand. And, as it happens, he has an alibi for both Thursday evening and Friday morning."

Inspector Coleridge nodded. "That's sound reasoning, Constable. How solid is his alibi?"

Daniel inwardly winced but held his ground. "He was seen by a neighbor on Thursday evening and then heard by the same neighbor on Friday morning. He lives alone, so she wouldn't have heard him moving about had he gone out."

"And how trustworthy is this neighbor?" Coleridge asked. "He might have asked him to lie."

"The neighbor is a respectable married woman who seemed surprised by my questions. She wasn't ready with the answers. I know that's not saying much, but I believe gut instinct is important in policing, and mine is telling me that she was being truthful, as was Mr. Sullivan."

"Gut instinct?" Deborah cried. "Is that the best you can do? My sister is dead, and you're citing your instinct as if it were some scientific instrument of detection."

"Calm down, Deborah," Inspector Coleridge said. "I happen to agree with Haze here. Gut instinct is not to be ignored when questioning the suspects. It may not be a scientific tool, but it has helped man avoid extinction for centuries."

Daniel wished he could thank the man for backing him up, but kept quiet, wishing only to be dismissed and go home. There was nothing to be gained here save humiliation.

"Had any strangers come through the village at the time of the murder?" Coleridge asked.

"Not that I know of, sir, but if they had, no one would have paid them any mind," Daniel said.

"Oh? Why's that?" Coleridge asked.

"Because it stands to reason that they would have seen them in the past. This was not a random crime. Whoever killed Mrs. Barrett had wished her dead for some time. They had carefully prepared and bided their time until the circumstances were just right, and they would have got away with the crime had Lord Redmond failed to detect the poison. It would have been the perfect murder."

"And who do you think is capable of committing the perfect murder?" Coleridge asked, his gaze thoughtful.

"Certainly not Shawn Sullivan or Miss Dawlish, who had no reason to murder her friend."

"And what of the missing ring?" Coleridge asked.

"I don't believe the theft of the ring was the motive for the murder. I think whoever took the ring did so more for sentimental reasons than financial ones. Perhaps they liked it, or simply wanted something that had belonged to Elizabeth Barrett."

"You mean like a memento?" Coleridge queried.

"Yes, of sorts. They might decide to sell it later on, once the crime has been forgotten about, but for now, they will enjoy possessing it."

"Finding the ring in someone's possession would be incriminating evidence," Coleridge suggested.

"Yes, it would be, but I think the murderer is a person of great daring. Also, someone who is knowledgeable about poisons. They would have had to know exactly how much would be enough to kill rather than just make Mrs. Barrett ill. Had she recovered, she'd have known exactly who'd tried to kill her."

"Unless she never made the connection," Deborah Silver said. "She might have thought something she'd eaten hadn't agreed with her or that perhaps she was suffering from severe morning sickness. Oh, I'm sorry, Jonathan," she said softly. "It was thoughtless of me to remind you of the child."

Jonathan Barrett made a dismissive gesture with his hand, but the pain was evident in his eyes.

"I'm afraid Deborah does have a point," Inspector Coleridge said. "Elizabeth might never have thought the sickness was anything more than indigestion or the effects of early pregnancy."

"In which case, the murderer is even more clever than I had initially thought," Daniel replied. "They would be able to bide their time and try again at a later date."

"But why?" Jonathan Barrett exclaimed. "Why would anyone want to kill her? What could she possibly have done to inspire such hatred?"

"That's what I'm trying to find out, Mr. Barrett," Daniel said. Despite his unease at being interrogated by Coleridge, he felt pity for Jonathan Barrett. The man was clearly suffering.

"Jonathan, if you suspect something or someone, now is the time to speak. I know you loved her, man, but if she had a lover or an admirer that she'd spurned, you must tell us. Time is running short," Inspector Coleridge urged.

Jonathan Barrett nodded. "There was someone." His voice was barely audible, and he averted his gaze and fixed it on the covered mirror, staring at it as if he could see his wife's reflection in it. "Michael Tanner."

"The painter?" Deborah asked, clearly surprised.

"Yes. Elizabeth met him in the spring. She'd gone to see his exhibition at the Royal Academy, and they got to talking. She was quite excited about it since she admired his work. I believe she saw him several more times after that," Jonathan Barrett choked out. "Privately."

"When would she have seen him?" Deborah demanded. "I always went to London with her. I was there when she met Mr. Tanner. She was awestruck, to be sure, but their meeting was nothing more than that of an artist and an admirer. They spoke for a few moments."

Jonathan Barrett looked like he was going to be sick. "They began to correspond and had arranged to meet. This was in May."

Deborah Silver's eyes flashed with anger. "You know why I didn't accompany her to London then," she snapped.

"No one is blaming you, Deborah," Jonathan said. "You had your own troubles to deal with, and I didn't want to burden you with the knowledge that Elizabeth might be having a relationship with this man."

"Did you ever confront her?" Coleridge asked.

Jonathan shook his head. "No. I was too afraid to. I hoped she'd come to her senses and forget about him."

"Had she?" Coleridge demanded.

"I'm not certain."

"How did you know your wife was meeting with this man?" Daniel asked.

Jonathan Barrett looked embarrassed. "I found his letters to her. I knew where she kept her correspondence and checked it from time to time."

"To be sure your wife wasn't cuckolding you?" Daniel asked cruelly.

"Yes, Constable, to be sure. I suppose I never felt secure in her love. It's a shameful thing to admit, but there it is."

"Oh, Jonathan," Deborah said on a sigh. "You poor, poor man."

"Mr. Barrett, is there any possibility that the child your wife carried wasn't yours?" Daniel asked carefully. He braced

159

himself for unbridled fury, but Jonathan Barrett only hung his head, his shoulders slumping with misery.

"Yes, there might be."

"No!" Deborah Silver exclaimed, bright spots of color staining her cheeks. "Lizzie would never. She might have admired this man for his artistic ability, but she would never stoop so low. Never!"

"Thank you for being frank with us, Jonathan," Coleridge said, his eyes warm with sympathy. "We need to speak to this Tanner as soon as possible. Constable, may I accompany you when you go to interview this man?"

"Would tomorrow suit?" Daniel asked. He had mixed feelings about Inspector Coleridge involving himself in the investigation. On the one hand, Daniel would have the benefit of his experience. On the other, he'd be forced to allow the man to take charge because of his superior rank, and if Tanner turned out to be the culprit, the inspector would take credit for solving the case.

"Yes. Shall we meet at the railway station at, say, ten?"

"I'll see you there, sir," Daniel replied miserably.

"Good man. Till tomorrow, then."

Having been thus dismissed, Daniel left the Barrett residence to make his way home.

Chapter 22

Jason set aside his book and gazed toward the window. The moon shone brightly, gauzy clouds sailing across its surface like the shreds of raw cotton he'd seen strewn across the fields after a skirmish at a Virginia plantation. The wispy white fibers had been saturated with blood where the dead and dying lay among the rows of plants, the wounded begging for water as the white-hot sun beat on their wool uniforms. Jason turned from the window, annoyed with his maudlin thoughts. The war had taken much from him, but it wouldn't take his peace of mind. He was in England now, half a world away from the setting of his worst nightmares.

Jason was just about to turn out the gas lamp when loud banging reverberated through the house. He jumped out of bed, pulled on his dressing gown, and ran downstairs, nearly colliding with Dodson, clad in his old-fashioned banyan, as he raced for the front door. Dodson unlocked the door and pulled it open. Katherine Talbot stood on the threshold, her pale face haunting in the moonlight.

"Katherine! What happened?" Jason cried as she exploded into the foyer. "What are you doing out on your own at this hour?"

"Jason, please come! She's dying. They both are." In her panic, she'd used his Christian name, an oversight that wasn't lost on him, but he'd savor his name on her tongue later. Now he was desperate to help her in whatever way he could.

"Who is dying?" he asked urgently.

"Alice Caulfield and her baby. Please, come quick."

"Give me a moment to get dressed and grab my medical bag," Jason said. "Did someone bring you here or did you walk?"

"John Caulfield brought me. He's outside with the wagon."

"I'll fetch your bag, sir," Dodson offered, already making for the stairs.

"No. There are items I need to add," Jason threw back over his shoulder as he overtook the butler and sprinted up the stairs.

He dressed in record time, pulling on the clothes he'd worn earlier and had left rumpled on the chair for Henley to deal with in the morning. Jason yanked open his bag and added several items he wouldn't normally bring when visiting the sick, then hurried back down, where Katherine was pacing the foyer floor like a caged tiger. He grabbed her by the arm, and they ran into the night, climbing into the wagon and squeezing in next to John Caulfield on the bench.

John Caulfield was silent, his gaze fixed on the road ahead. His jaw moved as he clenched and unclenched his teeth, silent tears sliding down his unshaven cheeks as he urged the horses to go faster.

"Tell me what's happening," Jason said to Katherine. "How did you come to be at the Caulfields' so late at night?"

Katherine looked like she was barely holding tears at bay. "Alfie, the Caulfields' oldest, ran all the way to the vicarage. He begged Father to come. Said his mother was in a bad way. I went with him."

Jason nodded. If the vicar had been summoned, the situation was grave. "Who else is with Mrs. Caulfield?"

"The midwife, Mrs. Gillman."

"Where are the younger children?" Jason asked, aware of how damaging it could be for children to see their mother's suffering and possible death.

"They're in the house. They were sent to bed, but, of course, they can still hear everything, and they're old enough to understand that something terrible is happening."

"Mr. Caulfield, after you bring us to the house, please take the children outside. All of them. They don't need to be traumatized by what they're about to see."

Katherine's mouth opened in shock, but she closed it and nodded. "Is there anything I can do to help?"

Alice Caulfield might be dead already, Jason thought, but didn't verbalize his thoughts for fear of further upsetting

Katherine. He hoped Alice had managed to hold on. These villagers were so stubborn. They should have called him earlier, but they wouldn't feel it right and proper to trouble him, especially not with something as common as childbirth. Only wealthy women had physicians attend them. Village women still relied on midwives, who knew their business most of the time but couldn't always save the mother or the child when the situation became dire.

As the wagon pulled into the yard, Jason helped Katherine down and strode into the house, heading directly for the bedroom. Animal-like moans came from behind the closed door, and three little faces were pressed to the balusters of the staircase, the pale cheeks tearstained and the mouths open in terror.

Alfie, who was no more than six or seven, sat on the bottom step, his face in his hands as he waited for his father to return. Jason walked into the bedroom, where Mrs. Gillman dabbed at Alice Caulfield's face with a damp rag while Reverend Talbot bent over her, speaking softly. Probably praying for her salvation.

"Please, step aside," Jason said.

"This woman is dying," Reverend Talbot said, spreading his elbows to prevent Jason from coming any closer to the bed.

"I'll be the judge of that, Reverend. Please, step outside," Jason demanded. "I'm a surgeon."

"I will not leave her in her hour of need," Reverend Talbot protested.

"Fine. Stay, but allow me to try to save her."

Reverend Talbot flashed Jason an angry look but moved aside, making it possible for Jason to approach the bed. Jason quickly removed his coat, tossed it over a nearby chair, and rolled up his sleeves.

"The child is lodged in the birth canal, yer lordship," Mrs. Gillman said quietly. "'As been for 'ours. She's bleeding bad."

"Mrs. Caulfield. Alice, can you hear me?" Jason said softly.

Alice moaned and opened her eyes, which were clouded with pain. "Aye, yer lordship," she whispered hoarsely.

"I'm going to examine you to see if there's anything that can be done to help you and the baby."

"God bless ye, yer lordship," Alice mumbled, and closed her eyes again.

Jason pressed his hands to the woman's stomach and moved them gently, ascertaining the position of the child, then pulled down the counterpane that covered her from the pelvis down, and slid his hand between her legs, making Reverend Talbot gasp with shock. Alice Caulfield's thighs were slick with blood, and she cried pitifully as Jason pushed his fingers as far as he could. He could feel the infant's head and, as he probed further, could make out the slimy length of cord wrapped around the child's neck. Alice Caulfield's glazed eyes stared at him as her lips moved soundlessly. She was barely conscious, the life bleeding out of her.

"Mrs. Gillman, clear the house immediately. I need to use the kitchen table."

"What?" she asked, leaning toward him as if she hadn't caught his words.

"Ask everyone to step outside and make sure there's nothing on the table."

Mrs. Gillman hurried from the room, probably glad to have someone else take on the responsibility for mother and child. Jason had no doubt she was an experienced midwife, but this was not a situation she had a remedy for. But he did.

"What do you mean to do, Lord Redmond?" Reverend Talbot demanded, stepping into his path.

"I mean to perform a cesarean section, Reverend. I could use your help in keeping the children and Mr. Caulfield calm. There's nothing more you can do here."

Jason expected Reverend Talbot to argue, but he nodded curtly and left the room, to Jason's great relief. Jason opened his bag and extracted the vial of laudanum he'd brought. He didn't have time to waste, so he dribbled a few drops into Alice's mouth, returned the vial to the bag, then lifted her up. Blood trickled down her bare legs and splattered onto the floor as he carried her through to the front room and laid her on the table, which was thankfully long enough to accommodate her. Had she been a taller woman, her legs would have been hanging off, making her even more uncomfortable. Mrs. Gillman stood off to the side, watching.

"I need hot water and clean towels," Jason barked.

She poured some water into a basin and returned to the bedroom to get the towels she'd prepared.

Jason quickly washed his hands, disinfected the scalpel he'd brought just for this purpose with alcohol, and pushed up Mrs. Caulfield's nightdress. Her stomach was heaving beneath his hands, the child kicking its legs as it slowly suffocated, but Alice was out, the laudanum having done its job. Jason swabbed her stomach with alcohol and sliced into her flesh with a sure, steady stroke. He heard Mrs. Gillman's sharp intake of breath, felt the cold air on his face as someone opened the door, but paid no mind to anything other than his patient. Jason cut through layers of fat and muscle until he reached the uterus, then very carefully made an incision, so as not to graze the child within. Mercifully, it was still alive, if only just. Jason sliced through the cord, unwound it from the child's neck, and lifted the baby out, giving it a gentle slap on the bottom.

There was a tense silence, broken only by Mrs. Gillman's nervous breathing and the beating of Jason's heart. He tried again, this time slapping a little harder. A few more terrifying moments passed until the baby finally cried out in outrage, its bottom lip quivering and revealing toothless gums. Exhaling in relief, Jason handed the child to Mrs. Gillman, who stood by with a clean towel. She took the child and laid it on the sideboard, ready to clean its mouth and nose, wipe off the blood, and swaddle it. The baby was fussing, but its soft cries were music to Jason's ears.

He checked Alice Caulfield's pulse. It was faint but steady. She would be all right as long as she didn't succumb to an infection. Jason extracted a surgical needle and silk thread from his medical bag, deftly threaded the needle, thankful that he could see the tiny eye by the faint glow of the oil lamp, and set it aside in preparation for suturing. It was only then that he noticed Katherine standing by the door, her eyes wide with shock, her face pale.

"Hand me a basin, please," he said to her. She did, and he buried his hands inside the unconscious woman, extracting the afterbirth and examining her uterus. Jason wiped his hands on a towel to clean off the blood, then picked up the needle.

"I need more light, Katherine."

Katherine instantly grabbed the oil lamp and brought it as close as she dared, lighting the woman's bloodied stomach. Jason went to work, neatly stitching the uterus before sewing up the incision in the stomach. After he finished and tied off the thread, he dabbed the area with alcohol, cleaned off the blood, and bandaged Mrs. Caulfield's stomach with wide linen strips until her entire middle was covered.

Mrs. Gillman approached him, a smile on her weathered face. "Ye've saved 'em both, yer lordship," she said in obvious awe. "This little mite owes ye 'is very life."

Jason looked at the baby, who lay peacefully in the midwife's arms. "He owes me nothing," Jason said. "No one does. Katherine, why don't you tell Mr. Caulfield he has another son while I get Alice back to bed before the children come back in. They don't need to see their mother like this."

He carefully lifted Alice Caulfield off the table and carried her back to the bedroom, where he placed her on the bed. The linens would need to be changed and she could use a clean nightdress before she saw her brood, but that wasn't his job. Jason looked at the sleeping woman and the infant Mrs. Gillman had placed next to her, and thanked God he'd arrived in time. He hadn't touched a scalpel in over two years, and it had felt surprisingly good to perform surgery again. He had been afraid he'd be rusty, but once he'd taken hold of the cool metal, everything else had fallen away, leaving behind only self-assurance and calm.

Mr. Caulfield stood in the doorway, his cap in his hands. "Yer lordship, I don't know 'ow to thank ye. I'm in yer debt for as long as I live." The man reached into his pocket and brought out several coins, but Jason waved his hand away.

"There's no need, Mr. Caulfield. I am happy to help. I'll come back tomorrow to check on your wife and the child. Send for me anytime if you think something is wrong," Jason said sternly. "Anytime," he enunciated, knowing full well that the man wouldn't wish to disturb him again tonight.

"Thank ye, yer lordship. I'll never forget what ye've done for us. Ye saved my children from losing their mum." Tears welled in his eyes as the reality of what might have happened washed over him. "Thank ye," he said again, with feeling.

"You are most welcome. I think you should all get some rest. You look exhausted, and the children need their sleep." John Caulfield nodded, as if in a dream.

"Please don't touch the bandage and give your wife something light to eat when she wakes. She'll be hungry after her ordeal. Goodnight, Mr. Caulfield. I'll see you in the morning."

Jason walked out into the front room, where Katherine was standing next to her father. She nudged her father lightly in the arm, giving him a pointed look that seemed to wake the man from his reverie.

"Both mother and child saved from certain death," the vicar said, his voice filled with awe. "Praise God for His mercy."

"It was Lord Redmond who saved them," Katherine said archly.

"It was God who made sure Lord Redmond was on hand and in possession of the necessary skills." Katherine glared at her father reproachfully but didn't argue.

"I did what I am trained to do," Jason said. "Now, I think you'd best be getting back to the vicarage. Miss Talbot looks weary."

Katherine threw him a grateful look. She looked like she was ready to drop, but she wasn't ready to leave just yet. Reverend Talbot walked out the door into the night, leaving Jason and Katherine alone in the front room.

"What you did tonight…" She didn't finish the sentence. "It was…" She shook her head in wonder as tears shimmered in her eyes, and as she looked up at him, his heart swelled with pride. He'd impressed her, and although he knew it was childish, it made him happy.

"I'll take ye home, yer lordship," John Caulfield said as he came back into the room. "Mrs. Gillman will see to the children."

"You stay with your wife, Mr. Caulfield. It's a clear night. I'll walk."

"Are ye sure?" John Caulfield asked.

"I am." Jason looked forward to the exercise. He needed to walk off the adrenaline rush coursing through his body before he could get to sleep.

Chapter 23

Wednesday, September 12

Daniel sat across from Detective Inspector Coleridge in an otherwise empty train carriage, wishing it would finally arrive in Charing Cross. Inspector Coleridge had been pleasant and forthcoming on the journey, talking about his time as a young peeler in London and then his rise through the ranks of Scotland Yard, but despite his friendliness, Daniel felt as if he were being lectured rather than spoken to as an equal—particularly when the inspector outlined the challenges the police force faced in the modern world and opined about the newest policing procedures and forensic discoveries that he was sure would change the process of detection forever.

Perhaps it was his own inadequacy and lack of prospects that made Daniel feel uncomfortable in the inspector's presence. He was a constable, but he wasn't of the police force, nor would he ever get to utilize the brilliant new methods police detectives were using to solve crimes. For as long as he remained in Birch Hill, he'd report to Squire Talbot, who had no interest in anything beyond a speedy resolution, not caring whether it was the right outcome or a travesty of justice. Squire Talbot wasn't an indifferent or a cruel man, but he was more interested in the prosperity of his estate than upholding the law. The role of magistrate came with his position, as it had done for his ancestors, who'd been in Birch Hill since before Sir Percival Talbot, whose tomb dominated St. Catherine's crypt, had ridden off to the Crusades in the thirteenth century. But Squire Talbot did not relish his position; he hated unpleasantness, and having a murder committed in his village was as unpleasant as it got.

"Have you heard of fingerprinting, Constable Haze?" Inspector Coleridge asked, interrupting Daniel's reverie.

"How does it work, sir?" Daniel asked, intrigued despite his eagerness to get on with the day's work.

"There's a civil servant in India, a Sir William Herschel, who's been requesting fingerprints and signatures on contracts for years. Others are beginning to adopt this method. You see, Haze, a man's fingerprints and handwriting are unique and can be used to identify him."

"Sorry, sir, but I don't follow," Daniel said. "Most people don't leave a note with their fingerprints and signature at the scene of a crime."

Inspector Coleridge smiled at him indulgently. "Oh, but they do, just not in the way you think. Let's suppose that a fingerprint could be lifted off a knife handle that had been used to kill a man. Then, we could take the fingerprints of our suspects and see which one matched. It's genius, really. Indisputable proof that the person had handled the murder weapon."

"But what if the knife used in the attack belonged to someone else, and the owner's fingerprints were already on the handle?" Daniel asked.

Coleridge looked stumped for a moment. "Well, then we would have to establish which of the people whose fingerprints are on the handle are the real culprit but being able to narrow down the field would make our job easier. We might go from having ten suspects to only two. Think of your own case for a moment. The murderer took the sapphire ring off Elizabeth's finger, which means that they had to touch her wedding ring in the process. If we were able to obtain their fingerprints from the ring, we'd be able to conclusively prove that they were the killer, should we have a match to one of our suspects."

"But what if the person wore gloves? Surely, they'd leave no fingerprints."

"You are right there, Haze. But what we have on our side is that the miscreants don't know about this ingenious new method yet and don't think to wear gloves when handling weapons or stolen goods."

Daniel nodded, wondering if fingerprinting would have helped him solve the murder of Alexander McDougal sooner. Probably not, since the murder weapon had not been left at the scene, but if they could have obtained fingerprints from the lid of the stone casket, they might have been able to narrow down the list of suspects considerably, except for one minor detail. The suspects in question would never have allowed themselves to be fingerprinted or to be treated like common criminals. They'd barely let him in the door and answered his questions; they'd hardly have permitted him to show up with whatever tools it took to take their prints. A method like that could only work for the police, Daniel thought bitterly.

"A photograph might have been helpful as well," Inspector Coleridge went on. "What can be more useful than a photograph of the crime scene and the victim? You can study it at your leisure and go back to it whenever you need, using it to either support or disprove your theories about the incident. No man can recall every detail from a scene he'd examined for only a few minutes, but now we have a permanent record of every footstep, every blood splatter, every wound inflicted on the victim. It's groundbreaking, don't you think?"

"Yes, I do. Do you have a photographer at your station in Brentwood?" Daniel asked.

"Indeed, we do. He joined our ranks only recently, but he's proving to be very useful."

"And your police surgeon?" Daniel asked.

Coleridge wrinkled his nose. "Not many surgeons relish the prospect of autopsying crime victims. Not a pleasant job, I'm afraid, Haze. Dr. Engle tends to turn to strong spirits when he finds it all too much. In truth, I don't think he'll be with us much longer. I'd like to see a younger man take over, someone who's open to new methods and isn't afraid to get his hands dirty, so to speak." Coleridge glanced out the window. "Ah, here we are. Charing Cross. Amazing how quickly the train gets one from place to place, isn't it?"

"Indeed," Daniel muttered as he reached for his hat and umbrella.

He was eager to confront Michael Tanner but worried about how the interview would proceed. This was his case, but

Coleridge was a senior officer in the police. Would he take the lead on the questioning, and if Tanner proved to be their man, would Coleridge take credit for solving the crime? He supposed it didn't really matter as long as justice was served, but some small, vain part of him longed to be the one to crack the case open. He needed to prove not only to himself, but to Sarah, that what he was doing was important, and to pave the way for his exit from Birch Hill. He needed several solved cases under his belt if he were to approach the Brentwood Constabulary about a position. Now that he'd spoken to the inspector at length, he realized how unprepared he truly was, and how much he still had to learn before making an attempt at bettering his situation. He was a country bumpkin, a parish constable who had neither a constabulary nor the skills needed to be a detective.

"Come on, then. Let's find us a hansom," Coleridge said once they'd stepped out of their compartment onto the platform and then followed the stream of departing passengers out of the railway station and into the street. "I get reimbursed for my expenses, so I'll see to the fare," he added, smiling at Daniel in a condescending manner. Not only did he not see him as an actual policeman, he assumed Daniel wouldn't get reimbursed for expenses incurred during an investigation. He was correct on both counts, which did little to improve Daniel's mood.

"Thank you, sir," Daniel muttered.

The street was swarming with fine carriages, dray wagons, and pedestrians. Street vendors called out their wares, and the appetizing smell of sausage rolls drifted toward Daniel as a man with a tray slung over his neck by a leather strap passed by, hoping to sell his inventory to people who'd just arrived by train and might want to fortify themselves before getting on with their plans.

Daniel wasn't really hungry, even though it was almost time for luncheon. He'd breakfasted at home, but he associated buying food from street vendors with his time as a London peeler, fond memories reinforced by the savory goodness of a hot pie on his tongue. Inspector Coleridge turned to watch the man's progress, then called out to him.

"Oi. Over here." He fished some coins out of his pocket and bought two sausage rolls, handing one to Daniel. "I confess, I can never resist. Reminds me of being a young bobby. I used to live on these, grabbing a meal whenever I could. I couldn't afford fancy dinners then, not on my wage."

Daniel accepted the roll gratefully. "Thank you, sir. I can never say no to one of these either."

"Eat up, then. It might take a few minutes to find a cab. This place is like a beehive," the inspector said, and took a large bite of his roll.

Daniel followed suit, savoring the spiced meat and flaky pastry. Whoever had baked these had to be nearby, since the rolls were still piping hot. He wished he had a pint to go with it, but now he was just being greedy. He was here to work, not to eat. After finishing his treat, he used his handkerchief to wipe his hands clean and pulled on his gloves, thinking how he could now touch anything he wanted without leaving his fingerprints.

Finally, an empty hansom cab approached and stopped when Inspector Coleridge waved it over. The men climbed in, and Coleridge gave the driver the address.

"I hope it won't take us an hour to get there," Coleridge grumbled. "I always forget how congested it gets closer to midday. Should have left earlier."

"Wouldn't have made a difference, sir," Daniel pointed out. "It's just as congested early in the morning, when everyone is making their deliveries for the day and clerks are heading to their offices."

"Yes, but at least the quality are still asleep, so their carriages are off the streets."

"Or they're just coming home after a night on the town, and their carriages are still out and about." Daniel wasn't sure why he was trying to prove his point, so he stopped talking and looked around, taking in the sights and sounds of the city. He loved it here, no matter how crowded, how dirty, how rich or poor the area was. London pulsed with life, and he pulsed with it whenever he was here, feeling invigorated and purposeful.

After a half hour of moving barely an inch at a time, Daniel felt more irritated than invigorated, but they were close to their destination, so they paid the cabby and walked the rest of the way. Michael Tanner lived in Notting Hill, an area of London popular with artistic types who had more talent than ready cash. The man answered the door himself, wearing a paint-splattered smock and a frown of displeasure on his handsome face. He had the kind of dark, brooding looks that seemed to appeal to women, his coal-black gaze jarringly intense in a face that hadn't seen too much sun.

"Good morning, gentlemen. How can I be of service?" Michael Tanner asked, his scowl making it clear that they were taking him away from something vastly more important than speaking to strangers.

"Go on," Coleridge said quietly. "It's your case."

Daniel stepped forward, grateful to the man for giving him his chance. "Mr. Tanner, I'm Constable Haze, and this is Detective Inspector Coleridge. We'd like to speak to you regarding the death of Mrs. Elizabeth Barrett."

Tanner's expression changed from irritation to sadness, his mouth drooping as he nodded in acknowledgment. "Please, come in. Sorry, the place is a bit of a mess. My maid's been visiting her sick mother, so I've had to fend for myself. Can I offer you some refreshment?"

"No," Daniel and the inspector said in unison.

The place resembled a midden heap, with dirty cups and plates and empty wine glasses cluttering every surface. The floor was filthy, and a layer of dust covered the unpolished surfaces of the furniture. The acrid smell of coal dust wafted from the parlor hearth, which looked to have been left upswept for days, the ashes a gray heap in a room where the curtains were still closed against the morning light. Michael Tanner hastily shut the door on the mess and ushered them toward the stairs.

"My studio is on the top floor," he explained. "We'll talk in there."

The studio was surprisingly clean and bright, the curtains open wide to let in the sunshine. Tanner invited them to sit on a purple velvet couch, positioning himself behind his easel and studying them as if they were the subject of a painting rather than representatives of the police.

Daniel's gaze drifted around the room, stopping on a portrait of a lovely young woman. Her luminous dark gaze made him uncomfortable, the intimacy it invited almost indecent in its frankness. A smile hovered about her lips, almost as if she were waiting to see if her message of seduction had been received. She wore a gauzy white gown in the Grecian style, the fabric doing little to hide the shape of her creamy breasts. Daniel felt an uncomfortable stirring in his loins and tore his gaze away, but not before he identified the subject of the painting, realizing with a jolt that he'd seen this woman only a few days ago.

"Haze," Coleridge prompted. "Are you going to keep woolgathering, or shall we start?"

"Of course. Sorry, sir," Daniel muttered.

"Was Elizabeth really murdered?" Tanner asked, his eyes fixed on Coleridge, whom he correctly assumed was the superior.

"Yes, she was poisoned with cyanide," Coleridge replied gruffly. "She wouldn't have died easily."

Tanner's eyes softened with pity. "No, I don't expect she would have."

Daniel cleared his throat and fixed his attention on the painter. "Mr. Tanner, how did you know Elizabeth Barrett?" The question sounded banal, but it was as good a starting point as any.

"We met at the Academy. She expressed her admiration for my work, and we spoke for a while," Tanner said. "I invited her to take supper with me, but she refused. She did, however, give me permission to write to her."

"Did you?" Daniel asked. He already knew that Elizabeth and Michael Tanner had corresponded, but he wanted to see if the man would answer truthfully.

"That very evening. Elizabeth responded promptly, and we arranged for her to come by the following week. She was interested in seeing more of my work."

"I hope the place was cleaner then than it is now," Coleridge grumbled.

"It was. I do apologize for the state of my lodgings, gentlemen. I'm not one for cleaning."

"Did Elizabeth Barrett tell you she was married?" Daniel asked, wondering how she could undertake to make arrangements without checking with her husband. Or maybe she had.

"Yes, she did."

"Did it not surprise you that a married woman would make an assignation with you and agree to come to your lodgings?" Coleridge asked.

"Why would it? Elizabeth said her husband was busy with some important case and wouldn't be home until late that evening. I wasn't looking to marry the woman, Inspector, so it made little difference to me how she managed it."

"How did your relationship with Mrs. Barrett progress?" Daniel asked, his gaze boring into the painter in the hope that his expression would give something away, but he seemed unperturbed by the questions.

"In much the usual way, Constable. She came by, I offered to show her some of my paintings, we came up here…" His voice trailed off, leaving Daniel and Inspector Coleridge to arrive at their own conclusions.

"Did you plan to seduce her when you invited her here?" Coleridge asked, unable to remain quiet.

"Of course. She was a beautiful woman. We had much in common, since she believed herself to be an artist. She was very passionate about her work."

176

The tone of Tanner's reply wasn't lost on Daniel. "She believed herself to be an artist?"

"I'm sorry. I suppose anyone who wields a paintbrush can call themselves an artist, but she was an amateur, a dabbler."

"Have you ever seen her work?" Daniel asked, leaning forward. If Tanner admitted to seeing Elizabeth's paintings, then he'd also be admitting to visiting her in Brentwood or Birch Hill, which would be a step in the right direction in this confounding investigation.

"No, I haven't."

"So, how do you know she was an amateur?" Daniel persisted, thoroughly annoyed with the man for getting his hopes up.

"It was the way she spoke about her work. You see, Constable, the difference between an amateur and a professional is actually quite simple. Elizabeth painted for pleasure, for the joy of painting and setting something she thought beautiful on a canvas. Professionals don't paint for joy; they paint for money, and for reviews from prominent critics, which lead to more money. We're jaded and angry, mad at the world for not appreciating our genius and being forced to paint banal subjects in order to make a living. I spend most of my time painting portraits of middle-aged matrons and puffed-up merchants in order to keep myself in food and coal. Art for art's sake doesn't pay, I'm afraid."

Daniel paid little attention to this tirade. He didn't care about Michael Tanner's artistic aspirations. From what he could see from the canvases in the studio, he was quite good, but that was neither here nor there, since his ability to paint had nothing to do with Elizabeth's murder— unless she'd insulted his art and wounded his ego, in which case, he most likely would have stabbed her with a paintbrush then and there. He seemed temperamental enough to do just that.

"Mr. Tanner, did you and Elizabeth Barrett become intimate?" Daniel asked, cringing inwardly. He hated prying into the poor woman's private life, but he had little choice, given the way she'd ended up.

Tanner didn't seem bothered in the least. "We did, but our affair fizzled out very quickly. You see, Elizabeth was more interested in art than in love. She was quite provincial at her core. She wasn't in love with her husband, but she cared for him and felt terrible about being unfaithful. I think she was also fearful that he would revoke her privileges or, worse yet, have her treated for hysteria by some overpriced Harley Street hack, who'd recommend locking her up in some institution or relieving her of her womb to calm her unnatural passions. Her fretting bored me, so I ended the relationship for her sake."

"Did she truly believe her husband would go to such lengths to get her under control?" Daniel asked. He'd heard of women suffering from hysteria, but he'd imagined them to be wild, unmanageable creatures for whom all other treatments had failed. Elizabeth Barrett didn't sound wild or unmanageable, but he supposed Jonathan Barrett might have thought differently, especially if he'd learned of the affair and had discovered that the child his wife carried might have been sired by another man.

"I don't think she did. I think she wanted to rant about the unfairness of it all, man's fear of women who dared to defy convention and pursue their passions, be they art or free love. I never met Jonathan Barrett, but he didn't strike me as an unreasonable man from what Elizabeth said about him. In fact, he seemed rather open-minded, encouraging his wife to pursue her interests and allowing her to travel to London without a suitable chaperone."

"Perhaps she did have a chaperone on those occasions," Inspector Coleridge said. "She usually came to London with her sister."

"If her sister had come to London with her, she must have had plans of her own, because I never met her after that first time at the Academy. I remember her well. Lovely woman. Sad."

"How did you and Elizabeth Barrett part?" Daniel asked.

"We parted as friends, Constable. Neither of us was in love, so it was easy enough to put an end to our meetings. I think Elizabeth was relieved. In fact, the last time we met, she came with a friend. A chaperone, if you will, in case things got unpleasant, which they didn't."

"When was this?" Coleridge asked.

"Toward the end of June."

"And who was this friend?" Daniel asked, wondering if she'd brought Shawn Sullivan along for protection.

"Miss Dawlish. Charming lady. That's her, right there," Tanner said, pointing toward the canvas. "We continued to see each other after Elizabeth and I ended things. Miss Dawlish agreed to model for me," he added. "She's a beautiful woman. Don't you agree?"

"Ah, yes, she is," Daniel said. The thought *and surprisingly sensual* sprang unbidden into his mind.

"Mr. Tanner, were you aware that Elizabeth Barrett was with child? About four months gone," Daniel added softly.

Michael Tanner's face transformed from a sneer of self-satisfied assurance into an expression of sorrow, his mouth opening in shock. "No, I didn't," he whispered. "Was it mine, do you think?"

"It's certainly possible," Coleridge boomed. "How would you have felt had she named you as the father?"

Tanner shrugged. "I wouldn't be the first man to impregnate a woman he's not married to. I'm sure Elizabeth would have tried to pass the child off as her husband's. Perhaps it was. How would anyone know for sure?"

"Her husband wouldn't be too pleased to discover he was raising someone else's bastard," Coleridge said spitefully.

"Her husband hadn't been able to give her a living child. Perhaps he would have been happy to have an heir and would have turned a blind eye to its questionable paternity. Besides, what makes you think he'd even suspect?"

"Jonathan Barrett is aware of your affair with his wife," Daniel said, not bothering to clarify how Barrett had come by the knowledge.

Tanner exhaled loudly and shook his head. "I suppose she must have confessed out of guilt and begged for his forgiveness. God, how utterly melodramatic. I expected better of her. Well, I suppose it made her feel better at the time but look where it got her."

"Mr. Tanner, where were you last Thursday evening and Friday morning?"

"Sleeping on a settee in my friend's studio. We had a bit of a party. There are at least five other people who can confirm I was there. One in particular," he added with a lewd grin. "Look, I had no reason whatsoever to murder Elizabeth. I liked her, desired her, and enjoyed her immensely while she was a part of my life, but I didn't love her, nor did I intend for our arrangement to become permanent. It was just a fling, Constable. And then it was over. I didn't know about the child, but even if I had, I wouldn't have done anything differently. It had nothing to do with me."

"Thank you for your candor, Mr. Tanner," Daniel said, rising to his feet.

Coleridge heaved himself off the settee and followed Daniel to the door and down the stairs.

"Shall we get some lunch?" Coleridge asked once they were back out in the street. "There's a decent place to get a beefsteak near here."

"Of course," Daniel agreed. He was getting hungry himself despite the sausage roll he'd inhaled earlier, and a beefsteak sounded enticing.

They walked for about ten minutes until Detective Inspector Coleridge spotted the place. It was small but cozy, the interior tastefully decorated in muted red. The wonderful smell of roasted meat wafting from the kitchens made Daniel's mouth water.

"You won't be disappointed," Coleridge said as the proprietor, who was clearly well acquainted with Daniel's lunch companion, showed them to a table by the window.

They ordered steak and fried potatoes, and a bottle of wine that Daniel strongly suspected was of French origin but carried no label. Coleridge either didn't realize it was contraband or didn't care. Before the food arrived, hot rolls with fresh butter were brought to the table, and both men helped themselves to the bread.

"Well, I hate to say it, Haze, but I think Jonathan Barrett is our man," Coleridge said once their lunch plates were placed in front of them and the waiter departed, leaving them to speak privately. Coleridge cut a piece of meat, put in it his mouth, rolled his eyes with obvious pleasure, and chewed thoughtfully.

Daniel tried the steak. It was delicious, and he took a moment to savor the first bite before replying.

"He certainly had a motive," Daniel agreed. "And it seems that Elizabeth Barrett did fear him to some degree, even though she didn't know he was reading her correspondence. Why mention the threat of being dragged to some women's physician to her lover if it wasn't real?"

Coleridge nodded. "Jonathan had opportunity too, having lived with the victim. He could have administered the poison any time he chose. Perhaps he was prepared to overlook the affair but couldn't stomach the thought of rearing another man's child."

Daniel nodded. "Yes, that appears to be the most plausible theory. And he could have purchased the poison in London, making the transaction impossible to trace. There are countless chemists in London. Obtaining the poison would have been a simple enough matter."

"To be frank, I can't say I blame him. Not that I would poison my wife," the inspector added with a rich chuckle, "but to see the woman you love betray you and then discover she's carrying a child that might not be yours would drive any man to extreme measures, especially one as proud as Jonathan Barrett."

"You think he definitely knew about the child, then?" Daniel asked. Jonathan Barrett's reaction to the news had seemed genuine, but given the depth of his wife's betrayal, he could have summoned grief and shock just by reliving what she'd done to him.

"Maybe not knew, exactly, but he might have suspected, or feared that a pregnancy would be the outcome of his wife's liaison with Tanner. I have six children, Constable. I always knew when my wife was expecting long before the news was confirmed. There are signs: fatigue, aversion to certain foods, hyper-sensitivity. I once told my wife that the venison was underdone, and she indulged in hysterics for a full half hour, carrying on as if her heart were breaking. When she finally calmed down, I said, 'So, it's like that, is it? When's this one due?' She hadn't even realized she was with child. That was with our youngest—Emily," he said, smiling fondly. "She's nearly thirteen now. Do you have children, Constable?"

"No," Daniel replied. "We had a little boy, Felix, but he died in an accident three years ago."

He wasn't sure why he'd told Coleridge about Felix. He rarely spoke of his boy, preferring to keep his grief private, but there was something paternal about the inspector that reminded Daniel of his own father.

"Oh, I'm so sorry," Coleridge said. "There's nothing more heartbreaking than losing a child. But there will be others," Coleridge said heartily. "Just be patient."

Daniel nodded, staring at his food. He had no wish to discuss his childlessness. "What do we do, sir?" he asked instead. "Do we arrest Jonathan Barrett for murder?"

"We have one more day until the inquest. I suggest we make sure of our assumptions. The man will hang for murder, so we'd best be sure he's the one that's done it."

How are we to make sure? He'll hardly admit to it, Daniel wanted to say, but this was his case and he had to figure it out for himself.

"I will attend the inquest on Friday and bring two men and a police wagon, should our man be pronounced guilty and need to be arrested. You don't have the facilities in Birch Hill to hold him until the trial, and anyway, he might try to flee."

"Thank you, sir," Daniel said. Coleridge was right. Jonathan Barrett could try to fight his way out of the Red Stag and flee before he could be arrested for the murder of his wife. Daniel was one man, and unless he had help from the villagers, Barrett could go free and start a new life on the Continent or maybe in the United States, where no one would care about his past. He could remarry and truly begin anew.

Coleridge finished his meal and took a long sip of wine, sighing with contentment. "The Brentwood police station is at your disposal should you need help, Constable Haze. Now, I think it's best we got back. I have another case I'm working, and you have proof to find." He waved away Daniel's offer of money and paid the bill. "It was my pleasure to work with you, Constable Haze. I hope you enjoyed your lunch."

"I have. Thank you, sir," Daniel said. "And thank you for the confidence you've shown in me."

Coleridge nodded in response and reached for his gloves. "Let's get back to Charing Cross, then. There's a train departing for Brentwood in forty minutes, and we should be on it."

The men walked out into the balmy afternoon and back to Charing Cross in silence, each lost in his own thoughts.

Chapter 24

Having cut Micah's lesson short, to the boy's great delight, Jason packed his medical bag with fresh bandages, alcohol, and wads of cotton, and headed out to the Caulfield farm on foot. The day felt unseasonably warm, making him wish he could remove his coat and walk in his shirtsleeves, but that wasn't the done thing, so he ignored the impulse and pressed on, enjoying the walk. The sky was a cloudless blue and the still-green trees that lined the lane threw dappled shadows onto the path. Birdsong filled the air, and fluffy sheep grazed in a meadow just visible through the trees, their white wooly shapes a stark contrast to the lush green grass. It was such a peaceful scene; it was easy to forget that only a few days ago, a woman had been murdered several miles from where he was walking.

As he approached the farm, he could see the Caulfield orchard just beyond the field, the trees dotted with shiny red apples. Several men were standing on ladders, picking the apples from the higher branches and filling basket after basket, which were then emptied into large wooden barrels. Full barrels were loaded onto wagons that stood at the ready, the horses munching on grass while they waited. Jason approached the house and knocked on the door, which was instantly opened by Alfie.

"Yer lordship," Mr. Caulfield exclaimed as Jason walked into the front room of the farmhouse, trailed by Alfie, who seemed frightened by the sight of his medical bag. "Please, come in. Can I offer ye a cup of cider?"

"I would love some after I've finished examining Mrs. Caulfield. How is she?" Jason asked.

John Caulfield beamed. "She's well, and the little 'un is right as rain. Suckling like a champ."

"I'm glad to hear that. May I see both mother and child?"

"Of course. Of course. Ye know the way, sir."

Jason knocked on the bedroom door and waited until Mrs. Caulfield replied before pushing the door open. She tried to sit up in bed but grimaced with pain and settled back down. The newborn lay next to her, swaddled in a cotton blanket, his face angelic in sleep.

"Yer lordship, I can't thank ye enough. What ye did for me and my baby…" Alice Caulfield gushed. "I thought for sure I weren't going to live to see this morning."

"May I examine you, Mrs. Caulfield?" Jason asked as he approached the bed.

She nodded, a flush spreading over her face and neck. Jason removed his coat and hat, rolled up his sleeves, and went to work, checking the incision, applying alcohol liberally to prevent infection, and changing the blood-soaked bandages. He decided not to embarrass Mrs. Caulfield by performing an internal examination. She hadn't given birth naturally, so there was really no need.

"You are to remain in bed for at least two weeks, Alice. If you try to get up too soon, the incision might open, which will not only be painful and set back your recovery but can lead to an infection. I'll come by every few days to check on you and change the bandages. Please, do not touch the incision without washing your hands thoroughly," he warned, knowing that Mrs. Caulfield would most likely try to take a peek at the scar and touch his neat stitching. "After the first week, you may get up very carefully, once every few hours should do it, and walk about the room for a few minutes. It will aid with recovery. If you have any severe pains or pus oozing from the incision, send for me immediately."

Mrs. Caulfield nodded. "Thank ye, sir."

"Now, may I see your handsome lad?"

She nodded toward the baby, barely able to hide her smile of pride. Jason rounded the bed and approached the child, taking in the even breathing, rosy cheeks, and partially open rosebud mouth.

"Your husband said he's nursing well."

"'E is, yer lordship. No problems there."

"Good." Jason reached out and placed his hand on the baby's chest. The child's heartbeat reverberated through his fingers—steady and strong.

"Sir," Mrs. Caulfield said shyly.

"Yes? Is there something you'd like to ask me?" he asked gently, knowing it wasn't easy for her to talk to a man about such intimate things as childbirth, especially a man she saw as her social superior.

"John and I got to talking this morn, and we'd like to name our boy after ye, if that's all right. We'd like to honor what ye've done for us."

Jason smiled at her, surprisingly embarrassed by her request. "I'm deeply honored, but if you're open to suggestions, may I propose Geoffrey? That was my father's name. He died in a railway accident three years ago, along with my mother, and as I have no son, it would mean a lot to me to know that someone carries his name."

"But ye'll have a son of yer own someday, my lord," Alice Caulfield exclaimed. "Of course, ye will. Why, there isn't a young lady within miles of 'ere who wouldn't be honored by a proposal from someone like ye."

Jason felt his face growing hot. Was the whole county speculating about his unmarried state?

Mrs. Caulfield smiled coyly, clearly seeing his embarrassment. "Geoffrey it is, then. A fine name for a fine little lad."

"Thank you, and now you and young Geoffrey should rest," Jason muttered.

"Is she all right?" John asked as soon as Jason stepped outside. "Is the child well?"

"They're both doing beautifully, Mr. Caulfield. You have nothing to worry about. I'll come back on Friday, after the inquest, to check on them both."

"Thank ye, sir, and God bless ye," John said. "Please, allow me to give ye something as a token of my gratitude. A cask of cider?" he asked, as he poured a cup of cider and handed it to Jason. "We make the best cider in the county."

Jason took a sip. The cider was cool and sweet, and slid down his throat easily. He could drink cups and cups of this stuff, especially on a warm day like today. "Perhaps a small one," he agreed, making John Caulfield very happy. "This really is wonderful."

"It's the apples, sir. These trees were planted by my grandsire more than fifty years ago and 'ave given us a fine 'arvest every year since. Why, people from all over the county order from us. Some are so eager for our fruit, they can't even wait till the apples ripen. Buy them green, they do."

Jason set down the empty cup and looked at John Caulfield as he absorbed his words. "What do people do with green apples?" he asked.

"I don't rightly know. I think they taste that much better when they're sweeter, but some like their apples sour, I reckon."

"Really? Like who?" Jason asked, his pulse quickening with a sense of foreboding.

"Like Moll Brody," he said with a sly grin. "Tart for a tart, I always say," he added unkindly. "And Mr. Todd. His wife makes applesauce that does wonders for 'is bowels, 'e says." John Caulfield must have realized the crudeness of his remarks and tried to cover his sentiments with a forced cough.

"And Mrs. Silver took a bushel off us," John Caulfield went on. "Said she likes them like that: crisp and sour. Makes a chutney from a recipe her mother had that had come from her own mother, who'd spent time in India when she were a young woman. Came for the apples in person nearly a fortnight ago, she did. I said we could deliver to Rose Cottage, no problem, but she said she wanted to see the apples first. Sample 'em, so to speak."

"Did she, now?" Jason asked, his stomach clenching with excitement.

"Oh, yes. Picked an apple right off a tree, she did, wiped it on 'er skirt, and bit into it, right there and then. Said it were perfect."

"How did she take the apples back?" Jason asked.

"Asked me to load the sacks in the dogcart. It were a tight squeeze, I'll tell ye that, what with the cart being so small, but she didn't seem to mind. Said she'd get to making the chutney that very afternoon."

"Thank you, Mr. Caulfield," Jason said, nodding toward the cup. "Your cider is truly one of a kind."

"I'll send that cask to ye, sir, as soon as there's more ready."

"I'll look forward to it," Jason said. He jammed his hat on his head, grabbed his medical bag, and headed for the door.

Chapter 25

Setting a brisk pace, Jason turned his thoughts to John Caulfield's seemingly innocent comments about Deborah Silver. Why would she buy green apples and then collect them from the orchard herself? Surely Jonathan Barrett had people who could do that for her. Perhaps she'd needed an excuse to get out of the house, have an hour to herself, but there were easier ways to accomplish that. And why not wait until the apples had ripened? Did the recipe call for apples that were sour? He wasn't an authority on chutney, but thought it was generally sweet rather than tart.

An idea was taking root in his head, but before he cast suspicion on the woman, he had to be sure his hunch was correct. As Jason walked up the drive, he saw Joe coming out of the stables, Micah at his heels. His red hair glowed like polished copper in the sun, his long, thin legs reminiscent of a newborn colt. Micah had grown by several inches over the summer, Jason realized, watching the boy. Before long he would reach puberty and be on his way to becoming a man, a thought that made Jason unexpectedly sad.

"I want to go for a ride, but Joe won't let me go on my own," Micah complained as soon as he spotted Jason.

"I thought Tom was coming over for a game of chess," Jason said. Micah and Tom had a standing arrangement on Wednesdays. Micah had taught Tom to play chess, thinking he'd have the upper hand over the novice, but Tom was proving to be a skilled opponent. He'd fallen in love with the game and was always begging Micah to play. He'd even taken on Jason and won once or twice.

"He said not to wait for him if he doesn't show. Sometimes he has to help his pa," Micah explained petulantly. "He says September is a busy time on the estate."

Jason had no idea what a gamekeeper's duties were from day to day, but if Tom had to help his father, Micah had to accept that. It wasn't so long ago that he'd helped his own father on the farm, working as hard as any adult.

"You'll have more time to play in the winter months," Jason said, hoping that would give Micah something to look forward to.

"I suppose. Can we go for a ride, Captain? The horses need exercising," he added for good measure.

"I don't see why not. What do you say we head to the abbey ruins?" Jason suggested.

"Really? That's where you want to go?" Micah asked, his eyes growing round with amazement. "That place is haunted. Tom said so."

"All right, we can go someplace else if you're scared," Jason said, smiling. He felt a little guilty at goading the boy, but there was nothing at those ruins save broken masonry and tall tales.

"I'm not scared of a bunch of old stones. Let's go," Micah cried defiantly.

"Let me get changed and put away my medical supplies, and then we can go," Jason said, heading toward the house.

"Will we be back in time for lunch?" Micah asked, trailing after Jason. "Mrs. D is making shepherd's pie. I like shepherd's pie."

"Of course, you do. It's meat and potatoes. What's not to like?" Jason replied, wondering if Micah's mother used to make the dish and that was why he liked it so much. Mrs. Dodson, being the clever soul that she was, asked Micah casual questions about his family and life on the farm and showered him with little kindnesses to make him feel more at home.

"I'm going to stop by the kitchen while you change," Micah announced. "I think I can smell scones baking."

Jason couldn't smell anything, but he was sure Micah had inside knowledge on what Mrs. Dodson was up to in her subterranean domain. If he said scones were baking, he was probably right.

Jason sprinted up the stairs and walked into his bedroom, surprising Henley, who was putting away clean shirts in the bureau.

"Good day, my lord," Henley said deferentially. "Is there anything I can help you with?"

"Micah and I are going riding."

"Very good, sir. You'll be needing your riding breeches and a different coat, then. I'll get you a fresh shirt as well. This one looks a bit wilted." He had a pained look on his face that only another long-suffering valet would relate to.

Henley hurried to the wardrobe and produced Jason's riding gear, then pulled a clean shirt out of a drawer, laying out the entire ensemble on the bed for Jason as if he were a child. "Shall I help you dress, sir?"

"Don't trouble yourself," Jason said, earning the usual look of scorn from his underused valet. "I have a different task for you."

"Shall I call on Miss Talbot again?" Henley asked, smiling slyly.

"No. I want you to take a message to Constable Haze."

"Yes, sir." Henley instantly brightened. The prospect of leaving the house and going for a ride always seemed to please him, especially if his task took him past the pub.

"You're not to stop at the Stag," Jason said.

Henley's face fell. "Yes, sir," he replied with much less enthusiasm.

Jason wrote a brief message, folded it, and sealed it with wax before handing the missive to Henley. The man was a curious sort, and Jason didn't want him reading what he'd written.

Henley slid the letter into the pocket of his waistcoat and turned to leave. "Enjoy your ride, sir."

Micah was already mounted by the time Jason came out of the house and walked toward his own horse. Joe handed him the reins and watched as Jason swung into the saddle with ease.

"Finally. Can we go now?" Micah said, frowning at Jason.

"Of course, but you might want to wipe the jam off your chin first, if you don't want to attract bees," Jason said. "How many scones have you had?"

"Just one," Micah replied, smiling angelically.

"Now, why don't I believe you?" Jason mused, wishing Micah had brought him one so he wouldn't have to wait for tea to sample Mrs. Dodson's delectable scones.

"We're going to the ruins," Micah told Joe, who remained stoically silent on the subject, looking after them as they cantered off down the drive.

Jason chuckled to himself. He knew exactly what Micah was doing. He hoped Joe would pass on the information to his nephew Tom. Micah wanted to impress Tom with his daring, even though the poor boy was in awe of Micah already. Tom had never been further than Birch Hill, while Micah had been a drummer boy during one of the bloodiest conflicts of the nineteenth century, spent a year in a Confederate prison, and then crossed the ocean in a luxury liner. But boys would be boys, and Micah wanted to show his friend that he wasn't afraid of some old legend.

"I'll race you," Micah called out as soon as they reached an open space. He took off, his laughter carried on the breeze.

Jason dug his heels into the mare's flanks and raced after Micah. It felt good to gallop across an open field. The wind caressed his face and he felt alive, every muscle in his body attuned to the animal beneath him, man and beast as one. They galloped for a few minutes, then slowed down, not wishing to tire out the horses too soon.

"Come on, then," Micah said. "Let's see those ruins."

Jason glanced up at the sky. The sun had been bright when they'd set off, but now it was obscured by gray clouds rolling in from the west. The air grew thick and moist, but they couldn't return home just yet. During the war years, Jason had learned to trust his instinct, and it had saved his life more than once. Today, his instinct was telling him to examine what was left of the abbey.

He turned his horse toward the ruins and beckoned for Micah to follow. It took them about a quarter of an hour to get to the place. The lone arch framed a window of leaden sky, the columns standing guard against intruders.

Micah brought his mare to a stop and sat staring at the ruins, his face set in lines of determination. "I suppose you mean to get closer," he said.

"I'm going to dismount," Jason said. "You can wait for me here, if you like."

Micah looked relieved, but then squared his shoulders and looked at Jason defiantly. "I'm coming with you."

They tied the horses to a tree surrounded by thick grass that the horses were sure to enjoy and walked toward the ruins, passing the spot where Elizabeth Barrett had breathed her last. Jason studied the ground leading up to what would have been the door to the abbey, but it had rained since last Friday, and any telltale tracks had been washed away. He wished he and Daniel had taken more time to search the surrounding area when Elizabeth Barrett's body was discovered, but time had been of the essence, and there had been too many onlookers to leave the body unattended while they scoured the grass.

The grass in the meadow was thick and lush, but once Jason and Micah reached the ruins, they had to tread carefully. The stones of the floor were slick with moss and rotting vegetation and stuck out at odd angles, upturned by protruding roots that had taken possession since the abbey had been destroyed centuries before. Bits of broken statuary and piles of stone that had once been part of the walls lay haphazardly strewn across the interior of the church. An altar, green with moss and crumbling after centuries of exposure to the elements, stood at the end of the nave, directly in front of the arch.

Micah stopped walking, his gaze pleading. "Let's go back," he whispered. "Please. This place gives me the creeps."

"You can return to the horses, if you like. I need a minute."

Micah was trembling, his freckles stark on his pale face. "I don't like it here."

"It's just stones, Micah. There's nothing else here."

"Tom said the ghosts of dead monks roam these ruins. Their spirits are restless because they died unshriven."

"The monks fled to France," Jason replied calmly. He had no idea what had happened to the monks when the abbey was sacked, but he didn't want Micah believing in malevolent ghosts, not when he had to live with ghosts of his own every day of his life.

Micah inched forward, never taking his eyes off the altar, as if he expected a long-dead monk to rise from behind the stone. "Tom said human sacrifices were performed here by the Pagans before the monks came and built their abbey. They kept the altar stone." Micah's voice faltered as he stopped dead, his muscles tense, ready for flight.

"Wait here," Jason said as he carefully stepped over the broken stones of the nave. Rusted iron latticework extended outward from the nave toward what would have been the north and south transepts, the only remnant of the rood screen that must have been quite impressive in its day if the elaborate iron arch that had fallen behind the altar was anything to go by. The latticework was covered with creeping vines and interlaced with the branches of saplings that had taken root inside the ruin. It was so thickly overgrown, Jason couldn't see what was behind it, but he continued on, certain there was something to find once he reached the altar.

He walked through the opening and stood before the altar, suddenly aware of the unnatural hush that permeated the overgrown space. For someone with superstitious beliefs, this would be the most haunted part of the ruins, the inner sanctum of the abbey, where the Pagan stone topped an altar that was shrouded in mysticism and had inspired stories of the occult. Jason had to admit that there was something spine-chillingly eerie about this part of the abbey, an otherworldly presence that seemed to guard the heart of the church, or maybe the stone that had been there for more than a thousand years. Jason took a step forward, refusing to give in to the spooky atmosphere. It was all superstitious nonsense, which made this the perfect place to hide something from prying eyes.

Jason studied what was left of the floor behind the rood screen, then carefully approached the altar. A loud gasp from Micah made him smile. He really was frightened, the poor lad, but he'd have to wait a few more minutes. Jason laid his hands on the ancient stone. The altar was solid and wide, long enough to accommodate a short person, should they be laid out on it. Jason could see why someone might think it had been used for human sacrifice, but it was nothing more than a hunk of gray stone. The top was cracked, a long gash running from one end to the other, filled with tufts of grass that had taken root in the narrow space. Jason removed his hands and walked around the stone, eager to see what he'd find behind it.

A pile of twigs and branches covered the ground behind the altar, the leaves withered. At first glance, there was nothing strange about the heap, but there weren't that many trees inside the ruin. How would the branches have found their way to that spot on their own? Even with a strong wind, they would have been strewn across the mossy floor, not laid in a neat pile just behind the altar. This pile of twigs looked man-made to him.

Jason shoved the branches aside with the tip of his boot, revealing something brown and coarse underneath. He bent down and pulled out an empty burlap sack. Then another. Beneath the sacking was a bunch of rotten apples, all of them cut in half. The apples were brown and slimy, their skins shriveled as they decayed, but Jason had all the proof he needed. There wasn't a single seed to be seen. Every apple had been cored.

Jason returned the sacks to their place, then covered the mound with the branches, intending to leave it as he'd found it until he could show Daniel the evidence he'd discovered. Turning slowly to face the nave, he stood still, listening intently. He couldn't see Micah from his vantage point, but his well-honed sense of self-preservation alerted him to danger. Jason retraced his steps, a shiver of apprehension snaking up his spine and making his breath come in short, urgent gasps. He couldn't see what was wrong but knew with unwavering certainty that he and Micah were no longer alone at the ruin.

Walking slowly, all his senses on high alert, Jason made his way toward the rood screen that hid Micah from view. The blood in his veins thundered in his ears and his mouth had gone dry, Micah's silence terrifying him more than any loud noise. He'd discounted Micah's cry a few minutes ago, thinking he was only being a scaredy-cat, but Micah must have cried out for a reason, hoping Jason would hear him and come to his aid.

Jason approached the rood screen from the side, so as not to appear at the center of the rood arch and expose himself to whatever was on the other side. He wasn't afraid for himself, his only goal being to retain an element of surprise in order to help Micah. All was deceptively quiet. Even the crows that normally circled above the crumbling arch were silent, the only sound the wind moving through the trees just beyond the empty windows. Jason found an opening in the wild foliage climbing up the iron latticework and peered out. It was imperative to discover what he was up against before showing himself.

Micah stood off to the side of the nave, his skinny body rigid with tension, his face greenish gray in the feeble light of the overcast afternoon. The nozzle of a pistol was pressed to his temple, the hand that held it steady and sure. The gun was a double-barrel Remington Model 95 Derringer, the weapon of choice for those who favored a gun small enough to conceal in a pocket or a reticule. Despite its toy-like appearance, it was a deadly weapon, especially when fired at close range.

Jason drew back his shoulders and prepared for battle as he left the safety of the rood screen and stepped out into the nave, eliciting a smile of satisfaction from Micah's assailant.

"Captain, help me," Micah cried.

"Micah, remain calm," Jason said, his gaze locking with Deborah Silver's unnerving stare. Her eyes were like bottomless holes in her pale face, her mouth pressed into a thin line. She wore a fashionable gown of apricot silk with a cream-colored lace fichu at the throat and matching lace at the cuffs, but instead of leather boots, her feet were clad in soft kid slippers, which was why they hadn't heard her approach, the footsteps silent on the heavy slabs of granite.

"Mrs. Silver, please let him go. Micah is not your enemy."

"No, he is not, but he's leverage against you, so I'm afraid I'll have to keep him hostage for a little while longer." Her voice vibrated with tension, but her hand didn't waver. "You are too clever for your own good, Lord Redmond. That dolt of a constable would never have figured it out."

"And what exactly do you think I've figured out?" Jason asked, stalling for time as his mind raced through his depressingly few options.

"You've been asking questions at the Caulfield farm."

"I went to the Caulfield farm to assist a woman in labor," Jason replied, as calmly as he could. "I delivered her child by cesarean section."

A spark of admiration lit Deborah Silver's eyes for just a moment, then faded. "Lucky for her the new Lord Redmond is also a surgeon. Not so lucky for me. You came here after calling at the Caulfield farm this morning. Clearly, you heard something while there that piqued your curiosity."

"Micah and I wished to explore the ruins. Didn't we, Micah?" Jason asked to distract the boy from his fear for even a moment.

"Yes," Micah squeaked.

"Is that why you were poking about behind the altar? Exploring? Stop playing childish games. It's beneath you, and it won't save you or him." She jerked her chin toward Micah.

"All right," Jason said. "Why don't we talk like adults, then? Why did you kill your sister?"

"Because she didn't deserve the life she had," Deborah Silver spat out. Her hand quivered wildly, making Micah shriek with terror as the barrel pressed harder into his temple. "She had it all: a husband who adored her, a comfortable life, and she was about to have a child that was probably fathered by her lover. And you know what? Jonathan would have accepted it as his own and would have loved it. Because he loved *her*. Always *her*. From the moment he saw her, I had become invisible. Inconsequential."

"Were you really so jealous of Elizabeth?" Jason asked softly. He didn't expect her to feel any remorse, but he hoped to keep her talking long enough for her to question the wisdom of killing two people in cold blood.

"I wasn't jealous; I was angry," Deborah exclaimed. Bright spots of color bloomed in her cheeks, and her eyes flashed with barely concealed hatred. "I had met Jonathan first. He'd courted me. Loved me. Wanted me for his wife. He'd come to the house to ask father for my hand in marriage, but then he saw her, just sitting there in the drawing room, reading a book, looking like an angel fallen from heaven—his exact words—and he forgot all about me. It was love at first sight, he said. His destiny. What a load of codswallop." Deborah Silver said with disgust.

"She wasn't even interested in him at first. You'd think he'd try to salvage his pride and marry someone who loved him and would have done anything to make him happy, but no, he kept pursuing her, trying to get into her good graces. He even asked me for help, the heartless bastard. Wanted me to put in a good word for him, and I did, because I had to pretend that I didn't care, that losing him had not devastated me. I had to stand aside and pretend to be happy for her when she married the man I adored, and then listen to her moan about how he suffocated her with his love. I had to watch as he showered her with gifts and often set aside his own needs to make her happy."

Deborah sucked in shaky breaths as if she'd forgotten to breathe during her angry monologue, and Jason couldn't help wondering if this was the first time she'd spoken the words out loud and allowed another person to see how she truly felt about Jonathan's betrayal and her sister's good fortune.

"But you were already married by that time," Jason reminded her. "Surely it no longer mattered what Jonathan Barrett did."

"Yes, I was, and regretting my decision to marry Anthony every day. He wasn't a cruel man, but he was weak and selfish, obsessed with his own interests and desires. He squandered everything we had on some moldy old books that he treated as the greatest of treasures, leaving us destitute in the process. He never had a thought to spare for his wife and son. In fact, he hardly noticed us. We were like pieces of furniture, something he had to walk around not to stub his toe. I barely managed to scrape enough money together to send Olly to school, so he would have the education and connections needed to forge his own future, since his father wouldn't lift a finger to assure it. I begged Elizabeth for help, and she gave me her monthly allowance to supplement the fees." Deborah's anger burned bright, but there was also pain in her eyes, and confusion. "Why did it all go so wrong for me?" she asked softly, shaking her head. "All I had ever done was try to please people and make them happy, but they never saw me. They took me for granted. Anthony took me for granted," she spat out.

"You killed him, didn't you?" Jason phrased it as a question, but it was more a statement of fact. He knew with unwavering certainty that Elizabeth hadn't been Deborah Silver's first victim.

"Yes. I tried it out on him first. And got away with it. No one suspected a thing. Anthony drank heavily; he wasn't in good health. When he dropped one day, no one batted an eyelash, not even the police. I suppose they must have checked for arsenic poisoning, but I would have never used arsenic. It's too obvious, too easily detected. I had used cyanide," she added, her chest swelling with pride.

"But why kill Elizabeth? What did you hope to accomplish?" Jason asked. He knew what he hoped to accomplish by asking her these questions. Deborah's arm was growing tired, her demeanor more erratic with every confession. He needed her to let down her guard long enough for him to take his chance.

"What I had failed to accomplish the first time. Jonathan cares for me, and he loves Olly. He offered us a home after Anthony died and has been paying Olly's school fees. I'll make him love me again. He'll marry me and give me what I should have had to begin with: a home, a family, and a future."

"Is it not against the law for a man to marry his deceased wife's sister?" Jason asked, wondering if Deborah Silver had ever considered the legal roadblock to her happiness. If she had, Elizabeth might still be alive.

Deborah laughed shrilly. "Laws are for people who don't have money," she spat out. "It's not illegal to marry abroad. Jonathan said so himself when the subject came up. A quick trip, and the deed is done. When I found out Elizabeth was pregnant again, I knew it was time to act."

"So, you bought the apples, removed the seeds, and made enough cyanide to kill your sister where she stood."

"It's easier than you think," Deborah replied with a snide smile. "A cupful of apple seeds is enough to manufacture a deadly dose." The gun was beginning to wobble, but Deborah kept it in place by pushing it even harder against Micah's temple. Micah was trembling, his blue gaze fixed on Jason and begging for help.

"How did you administer it?"

"I brought Lizzie some tea. It was a damp morning; I thought she'd be cold out here. I added enough sugar to disguise the taste, and she drank it and thanked me for my thoughtfulness. I stood there and watched her die, just as I had watched Anthony die. First, she was confused, unsure what was happening, then her eyes widened with shock once she realized that what she was experiencing was no random illness. Her hands shook violently, vomit streaming from that pretty mouth of hers and landing in a stinking heap at her feet. I watched her fall and saw the light go out of her eyes. I savored the moment of death, and I offered up my human sacrifice to the Pagan gods that are said to haunt this place, thinking maybe they'd be kinder than the cruel God who'd taken first my mother, then Jonathan, from me."

"Why did you take the ring?" Jason asked.

"Because it's valuable."

"But surely Jonathan Barrett would have recognized it had he seen you wearing it," Jason pointed out.

"I'm not that stupid, your lordship," she said, her tone mocking. "I won't wear it. I'll keep it for a time, then sell it should I have had need of ready cash. It would have been a terrible waste to bury it with her. Don't you think?"

"Were you still here when Davy Brody found your sister's body?"

Deborah chuckled. "Yes, I was here. I hid behind the rood screen when I saw the wagon coming. Brody thought she'd been killed by a demon. He was so frightened, I thought he'd soil himself, the poor fool." Deborah's smile faded, her gaze becoming flinty again. "And now that you know the whole truth, you have to die. No one will think to look for you here."

"Joe Marin knows we're here," Micah cried, his voice buoyant with hope. "Joe will come."

"Joe Marin won't dare set his foot here. None of them will. They think the place is cursed. Haunted. I'll hide your bodies behind the rood screen and no one, not even that nosy constable, will think to look there. No one will ever know what became of you, and no one will care. They might tip their hats and call you 'my lord,' but you'll never be one of them. You're a foreigner, and a stranger, despite your family ties. And this one here is nothing but an Irish peasant. You should have got yourself a dog if you wanted a pet."

Micah's eyes welled with tears at the cruel jab, and he lowered his gaze, staring at his shoes. Jason could have strangled the woman with his bare hands, but unfortunately, he couldn't get close enough to try without getting shot. Desperation welled up in his chest, taking his breath away as he realized that no one was coming to save them. Henley, that good-for-nothing reprobate who'd sell his mother for a pint, must have stopped at the Red Stag after all instead of going directly to Daniel's house as he'd been instructed to do.

Jason was on his own, and there were two options available to him. He could stand there until Deborah Silver grew tired of talking and started shooting, or he could charge her and hope that she let Micah go and fired on him instead. At close range, she was sure to hit him, even if she wasn't a very good shot, but depending on where the bullet entered, he may have a chance of survival, but only if Micah managed to get away. If not, Deborah Silver would use the second bullet to finish him off. It was worth the risk, but only if Micah knew what to do.

Jason shifted his gaze to Micah, sending a mental message to him, but all he saw in Micah's face was raw panic. If Deborah Silver fired at Jason, Micah would run to him instead of away from the ruins, leaving himself completely exposed.

"It won't work," Deborah said. "If you so much as move from that spot, I will shoot this rootless mutt in the head. And then, I will shoot you."

"So, what are you waiting for?" Micah suddenly shouted, taking them both by surprise. "If you were going to shoot us, you'd have done it by now. Or did you fancy a chat first?"

"Micah," Jason hissed in warning, but Micah's fear was egging him on. "I don't care if I die. Everyone I've ever loved is dead. Maybe I'll be better off. I'll get to see my ma and pa again, and my brother and sister." Tears streamed down his face as his eyes pleaded with Jason for understanding. He was sending a message of his own. He wanted Jason to tackle Deborah Silver as soon as she fired. There'd be a moment of confusion, precious seconds during which she'd have to turn her gun on Jason, enough time to charge her and knock the gun from her grasp. Micah was willing to sacrifice himself to save Jason.

Blind rage exploded in Jason, the last shreds of reason deserting him as he braced for impact. He pounced just as a loud crash reverberated through the ruins, the ground shivering beneath him as if something were about to come up through the broken stones of the ancient floor and swallow them all up. Deborah Silver's head instinctively whipped around, her eyes wild with fear, and her arm going slack. Several crows exploded into the sky, their screams bouncing off the broken stone and filling the ruins with noise.

Jason collided with Deborah Silver and grabbed for her wrist, but he was too late. The gun went off, the acrid odor of gunpower nearly overpowering the other smell, that terribly familiar metallic tang of blood. The gun fell from her grasp, falling into the grass between the broken stone slabs, the barrel still smoking. Micah staggered away, his face white with shock.

Deborah Silver was screaming and thrashing, her hair, which had come loose in the struggle, flying about her face. Jason tried to subdue her, but she was wild with rage, her pupils dilated with terror. She tore her hand from Jason's grasp and clawed at his face, going for the eyes. He managed to turn his head just enough to protect himself, but she dug her nails into his cheek, raking her fingers hard enough to draw blood. Jason grabbed her arms and slammed her against a column, knocking her momentarily senseless. There was blood on the shoulder and sleeve of her gown, but no sign of an entry wound. The blood wasn't hers, Jason suddenly realized, so it had to be his, but he felt no pain. He barely registered the arrival of Daniel Haze as he pressed the woman harder against the stone, desperate to punish her for everything she'd done.

"You can let go now, Jason." Daniel took hold of the barely conscious woman. "Let go and see to Micah."

"What?" Jason whispered, shaking his head in confusion. He finally released his vise-like grip on Deborah's arms and stared at Daniel. Had he been there all along? He hadn't heard him come. But then, he hadn't heard anything since the shot except Deborah's wild screams.

Turning slowly, Jason saw Micah lying on the ground, his face ashen, his coat soaked with blood. He was moaning softly, his lips moving as he stared at the open sky.

"Micah!" Jason cried. "Oh, Micah."

He sank to his knees beside the boy. Some primal part of him wanted to howl with despair, but the doctor in him instantly took over, taking Micah's pulse, carefully removing his coat so he could assess the severity of the wound. The sleeve of Micah's shirt was saturated with blood. Jason tore the fabric, exposing Micah's shoulders, chest, and arms. His skin was milk-white and as soft as the skin of a small child. The bullet had struck him in the upper arm, had penetrated the branchium, and was lodged perilously close to the humerus. Jason grabbed what was left of Micah's shirt and bound the wound as tightly as he could to stem the flow of blood. He had to get him back to Redmond Hall.

"Jason, take Micah home," Daniel said. He'd used his necktie to bind Deborah Silver's wrists. She had slid down the length of the column and was sitting on the ground, her head lolling from side to side as she moaned miserably. "I'm going to take her to the Brentwood police station. They'll know what to do."

"How long have you been here?" Jason asked. He yanked off his coat and used it to wrap Micah, then lifted the unconscious boy into his arms and held him close.

"Long enough to hear most of what she said," Daniel replied. He pulled Deborah Silver to her feet and pushed her in front of him, forcing her to stagger down the nave. "I toppled one of the columns to distract her. I'm thankful it worked. I thought of tackling her, but I was terrified the gun would go off and shoot Micah in the head."

"That was good thinking," Jason said. "You did the right thing."

"But Micah still got hurt," Daniel said mournfully. "Will he be all right, do you think?"

Jason nodded. "Thankfully, this is not a fatal wound. It will heal cleanly once I extract the bullet."

"Thank God," Daniel said, his relief obvious. "I would never have forgiven myself had Micah died because of my failure to act sooner."

Jason wanted to tell him that Micah's wound was no more his fault than the death of Felix had been, but this was not the time or place for that discussion. Micah would recover, and no amount of guilt or reasoning would bring back Daniel's son, but that was something Daniel had to work out for himself.

Deborah Silver would have killed them both, of that Jason was sure. She had too much to lose and nothing to gain had she allowed them to walk away from the abbey, so Daniel had saved their lives, and now he had the murderer of Elizabeth Barrett and Anthony Silver in custody. All in all, this was a favorable outcome.

It took a great deal of effort to get Deborah Silver onto the horse. She kept struggling and trying to slide off, but Daniel finally managed to get her to sit still, mounted behind her, and pressed his legs on either side of her to keep her from intentionally going over. Jason lifted Micah onto the second horse, then followed Daniel's example and mounted behind him, bracketing the boy with his own arms and legs. "Just hold on, Micah. Please, hold on," Jason whispered to him as he took off at a walk.

Micah slumped against him, pressing his uninjured arm against Jason's shoulder. His eyes were closed, but Jason could tell he was awake. "Does this mean I won't be able to have lessons for a while?" Micah muttered.

"Not a chance. The tutor is arriving next week, and lessons will commence immediately," Jason replied, encouraged by Micah's question. If he was trying to get out of doing his lessons, he wasn't in a bad way.

It took a long time to get home, but Jason didn't want to risk going any faster. The increased pace would have jolted the bullet and not only caused more severe bleeding but driven it deeper into Micah's arm. Micah's head was lolling against his chest by the time Jason brought the horse to a stop in front of the house. Joe came running, his mouth opening in shock when he saw that Micah was wrapped in Jason's coat and there was blood on Jason's hands and the sleeves and cuffs of his shirt.

"Take him," Jason ordered as he lowered Micah into Joe's arms. He dismounted and hurried on ahead, through the door that Dodson was holding open for him, the butler's eyes filled with incomprehension.

"Bring him into the dining room and lay him on the table," Jason called out to Joe before sprinting upstairs to get his medical bag.

He returned a moment later, ready to get to work. Mrs. Dodson was already in the dining room, crooning to Micah, who was mumbling something under his breath.

"Ma?" he called suddenly, bringing tears to Mrs. Dodson's eyes. "Ma, is that you?"

"You won't be seeing your mother just yet," Jason said as he quickly mixed a few drops of laudanum and water. He held the cup to Micah's lips, raising his head a little. "Drink up."

Micah drank the mixture and was out within seconds, his breathing becoming more even as he fell into a deep sleep. Jason tossed his bloodstained coat out of the way, then swabbed the wound liberally with alcohol. He disinfected surgical tweezers and very gently began to probe, searching for the bullet. Gasps from Mrs. Dodson didn't aid the proceedings, but he didn't ask her to leave. For some reason, her presence reassured him.

Dodson and Joe stood in the doorway, craning their necks to see what Jason was doing. He finally got hold of the bullet and pulled gently. The projectile was slick with blood and resisted Jason's efforts to extract it, sliding back into the cavity several times before he finally managed to get it out. A trickle of blood ran from the wound onto the white tablecloth, soaking into the fibers, the stain resembling a blooming rose. Jason cleaned the wound again, then covered it with a small wad of cotton and bandaged it before thoroughly washing his hands.

"Dodson, turn down Micah's bed, please," Jason called out over his shoulder as he lifted Micah into his arms.

"Sir, your face," Joe said quietly.

"What about my face?"

"It's bleeding."

"I'll see to it in a moment."

206

Jason carried Micah upstairs to his room, laid him on the bed, and carefully pulled off his riding boots and britches, leaving him in his drawers. Micah didn't stir. Jason covered him with the counterpane and walked over to the window, opening it a crack.

"What are you doing, sir?" Dodson asked, scandalized.

"The fresh air will do him good. It's too stuffy in here."

Dodson didn't bother to argue, but he did follow Jason to his own room. "Do you require assistance, sir?"

"No, thank you. If you'll just fetch my bag," Jason said as he studied his face in the mirror. Four deep scratches covered the right side of his face. He looked as if he'd been attacked by a panther or a mountain lion. He supposed in a way he had been. Deborah Silver had fought back like a wildcat in her desperation. She knew only too well what would happen if she were taken.

"Here you are, sir," Dodson said, handing Jason his medical bag.

Jason dabbed some alcohol on a ball of cotton and held it to his face. He sucked in his breath as the open wounds stung and throbbed for a few moments before the sensation began to fade. He didn't think he needed stitches. They would leave permanent scars and he was too fond of his face to walk around with stripes on his cheek for the rest of his life. But he'd need to cover the wounds for a few days at least to keep them clean before he could expose them to the air, which would aid in the healing process.

"Dodson, would you ask Mrs. Dodson for some honey, please?"

"Honey, sir?"

"Yes. A spoonful is all I need."

"I'll get it right away, sir."

When Dodson returned with the honey, Jason smeared some on the open wounds, then pressed a thick square of linen to the area.

"What are you doing, Captain?" Dodson asked, agape with curiosity.

"Honey has healing properties, Dodson. It prevents the wound from festering and keeps moisture at bay. It's also sticky, so it will keep the bandage adhered to my face until I'm ready to take it off."

"I see," said Dodson, who clearly didn't see at all. "Is that an American remedy?"

"I'm not sure," Jason replied truthfully. He suddenly felt drained and utterly depressed by the day's events. Deborah Silver had killed her husband, then cruelly murdered Elizabeth Barrett and her unborn child simply because she was jealous. He supposed people had killed for less, but Deborah's hatred must have run very deep to resort to such means.

"If there's nothing else, sir—" Dodson said.

Jason shook his head. As soon as the door closed behind the butler, Jason stripped off his filthy clothes, lay down on the bed, and pulled the counterpane up to his chin. He was shivering. He didn't think he'd be able to drift off, but the strain of the past few hours had caught up with him and he fell into a dreamless sleep.

Chapter 26

Daniel breathed a sigh of relief once he turned Deborah Silver over to Detective Inspector Coleridge. The ride to Brentwood had drained him, taking every ounce of strength and resolve to keep Deborah from unseating him and getting away. Once she'd come to accept that he wouldn't be so easily overpowered, she'd tried to sweettalk him into letting her go, but her pleas had fallen on deaf ears. By the time they'd arrived at the police station, Daniel was exhausted, both mentally and physically.

Inspector Coleridge called for a cup of tea and offered him some homemade scones, baked by the wife of the desk sergeant, then listened without interrupting as Daniel recounted what had happened at the ruins. The inspector was shocked by what had taken place, but also visibly impressed, both by Captain Redmond's skills of deduction and Daniel's rescue attempt; however, Deborah Silver refused to confess to her crimes, loudly proclaiming her innocence and crying that she'd been framed for the murder of her beloved sister, eliciting several sympathetic looks from the men at the station as she was taken down to the cells. Her guilt would still need to be proven beyond a reasonable doubt if Daniel hoped for a favorable outcome at the inquest.

Having finished his tea and bidden goodbye to the inspector, Daniel decided to take a detour to Redmond Hall on his way home. He needed to return Jason's horse, but he was also desperate to check on Micah and eager to speak to Jason about what had happened and how to proceed from this point on. Joe came out to greet him when he cantered up the drive and wordlessly took the reins, leading the tired horse away to be fed and watered.

Daniel walked up the steps and lifted the heavy brass knocker, announcing his presence. Dodson, his countenance impenetrable as ever, opened the door.

"Good day, Constable," Dodson said.

"Good day. I'd like to speak to Captain Redmond, please," Daniel said.

Dodson didn't budge. "His lordship is resting. Unless this is urgent, perhaps you can come back tomorrow."

Daniel nodded. "How's Micah?"

Dodson's expression softened. "Master Micah is resting comfortably. He will be all right," he added, in case Daniel hadn't already heard the same prognosis from Jason Redmond.

"Thank you, Dodson. Please tell the captain I will call on him tomorrow."

Dodson was about to shut the door when Daniel heard Jason's voice. "Let him in, Dodson."

Jason was coming down the stairs, looking like a pirate who'd survived a battle at sea. A large square bandage covered his right cheek, his dark hair was disheveled, and his shirt wasn't tucked into the waistband of his trousers. He was also barefoot.

"Pardon my appearance," Jason said. "I dressed in haste."

"Think nothing of it," Daniel replied. "I'm glad you are all right. *Are* you all right?" he asked carefully.

"Yes, I am. Please, come into the drawing room. I think we can both use a drink."

Daniel followed Jason into the room. They settled in the tufted leather chairs by the fireplace, sinking into their seats like two old men who'd had a rough day and needed desperately to get off their feet. Dodson wordlessly brought over the decanter of Scotch and two glasses and set them on the small table, making sure all was within easy reach. He added coal to the fire before leaving them to speak privately. Jason splashed Scotch into the glasses and passed one to Daniel, who took a large, warming gulp.

"Tell me what happened before I got there," Daniel said. "How did you come to be at the ruins, and how on earth did Deborah Silver know you were on to her?"

Jason leaned back in his chair, took a sip of his drink, and exhaled loudly, his weary gaze fixed on the leaping flames.

"I had been called to Caulfield farm by Miss Talbot to assist with a difficult delivery last night. I'll spare you the details, but mother and child are both well. I returned this morning to check on Mrs. Caulfield, and as I was leaving, John Caulfield and I exchanged a few words. He mentioned that Mrs. Silver had purchased a bushel of green apples and had taken them away herself, not something I would expect a woman of her station to do. Had Deborah Silver wished for apples, either John Caulfield would have been asked to deliver them to the house or a servant would have been sent to collect them, most likely a male servant, since to lift a bushel of apples would require physical strength. This got me asking why she would make the trip to the orchard on her own and take the apples with her when she left."

"I don't know. Please enlighten me."

"Apple seeds contain a high concentration of cyanide, and given that Deborah Silver was closely related to the victim and was the last person to see her before her death, other than Dulcie, I thought there was a strong possibility she had something to do with her death."

"Apple seeds can kill you?" Daniel asked, shocked to the core. He loved apples and had unintentionally swallowed his share of seeds over the years.

"A few seeds will not harm you, but a cupful will supply a lethal dose," Jason explained.

Daniel considered what Jason had just told him, but the facts still did not add up. "How would she have known that?" he asked. "And how would she have gone about extracting the poison?"

"I've never tried making cyanide myself, but I assume she ground them into a paste and then mixed it into her sister's tea, which she kindly brought to her. The tea would have looked murky and tasted bitter, but she'd added enough sugar to disguise the taste. The tea would have been lukewarm by the time she'd offered it to Elizabeth, but she must have known that Elizabeth wouldn't refuse to drink it, probably out of sheer politeness."

"But what were you doing at the ruins?" Daniel asked. "And how did she know to find you there?"

"I reasoned that she wouldn't have taken the apples back to the house. That would have been too risky, and she'd have needed a private place to work. So she brought the sacks to the ruins, dragged them behind the altar, where no one in their right mind would willingly go, and then cored the apples and extracted the seeds. She tossed the apples to the ground once she was finished with them and covered them with the sacks they'd come in. She then piled branches over them just in case, which was a mistake on her part, since that prevented animals from devouring the apples and consuming the evidence," Jason pointed out.

"And the seeds?"

"Once she returned home with the seeds, she must have ground them into a paste after everyone had retired and she had the kitchen to herself. Having prepared the poison, all she had to do was await an opportunity, which presented itself when Elizabeth went out to paint by herself early in the morning."

"But how did she know you were on to her?" Daniel asked again. "It's not as if you'd sent her a note telling her to meet you at the ruins so that she could watch you as you unearthed evidence of her crime."

"I wondered that as well, but the only explanation I can think of is that the ruins are clearly visible from Rose Cottage. I suspect Deborah Silver was keeping an eye on the place, just in case anyone came snooping around. She must have seen us arrive and dismount, and once she saw me heading toward the altar, she knew she had to act. It's probably common knowledge in the village that I had delivered Alice Caulfield's baby and had gone back to the farm this morning to check on my patients. She may have heard it from the servants."

Daniel shook his head in confusion. "All that makes sense, but I still don't understand how she would know how to obtain cyanide from apple seeds."

Jason considered the question. Daniel was correct. It was easy enough to poison someone with arsenic, although riskier, given that the police were on the hunt for arsenic murders, but cyanide was not a commonly used poison, and extracting it from apple seeds would not readily spring to mind if one was looking to poison someone. "What did Anthony Silver do for a living?"

"He was a don at Oxford, I believe," Daniel replied.

"What about Deborah and Elizabeth's father?" Jason asked.

"I don't know. I'll have to ask Jonathan Barrett when I speak to him tomorrow."

"I'd like to come with you," Jason said. "There are some questions I would like to put to the staff."

"Of course," Daniel said. He finished his drink and got to his feet. "I'll be off, then."

Jason gulped down the rest of his Scotch and stood as well. "This is one day I won't be sorry to leave behind."

"Please give my regards to Micah, and tell him he was very brave and selfless," Daniel said.

"You can tell him yourself when you see him next. It will mean a lot coming from you."

The two men stepped into the foyer, where Dodson was hovering, as usual. "Dodson, please have Joe take Constable Haze home."

"There's really no need," Daniel protested, but Jason cut him short.

"Given what happened the last time you decided to walk home, I'd say there's every need. I'll see you tomorrow, Daniel. Say, around ten?"

Daniel nodded. "Goodnight, Jason."

"Goodnight, Daniel."

Chapter 27

Thursday, September 13

Thursday morning dawned windy and bright, with fluffy white clouds scuttling across the pale sky and branches waving about like skinny arms. Jason had slept fitfully, dreaming of the ruins and reliving the scuffle with Deborah Silver again and again, the shot echoing in his mind as if the gun had been fired right next to his head. He rose early, dressed, and went down to the kitchen, where Mrs. Dodson was already hard at work, kneading the dough for the day's bread.

"Can I make you some coffee, Captain?" she asked, taking in his worn-out appearance.

"Please. Are there any scones left?" Jason asked. He hadn't bothered with dinner last night, but now he was hungry.

"One or two. You can have them, if you like, or I can make you a proper breakfast," Mrs. Dodson offered as she wiped her hands on a tea towel.

"Thank you," Jason muttered. "That would be wonderful."

Mrs. Dodson reached for a cast-iron skillet and set it on the range before taking a crock of butter and a bowl of eggs out of the larder. "This might not be the best time to mention it, but I suppose you should be told before she arrives. I've engaged a scullery maid."

Jason nodded. His mind wasn't on household matters, but it was important to Mrs. Dodson, so he tried to show interest. "I hope you'll be pleased with her work. How did you find someone so quickly?"

"I had a candidate in mind all along. Kitty's a good girl, hardworking and respectful. Her mother has been asking about a position for her for some time. They need the added income, I suppose. She's due to arrive any minute now."

Mrs. Dodson cracked two eggs into the pan, added a halved tomato, then cut two slices of bread and set them to toast before turning her attention to spooning coffee into a pot. Before long, Jason was presented with fried eggs, grilled tomato, toast, and a pot of coffee. He spread the bread with butter and dug in, grateful to be allowed to eat in the kitchen, where he had company.

"Kitty Darrow is a pretty little thing," Mrs. Dodson went on, her mind still on the new maid. "I wager Master Micah will take a shine to her."

"How old is she?" Jason asked between bites.

"Just turned fourteen."

"Shouldn't she be in school?"

"Not everyone can afford to send their children to school, Captain, not when the children can work and earn a wage. The Darrows have fallen on hard times since their mill closed. People don't mill their grain the old way anymore. There's a new mill near Brentwood, one that uses belts and gears, or some such nonsense. Everyone goes there."

"I see," Jason said, but he wasn't interested in mills. His mind was on Micah and the upcoming inquest. He finished his breakfast and pushed the plate away, sated. "I'm going to go check on Micah. Thank you for breakfast, Mrs. D."

Jason was just leaving when a fresh-faced girl was led into the kitchen by Dodson. She was short and thin, her raven-black hair scraped into a tight bun at her nape. She opened her eyes wide when she saw him, presumably astonished at seeing the lord of the manner eating breakfast in the kitchen.

"Good morning," Jason said, smiling at her. "I'm Captain Redmond."

"Kitty D-Darrow."

"Nice to meet you, Kitty. I'll leave you in Mrs. Dodson's capable hands," he said, and left the kitchen, heading upstairs.

He'd forgotten all about Kitty by the time he reached Micah's room. Micah was awake, watching him as he entered.

215

"How are you feeling?" Jason asked as he sat down on Micah's bed and reached out to touch his forehead. It was cool, and Jason breathed a sigh of relief. No fever meant no infection.

"I'm grand," Micah replied sarcastically, but his radiant smile took the sting out of his words. "You saved me. Again," he said softly. He reached for Jason's hand and clasped it, holding on tight. "Wait till I tell Tom I've been shot," Micah said smugly. "He'll never believe it."

"You can show him the entry wound. Once it heals," Jason added. "Would you like me to ask Joe to bring Tom here for the afternoon? I'm sure his parents will be able to spare him for a few hours."

"Would you?" Micah cried. "Oh, please."

"I'll see to it. Now I need to go out for a while. I want you to stay in bed. Understood? Mrs. Dodson and Fanny will look after you, and please don't abuse their generosity."

"You mean I can't eat a dozen jam tarts?" Jason glared at him, and Micah giggled. "I'll follow doctor's orders, I promise. To tell you the truth, I don't have much of an appetite."

"You must eat. Mrs. Dodson will make you a boiled egg and toast for your breakfast."

"Can I have some coffee?" Micah whined.

Jason considered this for a moment. He usually only allowed Micah to drink milk or tea, but this once wouldn't hurt. "All right. One cup with lots of milk."

"Thanks, Captain. You're a star."

"And you're cheeky," Jason replied with a chuckle, using the English term he'd come to like.

Micah's smile stretched wider. "I feel so awful, I might need Miss Talbot to come and minister to me as well," he moaned, giving Jason a conspiratorial wink.

Amused by Micah's matchmaking attempts, Jason wondered if there was anyone who wasn't aware of his feelings for

Katherine Talbot. "I'll have Henley take a note to Miss Talbot if you think you require additional care."

"If you keep sending that wastrel to deliver notes to your lady love, she just might develop feelings for him instead," Micah said, surprising Jason with his shrewd observation. "You know how she likes a charity case."

"That's enough from you," Jason said, trying to hide his smile. "Would you like me to bring you a book, or your schoolwork?" he added innocently. "This would be the perfect time to work on your Greek translation."

"A book will do," Micah grumbled.

"All right," Jason agreed, letting him off the hook.

**

Two hours later, Jason collected Daniel from his house and they drove to Rose Cottage in the brougham. Jonathan Barrett was still at his Brentwood residence, but before they spoke to him, Jason and Daniel planned to question the remaining staff, who'd been left behind to close up the house for the winter under Deborah Silver's supervision.

"Do you think Inspector Coleridge has informed Jonathan Barrett that his sister-in-law is in custody?" Jason asked as they approached the front door.

"I hope not," Daniel replied. "If Mr. Barrett questions her guilt, he might offer her legal counsel."

"Which is why we need to gather more evidence," Jason said.

When Dulcie came to the door, she looked pale and pinched, her eyes darting around nervously. "Constable, thank God," Dulcie exclaimed. "Ye got the message, then. Mrs. Silver didn't come 'ome last night. She went out in the afternoon and never returned."

Daniel looked confused. "I'm sorry, Dulcie, I never received a message, but don't worry, Mrs. Silver is quite safe," he reassured her.

"Is she in Brentwood, then?" Dulcie asked, brightening instantly. "She didn't say she were leaving. Just went out without a word. She seemed in a hurry, and she weren't wearing proper walking boots, just her satin slippers."

"She is, indeed, in Brentwood," Daniel said.

Dulcie breathed a sigh of relief, then looked from Daniel to Jason and back again. "If ye know she's not 'ere, then why 'ave ye come?"

"Dulcie, we'd like to ask you a few more questions," Jason said. "It will only take a few minutes."

"All right," Dulcie muttered, but clearly, she would have preferred that they leave. "I suppose ye'd best come into the parlor, then. It won't do to talk in the foyer." She led them into the parlor and invited them to sit, but remained standing herself, mindful of her station. She did keep sneaking sly glances at Jason's bandage, curiosity winning out.

Taking a seat on the pale green settee next to Daniel, Jason began. "Did Mrs. Silver go out after Mrs. Barrett left for the ruins last Friday morning?" he asked.

Dulcie thought about it for a moment. "She went out about an hour later. Said she were going for a walk."

"Did she take anything with her?" Daniel asked.

"I really couldn't say, sir. I was about my chores in the upstairs bedrooms," Dulcie replied.

"Who sees to Mrs. Silver's laundry?" Jason asked.

"Why, I do. There's just myself and Cook here at Rose Cottage, and she's not likely to be doing laundry, is she?"

"Have you washed any of Mrs. Silver's garments since last week?" Jason asked.

"I washed her unmentionables," Dulcie said, lowering her gaze. "As I do every week."

"What about her gowns?" Jason persisted.

Dulcie shook her head. "Gowns get ruined in the wash, sir. I usually spot clean them as needed."

"May we see Mrs. Silver's room?" Daniel asked.

Dulcie's cheeks flared with indignation. "Those are her private quarters. I'm sure I can't let ye in there. And I was just about to start packing her trunk."

"This is police business, Dulcie," Daniel said, even though he didn't have any official authority to search Deborah Silver's room, but Dulcie didn't know that.

"Suit yerselves, then," Dulcie replied. "Third door on the right."

Jason and Daniel ascended the stairs and entered the room. It was a typically feminine boudoir, decorated in shades of pink and cream. The patterned wallpaper matched the hangings on the bed, and the curtains were a muted mauve that picked up the colors of the thick carpet. Jason walked directly toward the wardrobe and opened the doors.

"What are you looking for?" Daniel asked.

"Evidence."

Jason meticulously went through each pocket, pushing his fingers all the way to the bottom and feeling for anything that might be an apple seed. He found what he was looking for in a walking gown of dark blue. Extracting several seeds, he placed them on his palm and showed them to Daniel. "This is the gown she must have worn when she cored the apples."

"The hem has mud and grass stains consistent with walking through the ruins," Daniel replied, "but a defense lawyer could argue that they're consistent with country living."

"Yes, that's true," Jason agreed. "And a few apple seeds don't prove anything in themselves."

Jason turned and surveyed the room, then walked toward the window and drew aside the curtains. The ruins were clearly visible in the morning light, the sun positioned high above the arch. "She must have been watching the ruins, frightened someone might come back to search the area."

"She had good reason to be. You'd figured it out," Daniel replied.

"We need to question the cook," Jason said as he allowed the curtain to fall back into place.

"You go on," Daniel said. "I'm going to search the room to see if I can find anything that might prove our case."

Jason returned to the ground floor to find Dulcie hovering by the stairs.

"Are ye finished in Mrs. Silver's room, sir?" she asked anxiously.

"Just about. Dulcie, I'd like to speak to Cook."

"Of course, sir."

Jason followed Dulcie to the kitchen. The pots and pans that hung from hooks above the pine table gleamed in the morning light, and all the surfaces looked freshly scrubbed. The smell of toasted bread hung in the air, but the fire in the range had been extinguished, probably because the two women would be leaving Rose Cottage today and returning to Brentwood with the trunks they had been left to pack. Jason briefly wondered if they had packed Elizabeth Barrett's things, but supposed it really didn't matter. A plump woman of middle years emerged from the larder, a look of astonishment on her face when she saw Jason.

"Good morning," Jason said politely. "I'm Jason Redmond."

"Gladys Watson," the woman replied, still staring up at him.

"I'd like to speak to you, Mrs. Watson, if that's all right," Jason said deferentially. "Shall we sit down for a moment?"

Mrs. Watson waited until Jason sat down at the table, then slid into a bench on the opposite side and folded her hands demurely as if she were in church. "How can I help you, sir?" she asked.

Jason noted her nervousness and smiled. "I need to ask you a few questions about the day Mrs. Barrett died," he said.

Mrs. Watson's eyes misted at the mention of her mistress, but she nodded, inviting Jason to proceed.

"What was Elizabeth Barrett like to work for?"

"She were a kind mistress. Always polite and considerate."

"And Mrs. Silver?" Jason asked. "What's she like?"

The cook shrugged. "She is haughty at times."

"Mrs. Watson, did Mrs. Silver ask you for anything on Friday morning?" Jason asked, keeping his tone casual.

"Like what?"

"Did you have any contact with her after breakfast?" Jason clarified.

"Not really. Mrs. Barrett usually approved the day's menu. I had little to do with Mrs. Silver before the death of my mistress."

"Did Mrs. Silver ask you to brew more tea after she had already breakfasted?" Jason asked.

Mrs. Watson considered the question. "She did. Said she fancied another cup of tea and asked me to brew it strong."

"And you brought her a pot of tea?"

"Yes, I brought it to the breakfast room."

"Was Mr. Barrett there?"

"No, he were still abed. Mrs. Silver was alone."

"Did she drink the tea?" Jason asked.

"She must have. The pot was nearly empty when Dulcie brought it back to the kitchen."

"Thank you, Mrs. Watson," Jason said. "You've been most helpful."

"Have I?" Mrs. Watson asked, looking confused.

"Yes, you have, and I'm most grateful."

Jason left the kitchen and went to find Daniel, who was just coming down the stairs, looking very smug.

"Did you find out anything from the cook?" he asked as they stepped outside into the cool morning.

"Nothing that can be used to convict Deborah Silver, but she did confirm that Deborah had requested more tea and asked for it to be brewed strong."

"Hardly a crime in England," Daniel replied.

"But it supports the timeline. Elizabeth went out, then Deborah had her breakfast and asked for more tea, which she must have poured into a container of some sort and taken with her when she went to the ruins to see Elizabeth. She'd have mixed the poison into the tea before offering it to her sister."

"Circumstantial," Daniel replied as they climbed into the brougham. "But this isn't," he announced with great pomp. He reached into his pocket and pulled out his handkerchief, from which he extracted a sapphire ring. "If Jonathan Barrett can confirm that this is his wife's betrothal ring, then we have our incriminating evidence. Lord, how I wish we could collect fingerprints from this," Daniel said wistfully. "Imagine being able to conclusively prove that the woman had handled the ring."

Jason considered this. "But is it really conclusive? She could say that Elizabeth had allowed her to try it on or something along those lines. Her fingerprints on the ring would not prove that she'd killed her sister; however, her possession of it after Elizabeth's death is certainly damning."

"Let's hope that this ring doesn't belong to Deborah Silver," Daniel said as the carriage began to move toward Brentwood.

Chapter 28

Upon arriving in Brentwood, Jason and Daniel called at the Barrett residence, only to be informed that Mr. Barrett had gone to the office and was expected to stay there for the remainder of the day.

"Joe, meet us by the offices of Barrett and Barrett," Jason called out as they set off on foot. There was a lot of traffic, so it probably would have taken longer to drive. Joe nodded as he looked in dismay at the stream of carriages and wagons clogging up the street.

Jonathan Barrett agreed to see them as soon as they arrived at his office. The clerk apologized for the delay profusely before leading Jason and Daniel into Jonathan Barrett's office. He was seated behind his desk, an official-looking document spread out before him. He looked up from his work and invited them to sit down.

"Thank you for coming in person, gentlemen," he said. He looked like a broken man, his eyes glazed with grief and his skin pale in the morning light streaming through the window. "I had a visit from Inspector Coleridge last night. He filled me in on the circumstances of Deborah's arrest. I hope your young ward will be all right," he added softly, his gaze passing over Jason's bandage. He winced as if he could feel the echo of Jason's pain. "So, it's true then," he said, nodding. "She killed my Elizabeth."

"She did," Daniel confirmed. "We are here to clarify a few points for tomorrow's inquest."

"Certainly. How can I help?"

"Did Deborah Silver ever have any exposure to chemistry or the making of poisons?"

Jonathan Barrett shrugged. "I really don't know. Her father had never expressed any interest in chemistry, as far as I know."

"And her mother?" Jason asked.

"I never knew Elizabeth and Deborah's mother. She was already deceased by the time we met. She had been the daughter of a civil servant. She'd had a governess growing up, of course, but I don't think she would have been taught chemistry. Do you?"

"Probably not," Daniel agreed. "But Deborah must have learned how to make the poison from someone."

Jonathan Barrett shrugged. He didn't seem to care where the poison had come from, only what it had accomplished and by whose hand it had been administered.

"I don't suppose it really matters," Daniel said. "Perhaps she'd consulted someone or had found a recipe in a book."

"Yes, that must be it," Jonathan Barrett agreed.

"There's one more thing, Mr. Barrett," Daniel said softly. "Is this your wife's ring?" He withdrew the ring from his pocket and showed it to Jonathan Barrett, who went even paler at the sight of it.

"Yes. That's the ring I gave Elizabeth the night I proposed. It had belonged to my mother. Elizabeth never took it off after that night, not even when she went to bed. Where did you find it?"

"It was in Deborah's jewelry box, hidden in one of the drawers and wrapped in tissue paper."

Jonathan Barrett shook his head. "I never imagined Deborah could be so brazen. I always thought her so meek. As a lawyer, I put a lot of stock in my good judgement, but I completely underestimated her. I trusted her and believed her to be devoted to Elizabeth."

"We often don't see those close to us clearly," Daniel said. "We see them as we want to see them."

"Yes, I suppose you're right," Jonathan Barrett agreed. "As was Arthur. He warned me about Deborah. He said I'd scorned her, and one day she'd make me pay for my callous behavior toward her."

Jonathan Barrett suddenly sat back, his expression changing from one of melancholy to one of a man who'd thought of something important and was eager to share it.

"Have you remembered something, Mr. Barrett?" Daniel asked.

"I don't know if this is relevant, but Elizabeth and Deborah's mother, Elspeth, lived in Delhi until the age of seventeen. Her father had been posted there shortly after Elspeth was born. She was close with her ayah, as she called her, and the family brought the woman back to England with them when they returned. Charita raised both Deborah and Elizabeth. Deborah, in particular, had been very fond of her."

Jonathan Barrett looked animated now, his expression almost feverish. "Yes, I remember now. Deborah mentioned it years ago, when we first met. Charita's mother had been a healer, as was her mother before her, but the family had fallen on hard times and Charita was forced to seek employment outside her village. She used her own natural remedies to treat illnesses and often administered them to the girls, with their parents' blessing, of course. Deborah said she'd found her mother's stories of India and Charita's foreign ways fascinating. It had always been her dream to visit India and learn more of its culture."

"Yes, that could explain Deborah's knowledge of toxins," Jason said, nodding. "Traditionally, healers were often the only source of medical assistance, especially for the poor. They weren't chemists, but they were well versed in the medicinal properties of plants. It's very likely that Deborah learned from her Indian nanny. Many poisons are used in medicine, so Charita might have unwittingly educated Deborah about their properties."

"Really?" Jonathan Barrett asked. "Poison is used in healing?"

"Yes. Rue, for instance, can aid digestion, reduce swelling, and improve circulation, but it can also be poisonous, and has been known to cause miscarriages. Women have been relying on rue for centuries to get rid of unwanted children."

Jonathan's eyes filling with sorrow. "I wish you hadn't told me that, Lord Redmond."

"Why? What has rue got to do with your wife's death?" Daniel asked.

"It had nothing to do with her death, but I'd always suspected that she was somehow relieved when she miscarried our children. For one mad moment, I even thought she might have wished to lose the pregnancies."

"And you now think she caused the miscarriages intentionally?" Jason asked.

"Both times Elizabeth miscarried, Deborah was on hand. She'd come to visit just before the sad events and stayed until Elizabeth recovered. I sensed an air of secrecy about the two of them, a camaraderie of sorts that wasn't always there, but I assumed they'd been brought closer by the unfortunate circumstances."

"There's no way to find out for sure if your wife intentionally caused the miscarriages, but given Deborah's feelings toward her sister, it's very possible that Elizabeth had known nothing of what was about to occur," Jason said, watching Jonathan Barrett's expression transform from utter desolation to some tiny glimmer of hope.

"You mean Elizabeth might have wanted our children?" he asked, his voice quivering with feeling.

"I really couldn't say, but I believe that Deborah hatched the plan to murder her husband some time ago and may have been paving a way for her future. She wished to be your wife, but I doubt she wanted to raise your children. She'd sent away her own son as soon as he was old enough. Besides, the children would be a constant reminder of her sister and a possible source of disagreement between you. Given her willingness to kill, it stands to reason that she might have slipped something into Elizabeth's food or drink, causing her to miscarry."

"If that's true, she killed two adults and three children," Daniel said, shaking his head in disbelief.

"Under the law, an unborn child has no rights, Constable Haze, so she wouldn't go down for the murder of my children, but Anthony Silver and Elizabeth had rights under Common Law, and I will defend them to the best of my ability. If there's nothing else, gentlemen, I'll see you at the inquest tomorrow. I'm afraid I've kept my clients waiting long enough."

"Well, I'll be damned," Daniel said as soon as they were out in the street again. "Do you really think she caused her sister's miscarriages?"

"I think that's certainly possible. If she knew how to extract cyanide, I've no doubt she was familiar with other toxins as well. In some ways, Eastern medicine is very advanced, even if their practices don't always coincide with those found acceptable in the Western world. And where there's poverty, there's always a desire to terminate unwanted pregnancies. Children are a strain on families who are already struggling to survive."

"A part of me hopes you're wrong," Daniel said, shaking his head in dismay. "If Deborah Silver intentionally caused her sister to lose her children, that would make her downright diabolical."

"I think she's already earned that description," Jason replied. "I think we have a solid case against Deborah Silver, even without a signed confession."

"I agree," Daniel said. "Let's go home."

Chapter 29

Friday, September 14

When Jason returned home from the inquest, he found Micah holding court in his bedroom. Tom was sitting next to him on the bed. Katherine Talbot was reading them a story, and Mrs. Dodson was caught red-handed in the act of depositing a platter of jam tarts on the bedside table, the pastries still hot from the oven and filling the room with a delectable aroma. Even Fanny and Henley were in on the act, doing Micah's bidding as if he were an invalid. Henley had been sent down to the library to fetch the chess set, and Fanny had been dispatched to fetch cups of milk to go with the tarts.

"Mrs. Dodson, please take the tarts back to the kitchen," Jason said.

"No," Micah wailed as he tried to grab a tart before the platter was taken away. "Tom would like one."

"You can have one each. The rest are going back. Really, Mrs. Dodson," Jason said, using his best reproving tone. "I did ask you not to overfeed him."

"But the poor mite is ill," Mrs. Dodson protested.

"He'll be a great deal more ill if he eats all of those."

Mrs. Dodson allowed Micah and Tom to take one tart each and took the platter away.

"How has the patient been?" Jason asked Katherine, who was doing her best to hide her amusement.

"Running everyone ragged and enjoying every minute of it."

"I'm in pain," Micah protested, but the twinkle in his eye did little to support that statement.

"I could use a drink," Jason said. "Would you like one?"

"No, but a cup of tea would be most welcome." Katherine marked her place in the book and followed Jason from the room.

"I'll join you in a cup of tea, then," Jason said. He'd have a drink later. A large one.

Once they were settled in the drawing room with a tea tray between them, Katherine asked the question he'd been dreading. "Can you tell me what happened at the inquest?"

Jason nodded. He had no wish to speak of it, but she deserved an answer, and the inquest would be the talk of the village for the next few months, so she'd hear all the gory details anyway.

"It was all over very quickly. Constable Haze presented the physical evidence and I shared my medical findings, but Deborah Silver condemned herself the moment she opened her mouth. She proudly admitted to causing her sister's miscarriages in the hope that Jonathan Barrett would set her aside. Once her own husband, whom she'd poisoned with cyanide a year ago, was safely out of the way, she had decided it was time to pave the way for her second marriage. She'd made sure Jonathan was made aware of Elizabeth's affair with Michael Tanner by mentioning their correspondence to each other and threw herself wholeheartedly into comforting him after Elizabeth's death. Having been on the verge of an engagement prior to his marriage to Elizabeth and united in their grief, she was sure Jonathan would turn to her for solace and ask her to marry him."

"Do you think he would have?" Katherine asked.

Jason shrugged. "I really don't know. Perhaps. If he ever harbored any affection for Deborah, it's been replaced by a burning hatred."

Katherine shook her head in wonder. "He knew his wife had been unfaithful to him and might have been carrying another man's child, and still his love for her never wavered."

"Love can be inexplicable, which is what makes it so precious," Jason said, his thoughts turning to Cecilia and Mark. Would he have been able to forgive her infidelity if she'd wished to pick up where they'd left off before he went off to fight for the North? He wasn't so sure, but he'd never loved her as obsessively as Jonathan had loved his Elizabeth.

"What was the verdict?" Katherine asked as she set her teacup on the table with a soft clink.

"I'm not an expert on British law, but it is my understanding that Squire Talbot, in his role as magistrate, cannot pass a sentence in a murder case. Deborah Silver will be incarcerated until the assizes in Chelmsford, at which juncture she will be tried and sentenced."

"Do you think she will be hanged?" Katherine asked, her voice catching slightly.

"I can only assume it will be either the noose or the madhouse for her."

"If it were me, I'd rather be hanged," Katherine said, surprising Jason with her vehemence.

"Really? Why?"

"I visited a lunatic asylum with my father once. I couldn't sleep for weeks after that. My worst imaginings could never live up to the horror and cruelty I witnessed in that place. Death is a mercy when compared with a life in captivity being treated like an animal that's gone mad. I wouldn't wish that on anyone, not even a woman who'd killed two adults and three unborn children."

"Jonathan Barrett is determined to see her hang," Jason replied. "He wants justice for his wife."

"I've no doubt he'll get it," Katherine said. "The Barretts are well connected, and I suppose Arthur Barrett can represent the prosecution, given that he's a trial lawyer. What will happen to Deborah Silver's son, do you think?"

"Jonathan Barrett has agreed to act as his guardian until he comes of age. He said it's what Elizabeth would have wanted. That's an admirable thing to do, given the circumstances."

"Yes. He's an honorable man. I hope, in time, he'll find happiness with someone who genuinely cares for him," Katherine said sadly. "Well, I must be getting on. Father will be wondering what's become of me."

And he'll be wanting his luncheon, Jason thought sourly. The poor woman was a martyr to her father's needs, where a competent housekeeper would be able to set her free.

"Will I see you on Sunday?" Jason asked, trying to keep the hope out of his voice.

"Father's expecting the bishop to luncheon after the service. I'm afraid I will be rather busy."

"Tuesday? Will you be visiting the sick?"

Katherine nodded, but her gaze held no conviction. "Perhaps we'll meet in the lane."

"Yes, perhaps," Jason agreed, already knowing he'd be haunting the lonely road in the hope of catching a glimpse of her.

"Good day, Captain."

"Good day, Miss Talbot."

Epilogue

December 1866

The ballroom glowed with hundreds of candles, the room festive with boughs of holly and red ribbon in anticipation of Christmas, only two days away. Dancing couples swirled in a colorful kaleidoscope, the music spilling out onto the patio, where some guests had retreated for a breath of fresh air. The whole village had turned out, as well as some prominent families from the county whom Jason had met for the first time that evening. Jason wished Micah could have been there, but children had not been invited to the ball, and Micah, despite his displeasure at being left out, was looking forward to Christmas. Jason had a wonderful surprise in store for him and hoped it would work out exactly as he had planned.

Taking a break from dancing, Jason helped himself to a cup of punch and watched the dancers, smiling as Miss Talbot whirled past with her cousin Oliver Talbot, followed by Shawn Sullivan, wearing a waistcoat embroidered with golden butterflies, and Fanny, who looked lovely in a blue frock. Jason had tried to fill Katherine's dance card with only his name, but she'd informed him that he could have only two dances. It was up to him which, so he'd chosen a waltz and a quadrille, the latter to come later in the evening. Miss Talbot looked enchanting in a gown of pale peach. Her hair, normally worn parted in the middle and pulled into a modest bun at her nape, had been curled to frame the face, the rest twisted into an intricate chignon and decorated with a silk flower that matched her gown.

Jason's gaze followed Daniel and Sarah Haze as they moved past. Sarah's face, which had filled out a little since Jason had first met her, was serene as she looked up at her husband, her bosom straining against the tight bodice of her gown. Jason smiled to himself. He couldn't be sure, but he thought Sarah might have some happy news for Daniel in the new year. It was just a hunch, but he hoped he was correct. He knew how happy the prospect of a child would make his friend. The dance ended and Daniel came to stand next to Jason, his eyes bright behind the lenses of his spectacles.

"I have some news," he said, barely able to suppress the grin that spread across his face.

"I thought you might," Jason replied, smiling back.

Daniel looked momentarily taken aback but dismissed whatever had surprised him and continued. "Detective Inspector Coleridge put in a good word for me with the head of the Brentwood constabulary following the Elizabeth Barrett investigation. I've been offered the position of inspector, Jason. Not even a sergeant—an inspector!" he exclaimed.

"I'm very pleased for you, Daniel," Jason said. "You will make an excellent inspector. In fact, you already are an excellent inspector."

"There's more," Daniel said, grinning from ear to ear. "If you have any interest in assisting the police in a more official capacity, they'd like to offer you the position of police surgeon."

Jason stared at Daniel. He had not been expecting that. "Can I think about it?" he asked.

"Of course. In fact, you don't have to accept the job if you don't want to. You can consult on cases, if you so choose."

Jason nodded. He might prefer that option to becoming a full-time police pathologist. He was just about to say so when a uniformed constable entered the ballroom, his gaze searching the room until it alighted on Daniel and Jason. He made his way toward the two men, the look on his face grim and determined.

"Constable, what's happened?" Daniel asked.

"You're wanted, sir. A body has been discovered at the old mill in Elsmere. The circumstances are suspicious."

"Do you know who the victim is?" Daniel asked.

"It's Frank Darrow, sir."

"I'll come with you," Jason said, following Daniel as he cut through the crowd. "Is Frank Darrow related to Kitty Darrow?" he asked, once they had retrieved their coats, hats, and gloves.

Daniel nodded. "He's her father. He used to be the miller before the mill shut down. Constable, where was the body found?" he asked, turning to the young man.

The constable looked uncomfortable for a moment, then replied in a barely audible whisper. "He's been stripped naked and tied to the wheel."

"Good God," Daniel exclaimed. "That's positively barbaric. Who'd do such a thing?"

"I have a feeling we're about to find out," Jason replied as he followed Daniel out into the night.

The End

Please turn the page for an excerpt from Murder at the Mill

A Redmond and Haze Mystery Book 3

Notes

I hope you've enjoyed this installment of the Redmond and Haze mysteries. I have several more planned.

I'd love to hear your thoughts. I can be found at irina.shapiro@yahoo.com, www.irinashapiroauthor.com, or https://www.facebook.com/IrinaShapiro2/.

If you would like to join my Victorian mysteries mailing list, please use this link.

https://landing.mailerlite.com/webforms/landing/u9d9o2

An Excerpt from Murder at the Mill
A Redmond and Haze Mystery Book 3

Prologue

The moon hung low in the nighttime sky, its fat belly skimming the tops of the elms that stood like a row of silent sentinels in the distance. Silvery light bathed the meadow and danced on the inky waters of the river that had once been the source of the family's income but now flowed over the stationary wheel of the mill, gurgling and rushing past, its current as strong as ever. Wooly clouds moved at a stately pace across the star-strewn sky, obscuring parts of the moon and throwing wild shadows on the frostbitten countryside.

Sadie Darrow stopped the dogcart and looked out over the haunting scene, her nerves as frayed as the cuffs of her coat. She'd been alone since suppertime, washing up and then darning shirts and socks by the fire. Frank and the boys had left hours ago, but only Jimmy and Willy had come back, drunk and subdued, and had gone to bed after muttering something about Frank staying for another round.

She should have gone to bed and left Frank to fend for himself; he was a grown man, after all, but something had made her pull on her threadbare coat and worn boots and set off into the night in search of her husband. He hadn't been at the Queen's Arms, nor had she seen him ambling along the lane that led toward their house. So, she'd come to the mill, hoping he'd staggered to the old building to sleep off the drink on the moldy old cot that had been there since the days when the mill had been a thriving concern and not the derelict relic it had become in the last few years.

A thick cloud that had momentarily obscured the moon passed, leaving the meadow and the mill bathed in moonlight. Sadie squinted, her gaze drawn to the wheel. Something was lying across it, something long and thick. Climbing out of the cart, she hurried toward the deserted building, her boots crunching on frosty grass, her gaze glued to the odd shape on the wheel.

A strangled scream tore from her chest as her mind finally accepted what her eyes had been seeing all along. A naked man was strapped to the top of the wheel, his head thrown back, his eyes wide open as if he were stargazing. His skin was bluish with cold, his body arched to fit the shape of the wheel, the stiff rod of his manhood pointing straight at the sky.

Sadie clapped a hand over her mouth as she stared at her husband's slack face, and then she smiled, ever so slightly, before turning away and going for help.

Chapter 1

Thursday, December 20, 1866

Inspector Daniel Haze shivered, as much from the bitter cold as from the sight that had greeted him when he'd arrived at the mill. Constable Pullman, who'd come to fetch him from Squire Talbot's Christmas ball, stood on one side, Captain Jason Redmond on the other, all three men speechless in the face of the crime scene, for there was no doubt this had been a crime, and a gruesome one. A second constable, a young man of about twenty with just a hint of a fair moustache, was stepping from foot to foot and rubbing his hands, having had to stand watch over the body until the inspector and the surgeon had arrived.

"Well, what do you make of this?" Daniel asked as he turned toward Jason, whose head was tilted to the side as if he were looking for something in particular.

"I won't know anything for certain until I examine the body," Jason said quietly, "but I think it's safe to assume this wasn't an accidental death."

Daniel looked around, scanning every inch of ground. There was nothing to see. The grass glittered in the moonlight, the stalks petrified with cold. There were no obvious footprints or signs of struggle. He looked around for the dead man's clothes but couldn't see them anywhere. Perhaps whoever had done this had left them inside the millhouse or had taken them away as a precaution or as a souvenir of the night's events.

"Have you ever met the man?" Daniel asked. "His daughter works in your kitchens, doesn't she?"

"Yes, Kitty's been working at Redmond Hall since September, but I've only ever seen her brothers. They come to collect her on her afternoons off. Nice chaps. Quiet," he added thoughtfully.

"From what I hear, Frank Darrow was anything but quiet, but I never met the man in person."

"Let's get him down, shall we?" Jason said, setting down his medical bag and walking toward the immobile wheel.

"How do we go about it, guv?" asked the young constable, whose name was Ingleby, looking at the corpse with ill-concealed distaste.

"Someone will have to hold the wheel to make sure it doesn't shift, and two people will have to climb up and cut him down. Any volunteers?" Daniel asked, looking from one constable to the other.

"I'll hold the wheel," Constable Ingleby said eagerly.

"I'll go up, but I'll need one of you to help me," Constable Pullman said.

"I'll go," Jason said, but Daniel held up a hand to stop him. "It's my case, it's my responsibility. I'll ask you to hold my things," Daniel said, taking off his woolen coat and top hat. He was still in evening clothes, his white shirt and silk scarf stark against the black broadcloth of his jacket.

"Be careful, Daniel," Jason called out as Daniel walked toward the wheel, followed by the two constables, who disappeared inside the millhouse and emerged a few minutes later, carrying a ladder, which they propped up against the wooden hub of the wheel. Daniel went first, followed by Constable Pullman.

"Hand me the blade," Daniel called out.

Constable Pullman pulled a pocket knife out of his coat pocket and handed it to Daniel.

Taking hold of the knife, Daniel sawed through the rope that bound Frank Darrow at the ankles, then carefully shifted his weight to get easier access to the man's wrists.

"Constable, I will pass him to you headfirst," Daniel said. "Grab him under the arms and carefully begin to make your way down."

"As you say, guv," the constable replied, but the confusion on his face was a testament to the impracticality of Daniel's plan.

Daniel pulled the man by the arm until the upper body was hanging off the wheel. Just as the constable reached for the dead man's torso with his free hand, the body slid downward, knocking both Daniel and Constable Pullman off the ladder and sending all three hurtling to the ground. The constable cried out as the dead body landed on top of him, followed by Daniel, who knocked his head against the dead man's shoulder and banged his knee painfully on the hard ground.

"Are you all right?" Jason exclaimed as he rushed toward the heap of body parts. "Constable?" he called out to the poor man. The constable's helmet had slid forward and was obscuring his vision, which was probably a blessing since Frank Darrow's torso was right in front of the constable's face, his erect penis nearly in the constable's mouth. Constable Ingleby stood off to the side, frozen with horror.

Daniel sprang to his feet and adjusted his spectacles, which were miraculously still intact, if on a bit crookedly, gasped when he saw the position of the body, then grabbed the corpse by the arms and pulled, moving the man's private parts downward just in time for Constable Pullman to push up his helmet and look about.

"Got the wind knocked out of me is all," Constable Pullman grumbled as he crawled out from under the body, leaving Frank Darrow's remains sprawled on the ground.

"I hope our little tumble doesn't interfere with your conclusions," Daniel said as he looked up at Jason, who was trying hard to hide the twitching of his lips and the amusement in his eyes.

"It shouldn't. Let's get him to the morgue," he said, mastering his mirth.

The two constables lifted the corpse by the arms and legs and carried him, with great difficulty and much huffing and puffing, toward the police wagon.

"He's one heavy sod," Constable Ingleby muttered.

"A dead weight, one might say," Constable Pullman replied between intakes of breath.

The constables deposited him on the floor and invited Jason and Daniel to follow. They climbed into the wagon and sat on either side of the corpse, Daniel wincing slightly as the door slammed behind them and was locked from the outside. The only source of light was the barred windows, which let in narrow shafts of moonlight that fell on the milky-white body on the floor. Daniel had a strange urge to cover up the body but had nothing save his coat, which he wasn't about to remove. The temperate inside the wagon was as arctic as it had been outside. He looked down at the dead man and pushed his spectacles up his nose as they began to slide downward. "This is my first case as an inspector for the Essex Police," he said dreamily. "Is it wrong to be excited?"

"Not at all," Jason replied. "I have no doubt you'll get justice for Frank Darrow."

"I hope so," Daniel said. "I hope so."

Chapter 2

The morgue, or the mortuary, as the desk sergeant on duty at the station referred to it, was located in the basement of the building. The walls were covered in white tiles from floor to ceiling, and several gas lamps were affixed to the walls at dual intervals, giving off a sickly yellow light. There was a stone table, complete with a hole at the center for drainage, and several cabinets equipped with surgical tools, bowls, and beakers. There were also a washbasin, soap, and a towel provided for the surgeon's use, as well as a coatrack to hang one's coat and hat before getting down to business.

"Dr. Engle left his apron," the sergeant said, pointing to a bloodstained apron that hung on a hook behind the door. "You're welcome to use it."

"Thank you," Jason said, trying not to show his distaste.

Removing his outer garments, he hung them up on the coatrack, then unwound his cravat and stuffed it into the pocket of his coat. He then reached for the apron. It wouldn't do to return to Redmond Hall covered in blood and gore, especially if he happened to come across poor Kitty, whose father he was about to disembowel. As Jason prepared to begin the autopsy, he wondered if Kitty had been informed. She hadn't been at Squire Talbot's Christmas ball, not having been invited along with all the other villagers because she didn't come from Birch Hill.

Kitty Darrow was from Elsmere, a village several miles north of Brentwood. Jason hoped that whoever broke the news to her would be gentle. Kitty was a shy, quiet girl of fourteen who felt the most comfortable with Mrs. Dodson, who was not only both cook and housekeeper but also Redmond Hall's mother hen and treated Kitty more like a daughter than a scullery maid. Jason's young ward Micah was quite fond of Kitty as well. He still admired Fanny, the upstairs maid, whose fair curls and large brown eyes had probably attracted many a young man, but Kitty was closer to his own age, and he tried hard to befriend her and win her approval, as any eleven-year-old boy would.

Kitty had never mentioned her father to Jason, but then their paths didn't often cross, and when they did, Kitty usually mumbled something in response to his greeting and scurried away. Jason would always be an American commoner in his own mind, but to those around him, he was Lord Redmond, master of Redmond Hall and heir to the profitable estate that had been left to him by his titled grandfather. Few noblemen would soil their hands with the blood of peasants, but Jason was a trained surgeon who'd performed countless postmortems during his medical training in New York and then life-saving surgeries near the battlefields of the American Civil War. He was happy to help the police, and especially Daniel Haze, who'd become his closest friend in England.

"I'll stay, shall I?" Daniel asked as he positioned himself at the corpse's feet for a better view.

"Of course," Jason replied. He laid out the supplies he'd need on a small table near the stone slab and turned to the body.

"Are you going to start cutting now?" Daniel asked. He seemed torn between curiosity and apprehension.

"Not just yet. I will see what I can learn from the body's external appearance first."

"Right," Daniel said, visibly relieved. "Eh, Jason, why does his, eh…?" Daniel faltered, but having followed the direction of his gaze, Jason understood the question.

"This is what's known as a death erection," Jason explained. "It happens most frequently when a man dies by hanging, since there's pressure from the noose on the cerebellum, but it's possible that the killer had applied pressure to the back of the victim's neck, producing a similar effect."

"You don't think he was killed while in the act?"

Jason cocked his head to the side, considering the question. "He may have been. I'll know more once I've finished."

Jason carefully examined Frank Darrow from head to foot before rolling the corpse over onto its stomach. Using his fingers to part the hair, he checked for bruises and lacerations to the scalp before making his way down and checking every inch, then returned the body to its original position on its back.

"What do you reckon?" Daniel asked.

"There are no obvious wounds," Jason said. "Not a mark on him save these bruises on his shoulders and back of the neck, but they're not what killed him. The marks on the ankles and wrists are from the ropes and were inflicted postmortem."

"So, how do you think he died?"

"That's what I'm about to find out."

Jason picked up a scalpel and made a Y-shaped incision in the man's chest and stomach, then pulled apart the flesh to reveal the ribcage and the bowels.

A strangled cry came from Daniel Haze. "If you'll excuse me," Daniel choked out. "I'll just wait outside."

Jason chuckled to himself and continued with the autopsy. It'd been a while since he'd performed a postmortem, but some things weren't easily forgotten once learned. He spent the next several hours completely immersed in the process, determined to discover everything he could about Frank Darrow and the life he'd led before winding up on the slab in the Brentwood station mortuary from his remains.

By the time Jason emerged into the corridor, a faint pink haze could be seen through the high window of the basement chamber, the impenetrable black of the night replaced by a murky gray that was growing lighter by the minute. Jason pulled out his watch and checked the time. It was just past seven in the morning, and he'd been awake for more than twenty-four hours.

Daniel, who'd been dozing in a hard wooden chair beneath the window, woke with a start and stared at Jason, his eyes clouded with confusion.

"Good morning," Jason said softly, giving Daniel a moment to recollect exactly where he was and why.

"Good morning. Are you finished, then?"

"Yes."

Jason was just about to share his findings with Daniel when Detective Inspector Coleridge, Daniel's superior, appeared at the end of the corridor, still dressed in his coat and hat. Snowflakes dusted the shoulders of his dark-gray coat and luxurious fur collar and decorated the brim of his bowler hat.

"Gentlemen," Coleridge boomed as he approached. "I've just been informed. Extraordinary," he said, shaking his head. "Nearly thirty years as a policeman and I've never heard of such a thing."

"Someone certainly has a good imagination," Jason said, recalling the sight of Frank's naked body glowing in the moonlight.

"Do we have a cause of death?" Coleridge asked as he yanked off his gloves.

"Frank Darrow died by drowning."

"What?" Haze and Coleridge asked in unison, their mouths agape with shock.

"He died by drowning."

"What brings you to that conclusion?" Coleridge demanded.

"The victim did not have any visible wounds on his body except for some bruising along the shoulders and the back of the neck, and his lungs were full of water. My theory is that someone held him down in the river until he drowned. After death occurred, they undressed him, tied him to the wheel, and then shifted the wheel so the body was positioned along the top and more clearly visible, which I think was the objective."

"But why?" Daniel asked, his mouth forming a moue of distaste.

"To kill him wasn't enough. The murderer clearly intended to humiliate him as well," Jason theorized.

"Was he in good health otherwise?" Daniel asked.

"Judging by the state of his liver, he was a heavy drinker, and he'd ingested quite a bit of ale immediately before his death. Otherwise, he was in fine health."

"How long has he been dead?" Detective Inspector Coleridge inquired.

"It's hard to say, given that he was left out in the cold, but if I had to guess, I'd say about three hours."

"Who found the body?" Coleridge asked.

"His wife, Sadie Darrow, arrived at the mill sometime before midnight. Seems she had been out looking for her husband. Then the oldest son, James Darrow, reported the crime to the sergeant on duty about half past twelve."

"Well, Haze, this is what I believe they refer to as a trial by fire," Detective Inspector Coleridge said, a smile of amusement just visible beneath the waxed moustache. "Your first official case with the service, and it's a corker."

"I won't let you down, sir," Daniel said, drawing himself up to his full height and squaring his shoulders.

"I have every faith in you. Now, go home, change out of those clothes, have some breakfast and a strong cup of tea. You have a long day ahead of you."

"Yes, sir," Daniel replied.

"Constable Pullman will take you gentlemen home in the police wagon. It's snowing out there, so you'll have a deuce of a time finding a hansom to take you all the way to Birch Hill."

"Thank you, sir," Daniel said. "Shall we?" he addressed Jason.

Jason nodded, too tired to speak.

Chapter 3

"Daniel, where have you been?" Sarah exclaimed when he finally walked into the house, his coat and hat dusted with snow and his shoes leaving wet tracks on the polished floor. "I was so worried."

"I'm sorry, my dear, but there's been a murder."

Sarah's hand flew to her mouth. "A murder? Where? Was it anyone we know?"

"At the old mill near Elsmere. A man by the name of Frank Darrow. His daughter, Kitty, works as a scullion at Redmond Hall."

"Oh, that poor girl," Sarah said. "How dreadful to lose a parent so suddenly and violently. How was he killed?"

"He was drowned," Daniel said, intentionally omitting the racier details. There was no need for Sarah to know the rest, at least not this morning. "I'm afraid I must go out again as soon as I've changed and eaten."

"Of course," Sarah said, nodding. "I understand. I'll tell Cook we're ready for breakfast."

"Haven't you eaten?"

"I was waiting for you," Sarah said shyly. "Would you like your eggs fried or boiled?"

"Fried. Are there any kippers?" Daniel asked.

Sarah made a face of distaste at the mention of the kippers. "I'll tell Cook to make some. You must be exhausted," she said, laying a hand on his chest. "My poor dear."

"I am rather tired," Daniel admitted, smiling down at her. "Who brought you home from the ball?"

"Captain Redmond's driver brought mother and me home. It was a tight squeeze in the brougham, what with Mr. Sullivan, Miss Talbot, and the vicar, but we were grateful for the ride, as I am sure was Miss Talbot. Trudging home in satin slippers would not have been pleasant."

"No, I don't suppose it would be," Daniel said, trying to suppress a yawn.

"Go on. I'll tell you the rest later," Sarah promised.

Daniel sighed and nodded wearily. He had no interest in village gossip but was glad to see Sarah so animated. It hadn't been that long ago that she'd spent her days reading or staring out the window, her mind trapped in the recurring nightmare of their son's death. He'd happily listen to her recite the day's menu or a list of preserves in the pantry just to hear her speak and to know that she was engaged with the world, and their life. They would forever mourn Felix, who'd been nearly three at the time of his death, but life went on, and now, three years later, they were finally beginning to repair their fractured relationship and find their way forward.

Daniel made his way upstairs, where he shaved, washed his face, and combed his hair. He then changed into a clean shirt, put on his favorite suit of brown tweed, and returned downstairs. Sarah was already in the dining room, a cup of steaming tea before her.

"Come and sit down," she invited. "Tea?"

"Please."

Daniel accepted a cup of tea, added milk and sugar, and sighed with contentment after taking the first sip. He hadn't realized how thirsty he'd been. A few moments later, Tilda brought in a tray laden with two plates of fried eggs, toast, butter, marmalade, and a dish of kippers.

"Can you tell me more about the case?" Sarah asked as she buttered her toast.

Daniel shook his head. "I'd really rather not talk about it. It's bizarre, to say the least, and the details would only upset you."

Sarah lowered her knife and fixed him with an accusing stare, one eyebrow raised in astonishment. "Surely you won't keep the details from me, now that you've told me that."

"Sarah, it's gruesome. Do you really wish to hear the rest?"

"Indeed, I do," Sarah replied, lowering the eyebrow marginally.

Daniel quickly filled Sarah in on the particulars, leaving nothing out. It helped to talk about it, since it was a way to organize his thoughts, but he still thought Sarah would have been better off not knowing the grisly details.

"Good Lord," Sarah exclaimed. "That must have taken some doing."

"Yes. I think it's safe to assume this wasn't a random attack. The man must have truly infuriated someone to elicit this kind of a response."

"Is that what this is? A response?" Sarah asked.

"It must be. If you were to murder someone, why would you go through the trouble of taking off their clothes and mounting them up on that wheel?"

Sarah nodded. "If it is a response, it's one of Biblical proportions."

"I'll say. Except our murderer is not divine. He's just a man who was angry enough to go through the trouble of humiliating Frank Darrow, even in death."

"Where will you start?" Sarah asked as she took a bite of her toast.

"I'll start with the family. See if they can shed any light."

Daniel finished his breakfast, gulped the rest of his now-tepid tea, and got to his feet. "I have to go," he said apologetically.

"Will you be home for dinner?"

"I hope so," Daniel said. "That all depends on what leads the family can provide."

"Thank you, Tilda," Daniel said to the servant, who handed him his coat, hat, and gloves. He grabbed his walking stick from the stand near the door and headed out into the overcast morning.

Elsmere was a typical English village, similar in appearance and layout to Birch Hill. The two most important establishments of the village stood directly opposite each other, separated only by the village green. Daniel decided to forgo the church for the moment and stopped into the Queen's Arms, where Frank Darrow must have worshipped regularly, given the state of his liver and his level of inebriation at the time of his death. The barkeep looked up as Daniel walked in, as though surprised to see a customer so early in the day.

"Good day to you," Daniel said. "I'm Detective Haze of the Brentwood Constabulary. Would you kindly direct me to the Darrow house?"

The barkeep looked furtive for a moment, then forced a smile onto his craggy face and nodded. "Of course. It's about a mile from here. Just follow the road westward. You can't miss it. So, it's true, then?" the man asked, his eyes dancing with morbid curiosity. "We heard Frank was found dead, but Sadie is keeping mum, and no one has seen the boys yet this morning."

"It's true that Frank Darrow is dead," Daniel replied. He wasn't about to offer up any further information. Not yet. "Thank you for your help."

He'd question the barkeep later, once the public house officially opened for business and the regulars began to speculate, doing some of the legwork in Daniel's stead. They'd know something of Frank Darrow's life and associates, and their theories, even the barmy ones, could prove useful, particularly since Daniel had not known Frank personally and would have to rely solely on the say-so of others.

Daniel followed the man's directions and drove the dogcart west until he saw a shabby two-story farmhouse in the distance. A thin plume of smoke wound into the nearly white sky, and several chickens pecked in the yard, trying to find something to eat beneath the thin layer of snow. A mangy dog barked wildly when Daniel turned off the road and drove into the yard, stopping before the door. A slim young man of about twenty stepped outside.

"What ye want 'ere?" he asked rudely. He looked pale and tired, and his eyes were red-rimmed, as if he'd been crying.

"I'm Inspector Haze," Daniel said as he climbed down from the cart. "I am investigating your father's death. Are you James Darrow?"

"I am," the young man replied. "Come in, Inspector."

Daniel followed the young man into the house. The smell of bacon and toasted bread filled the small space, making Daniel wish someone would open the window and air the place out. A woman he presumed to be Mrs. Darrow sat by the window, darning a shirt, while another young man, this one a bit younger than James, sat at the table, a book open in front of him.

"Good morning," Daniel said awkwardly, knowing it was anything but a good morning for this family. "I'm Inspector Daniel Haze. I'm very sorry for your loss."

"Thank you, Inspector," the woman said.

"Mrs. Darrow, I presume?" Daniel asked.

"I'm Sadie Darrow, and these are my boys, Jimmy and Willy. Please, have a seat, Inspector."

Sadie Darrow was probably no older than forty, but she could have easily passed for someone much older. Her brown hair was liberally threaded with gray, and her dark eyes looked sunken and dull, her skin sallow. She wore a threadbare gown of faded brown wool, and her boots were scuffed and probably worn through. Her hands, which might have been delicate had she been born a lady, were red and work-roughened, the nails bitten to the quick.

"Thank you." Daniel took a seat at the table, across from Willy, and waited for Mrs. Darrow to join them. Jimmy remained standing but moved toward the hearth, where Daniel could see him.

"Mrs. Darrow, can you tell me what happened, starting with the last time you saw your husband alive?"

Sadie Darrow nodded. "Frank and the boys came 'ome 'round 'alf past six."

"Where did they come from?"

"Since the mill closed—that'd be five years ago now—they've been working for Graham and Sons Coal Dispensary. From eight in the morning till six in the evening, six days a week. And I char for the Hollingsworths, the other side o' the village, three days a week," Sadie added, even though Daniel hadn't asked her about herself. "So, as I were sayin', they came 'ome 'round 'alf past six and we 'ad supper. After supper, Frank and the boys went to the Queen's Arms. That'd be the last time I saw Frank alive."

Daniel turned to Jimmy. "What happened when you got to the Queen's Arms, Jimmy?"

"Nothin'," Jimmy said, shrugging. "We had us a few pints, chewed the fat with a couple o' mates, and gone 'ome."

"And your father?"

"'E stayed behind."

"Why?"

"Said 'e weren't ready to go 'ome. His mate, Elijah Gordon, offered to stand 'im another round."

"What time was this?" Daniel asked.

"'Round nine or thereabouts. Right, Willy?"

"Yeah, 'bout that," Willy agreed. He looked a lot like his brother but was a little stockier and shorter than Jimmy. Both young men had the look of their mother about them.

"What happened then?" Daniel asked.

"We got back and went to bed. Ma was gettin' ready for bed too," Jimmy said.

"What made you go out and look for Frank?" Daniel asked. "Did you normally go looking for him if he failed to come home by a certain time?"

252

"No, but Elijah Gordon 'as always been bad news. 'E'd stand Frank a pint, then expect one in return, and so it went until Frank had run up a tab it'd take him months to pay off. Then 'e'd come 'ome so drunk, 'e wouldn't be able to go to work the next day and lose wages. And Mr. Graham, that's 'is employer, 'ad already threatened 'im with dismissal."

"So, you went to fetch him home?" Daniel asked.

Sadie nodded. "When I got to the Arms, Tony Parks told me Frank had left an 'our or more since. Elijah were still there, but 'e were too pissed to talk to."

"So, what did you do?" Daniel asked.

"I 'adn't seen Frank walking down the lane, so I went to the mill."

"Why?" Daniel asked. He couldn't begin to fathom why a man who'd been drinking for several hours would go to a derelict mill in the middle of the night rather than make his way home.

"Because 'e went there sometimes. 'Specially when 'e were drunk. He missed the place. It'd been in 'is family for generations before 'e were forced to close it. Sometimes 'e even slept there."

"When you arrived at the mill, did you see anything out of the ordinary?"

"Ye mean besides my 'usband strapped to the wheel with his prick pointing skyward?"

"I mean like evidence of a struggle or someone still in the vicinity," Daniel amended patiently.

"Nah, nothin' like that."

"What did you do then, Mrs. Darrow?" Daniel asked softly, feeling guilty for forcing the woman to relive what had to be one of the worst moments of her life.

"I returned 'ome, roused Jimmy, and told 'im to go get a policeman right quick."

Daniel turned to Jimmy. "Is there anything you wish to add?"

Jimmy shook his head. "I went straight to Brentwood, to the station."

"Can you think of anyone who might have wanted to harm Frank?" Daniel asked, looking at all three Darrows in turn.

"Frank was not what ye'd call an amiable man," Sadie said, "but I can't think of anyone who'd do that to 'im. It were awful, seein' 'im like that."

"So, what kind of man would you call him?" Daniel asked.

"Selfish," Sadie replied instantly.

"Jimmy? Willy?" Daniel prompted.

The young men shook their heads, but not before Daniel noticed the sheepish look on Jimmy's face.

"Jimmy, I need to know the truth," he said sternly.

"Well, I don't think this 'as got anythin' to do with 'is death, but Mr. Graham sacked 'im last night."

"What?" Sadie cried. "Why?"

"'Cause 'e were insolent to the overseer. Called 'im a worthless sod, and worse." Jimmy looked at his mother apologetically. "Sorry, Ma, but we didn't want to upset ye."

"I can't be any more upset than I already am," Sadie replied. "What about ye two? Ye still got a job to go to?"

"We're all right," Jimmy said. "We'll go to work on Monday."

Sadie nodded, and Daniel could almost feel her relief. This was not a family that could afford to lose wages.

"What about Kitty? Has she been told?" Daniel asked.

"Kitty doesn't know, unless someone else told 'er," Jimmy said.

Sadie suddenly looked up, searching Daniel's face as if she'd thought of something important. "How'd 'e die, Inspector? Surely 'e didn't freeze to death."

254

"He drowned, Mrs. Darrow."

"Drowned?" she echoed.

"Yes. There was water in his lungs."

"Ye cut 'im open?" Willy cried.

"I'm sorry, but yes. We needed to know what killed him."

"Ye had no right," Willy sputtered, color rising in his cheeks as he looked from his mother to his brother. "Ma, tell 'im. They 'ad no right!"

"What's it matter now, Willy?" Sadie said, laying a hand over her son's.

"It matters. It's wrong to butcher a man as if 'e were a sheep carcass," Willy protested.

"It's all right, son," Sadie said, her tone soothing. "It's all right."

"Is there anyone I can speak to who might know what Frank had been up to in the days leading up to his death?" Daniel asked.

"Talk to the barkeep at the Arms," Sadie muttered. "Tony Parks saw a lot more of my 'usband than I did."

"Thank you," Daniel said, rising to his feet. "I will keep you apprised of our progress on the investigation."

Sadie nodded, but her sons remained silent, their gazes unbearably sad.

Printed in Great Britain
by Amazon